OPPOSITES ATTRACT
BUTCH/FEMME ROMANCES

By Meghan O'Brien

Infinite Loop

The Three

Thirteen Hours

Battle Scars

Wild

The Night Off

The Muse

Delayed Gratification: The Honeymoon

Camp Rewind

Her Best Friend's Sister

The Sex Therapist Next Door

By Angie Williams

Mending Fences

Last Resort

By Aurora Rey

Built to Last

Crescent City Confidential

Lead Counsel (Novella in *The Boss of Her*)

Recipe for Love: A Farm-to-Table Romance

The Inn at Netherfield Green

Ice on Wheels (Novella in *Hot Ice*)

The Last Place You Look

Twice Shy

You Again

Cape End Romances:

Winter's Harbor

Summer's Cove

Spring's Wake

Autumn's Light

Visit us at www.boldstrokesbooks.com

OPPOSITES ATTRACT
BUTCH/FEMME ROMANCES

by

Meghan O'Brien, Aurora Rey, and Angie Williams

2021

OPPOSITES ATTRACT: BUTCH/FEMME ROMANCES
An Epiphany in Flannel © 2021 by Meghan O'Brien. All Rights Reserved.
Follow Her Lead © 2021 by Aurora Rey. All Rights Reserved.
Just As You Are © 2021 by Angie Williams. All Rights Reserved.

ISBN 13: 978-1-63555-784-8

This Trade Paperback Original Is Published By
Bold Strokes Books, Inc.
P.O. Box 249
Valley Falls, NY 12185

First Edition: June 2021

CREDITS
EDITOR: SHELLEY THRASHER
PRODUCTION DESIGN: STACIA SEAMAN
COVER DESIGN BY TAMMY SEIDICK

CONTENTS

FOREWORD

What is a butch? What is a femme?

Three BSB authors envision these distinctive types of female partnerships in this collection of novellas. And while reading about a business executive and her dance instructor, a mechanic and a software engineer, and a trucker and a waitress, you can experience a broad range of takes on this type of pairing.

Pioneer novelist Lee Lynch comments on butch/femme couples: "There was never a question in my mind that I was butch; all I had to do was consider the women who attracted me."

Responding to Lee's comments, Aurora Rey, author of the first novella in this collection, says, "Jude knows she's attracted to femmes, but she assumes the carefree, playful Gabby isn't her type. Until, of course, she falls for her."

Iconic novelist/editor Katherine V. Forrest defines the butch and femme phenomenon as "an idealized and complementary view of women in which butch women live out an innate instinct to cherish and primarily protect a femme partner, and femme women, in return, cherish and primarily nurture their butch partner."

Angie Williams, who has written our second novella, can relate. "This quote is perfect for my story because it's basically the lesson Dylan has to learn. Being butch is more about who you are than what you know."

Finally, poet/novelist/activist Lesléa Newman states succinctly, "A femme is velvet-covered steel and a butch is steel-covered velvet."

And in response, Meghan O'Brien reveals the core of her novella. "While Maisie (the femme) is young, inexperienced, trapped under the thumb of her parents, she takes several bold steps toward self-discovery, inspired by Aiden—an outwardly tough, masculine-presenting trucker who's the more emotionally open and even vulnerable one as they're establishing intimacy."

We hope you enjoy these stories and that they broaden your perspective on butches and femmes.

Shelley Thrasher, Editor

FOLLOW HER LEAD

Aurora Rey

CHAPTER ONE

Jude moved yet another business plan to the "no" pile and started on the next. Some days, looking for the next breakthrough idea or promising startup felt like searching for the proverbial needle in a haystack. She loved working with scrappy young companies, but finding the right ones could be exhausting. At the sound of her name, she looked up from the stack to find her assistant Muriel hovering in the doorway.

"SoundSense rescheduled their meeting to four o'clock, your mother wants to know if you plan to be at Cora's baptism this weekend, and the Krewe of Artemis woman called. They're getting the playlists ready for the ball and asked if you've selected your song for the opening dance."

She filed the details away, adjusting her calendar in her mind and adding items to her mental to-do list. Until the last bit, which made her brain blip as though Muriel had switched to another language mid-sentence. "Dance? No one said anything about a dance."

Muriel folded her arms and gave Jude a bland look. "Ms. Benoit, what do you think happens at a Mardi Gras ball?"

She blew out a breath. "I knew there'd be dancing. I'm not an idiot. I just didn't realize I'd be required to participate."

Muriel pressed her lips together, clearly suppressing a smile. "Are you stodgy about it or do you have two left feet?"

Ugh. Both. "Neither."

"Because I'm pretty sure your entire image and reputation are based on you being good at everything."

This time, the breath came out as more of a growl. "That's not true."

No reply, just an infuriatingly quirked eyebrow.

"I prefer to focus my time and energy on things I do well. That's not the same thing." She considered herself a selective perfectionist, selecting to avoid things that made her feel incompetent.

Muriel unfolded her arms. "Aren't you old money, high society? Don't dance lessons come with finishing school or wherever it is you learned how to be charming and proper?"

Jude pinched the bridge of her nose. She wanted to be offended, but it was hard to take offense at the truth. She *had* gone to finishing school, complete with dance lessons. The whole experience had bordered on torture, but the absolute worst was being forced to fumble through waltzes and foxtrots. With boys. As the follower.

"Oh, come on. I tease you about your posh childhood all the time. Don't get stuffy on me now."

She shook her head. The teasing didn't bother her. No, but the very real possibility of making an absolute fool of herself in front of several hundred members of the New Orleans queer community did.

"Jude, you look legit freaked out right now. What's going on?"

She imagined herself in a tux, stepping on the feet of a faceless woman in an elaborate gown. Everyone would stare. They'd whisper and laugh behind their hands. In the span of five minutes, she'd plummet from being the angel investor who brought progressive and minority-run businesses to the next level to a bumbling klutz. And she'd be humiliated. "Is it too late to back out?"

Muriel came the rest of the way into the office and sat in one of the chairs across from her desk. "You don't want to back out."

She didn't. Being named Majesty of the Krewe of Artemis was a huge honor. It recognized her work in the community as well as her status as one of the highest-profile lesbian professionals in the city. But the thought of taking center stage for the ball's opening dance gave her an almost crippling feeling of dread. "Is it absolutely necessary?"

"Pretty sure they're not going to change the tradition, even for you."

Especially since the spirit of the krewe was putting a queer spin on old traditions. It was why they crowned a Majesty, instead of a king and queen, in the first place.

"What about dance lessons? We could get you dance lessons."

Her mind conjured up Tyson Banks, the boy she'd been paired with week after week, during the dance lessons her mother had insisted she take. His sweaty hands and endless talk about waterskiing in St. Croix. His listing of the girls he'd rather be paired with.

"I bet I could find a beautiful woman willing to take on a private student."

Jude blinked away the memory of Tyson and allowed a different, more appealing image to take root. A leggy blonde in a leotard and high heels coaching her in the privacy of an otherwise empty studio.

"You're considering it. I can tell."

She didn't have a lot of options. And private lessons—leggy blonde or not—were far less daunting than a class. Even one filled with other queer people. "Maybe."

"How about I do some research?"

She paused her simmering anxiety long enough to focus on Muriel and the fact that she'd be utterly lost without her. "I'm pretty sure that isn't in your job description."

Muriel didn't miss a beat. "My job is to keep the company running smoothly. You not being a massive ball of stress makes that a hell of a lot easier."

In addition to being impeccably competent, she also managed to keep Jude in her place. "Point taken."

"Besides, having you look like an idiot would be bad for business."

Without giving Jude a chance to reply, she vanished in the direction of her office. Jude stared at the now-empty doorway, then back at the stack of business plans. She opened one and read the executive summary. But for all the pride she took in having razor focus, her brain flitted from one mortifying scenario to another.

She pressed on, gleaning enough to know the business plan for Queer and Far deserved another read. She moved it to the maybe pile and started on the next. After about twenty minutes, her rational brain returned. It was fine. It was going to be fine.

Like it or not, she would have to dance in front of people. She'd taken on objectively more daunting tasks with much higher stakes. And less prep time, to be honest.

She'd tackle this situation like anything else. She'd face it head-on, and she'd conquer it. And unlike some business deals, with make-

or-break windows in the forty-eight-hour range, she had five weeks. She could learn anything in five weeks.

❖

Gabby studied the woman who'd insisted on meeting in person to discuss the arrangements for private lessons. Younger than she expected from their initial conversation, the woman was every bit the efficient and slightly uptight executive assistant. "You know, we could have taken care of this over the phone."

The woman, Muriel, shook her head. "I needed to meet you, see the space for myself."

"Is your boss, like, the governor's kid or something?" It sure had the feel of a Secret Service sweep. Not that she'd ever experienced one of those firsthand.

Muriel laughed. "No, no. Nothing like that. She's not crazy about the whole dance-lesson thing. And since I'm the one who talked her into it, I wanted to do my due diligence."

"Due diligence?" Maybe she was being punked.

Muriel winced slightly but continued to smile, like she realized how absurd she sounded. "I'm trying to make sure it won't be something we'd both regret."

She was pretty sure Muriel meant her boss and herself, but the exchange made her wonder if agreeing would turn into something she'd regret, too. "Nervous or cranky?"

"Yes."

At least she had a sense of humor about it. "I can work with that, as long as she takes the time we have together seriously. No amount of lessons will help someone who refuses to try."

Muriel shook her head. "Oh, no. If anything, she'll try too hard. Jude doesn't do well with failure."

Should she admit that the longer they talked, the less inclined she was to do this? "Well, I can't promise she'll be graceful, but I've never had someone not able to learn the basic steps."

That reassurance earned her a serious nod. "I'll take it."

"Okay, then." She'd lost track of who was trying to convince whom.

"And the whole lesbian thing isn't a problem? I really don't want that part to be awkward."

She shouldn't out herself. Being a professional dancer meant she could and should be perfectly happy to dance with a partner of any gender. Or gender identity. Or age or race or size, for that matter. But her invisible queerness irked her more than any professional slight. "Not that it matters, or should matter, but I happen to be queer, too."

"Oh." Muriel managed to look surprised, cowed even, but also slightly pleased. "I'm sorry. I didn't mean to—"

She lifted a hand. Point made, she had no need to belabor the matter. "No need to apologize."

"All right." Muriel nodded with more enthusiasm than the disclosure warranted. "I think we're good to go. I have Jude's schedule. I'd love to get on your calendar as quickly as possible since we have only a few weeks."

She started in the direction of her planner but stopped. "Don't you want to discuss price first?"

"If you can get Jude through this without making a fool of herself, you can name your price."

A small part of her was tempted to inflate her rates just to see if Muriel would bat an eye. But even though this whole arrangement might warrant hazard pay before it was all said and done, that wasn't her style. She picked up her appointment book. "Are you looking for days, evenings, or weekends?"

Muriel poked at her phone. "Oh, definitely evenings. Weekends are fine, too. But no chance in hell am I getting her to leave work in the middle of the day."

Great, so uptight and a workaholic. "Unfortunately, that's when most of my group classes are, so our options will be somewhat scattered, if not limited."

"We'll take what we can get. And I might be able to squeeze in a morning or two if she doesn't have meetings."

Something gave her the impression that was Muriel's take on it more than—what was her name, again? Oh, Jude. "Let's see what we can do."

By the time Muriel left, they'd scheduled eight lessons over the next two weeks, two hours each. Muriel had pressed for more, but she wanted to make sure Jude actually showed up and was a willing student before going through the trouble. Muriel insisted on prepaying, saying that would make Jude think of it as an investment more than an obligation.

The choice of phrase struck her until Muriel handed her the check. Benoit Capital, Benoit being the last name Muriel had given for her new student. Even without knowing the specifics, she heard the words big money loud and clear.

Muriel thanked her, then gave her a card with both Jude's and her cell numbers. "If it's a scheduling thing, text or call me. But don't hesitate to reach out to Jude with special instructions or anything else. She might bark, but I promise she won't bite."

Gabby shook Muriel's hand and watched her leave. She looked at the card again, then the check. Muriel's parting words bounced around in her brain. Maybe she should have inflated her rates after all.

CHAPTER TWO

Jude pulled into the parking lot and allowed her lip to curl. *Really, Muriel? A strip mall?*

She'd tried to make a case for paying the instructor to come to the office, but Muriel had insisted it wouldn't do. Not enough space, not the right floors. Like she'd become a dance expert or something. Or maybe she'd asked and the instructor had refused and Muriel had kept that fact to herself so Jude wouldn't go into this nonsense even more irritated than she already was.

No matter. She was here now, whether she liked it or not.

She pulled into a vacant spot and headed toward the glass door with the Step To logo on it. Inside was a waiting area of sorts, with a reception desk and several chairs. There was also a row of hooks and a wall of cubbies, ostensibly where people could leave their things while fumbling or prancing around the dance floor. She instinctively wanted to find fault, but the area was tidy and every inch of space well used.

"You must be Jude. Hi. I'm Gabby."

Jude turned. Gabriella Viard was not the leggy blonde of her imagination. Her dark hair and curvy frame were a lot closer to Jude's actual type. In fact, Gabby was exactly her type, the kind of gorgeous that could make her forget why she was dreading this dance so much in the first place. That might make this whole experience a bit more tolerable, but it also might make it more uncomfortable. Either way, it would have been helpful if Muriel had given her a heads-up. She extended her hand. "It's nice to meet you."

Gabby shook her hand, but her eyes danced with humor. Was Gabby laughing at her? Even before they started dancing? "Thank you for fitting me into your schedule on such short notice."

Gabby waved away the thanks. "With the exception of people taking classes for fun, most people realize they need to know how to dance on fairly short notice. Even people getting married seem to lose track of having a first dance until the eleventh hour."

The comment was clearly made to make her feel better, but it didn't. "I assure you I only found out about this particular obligation this week."

"And what exactly is this obligation? Your assistant didn't say." She heard a trace of humor in Gabby's voice. Again.

"It's for a Mardi Gras ball. Not just the ball, though. The opening dance. Which is a big deal, apparently, since I'm, you know…" She wasn't sure where all the awkward had suddenly come from.

"On the court?" Gabby's tone had turned encouraging.

She let out a sigh that she just barely managed to keep from being a growl. "I'm the Majesty. Sorry. It's a big honor, but it feels strange using that word in reference to myself."

Gabby laughed then, a rich and sexy sound that had the potential to be even more distracting than her looks. "I totally get it. Cool in theory, weird in practice. Is it Artemis?"

Muriel had mentioned that Gabby was queer as part of her pep talk before tonight's lesson, but hearing her reference Artemis sent a wave of relief through her. "It is."

Gabby's eyes lit up. "That's so cool. I've never been to the ball, but I go to the parade every year."

Jude relaxed and, for a second, forgot why she was having this conversation. "Well, the ball has a big, splashy first dance, and that falls to me."

"Okay. We can work with this. Do you have any dance experience, or are we starting from scratch?"

Starting from scratch would probably be easier than what she brought to the table. "Let's just say the experience I do have isn't going to be helpful."

Gabby looked her up and down in a way that threatened to have Jude sweating with something that had nothing to do with discomfort. "Let me guess. TDL."

"Excuse me?"

"Traumatic dance lessons. Quite common here in New Orleans, especially for queer folks who grew up in families with money."

Jude laughed despite herself. "Yes. That's exactly what I have."

Gabby angled her head but kept her expression serious. "Sweaty boy or mean teacher?"

She nodded. "Yes."

"I promise this will be nothing like that."

Well, that was a step in the right direction. "Thank you."

"Why don't we head into the studio and get started?" Gabby's smile seemed to hold mischief and the promise of something Jude couldn't quite identify.

"For the next two hours, you're the boss."

"I do love being in charge."

Gabby led the way from the reception area to the main part of the studio, giving Jude a view almost as enticing as the one from the front. She allowed herself exactly two seconds to enjoy it before shutting it down. She wasn't here to send her hormones on a field trip. This was work. Different from the work she was used to, but work all the same.

Forcing her gaze from Gabby's luscious backside gave her the opportunity to soak in other details of the room. Larger than she expected, bright but without the harsh glare of fluorescent lighting. "This is nice."

Gabby turned, brow raised. "You sound surprised."

Open mouth, insert foot. Did that count as a dance move? "It's just more space than I was expecting. Strip malls always fool me."

She hadn't meant that to come out judgy, but it did. Gabby definitely picked up on it. "Not the most glamorous, but affordable for me and convenient for my students."

Great. She'd managed to come across as an ass and insult Gabby personally. Interesting that she was the owner and not just an instructor. Muriel had failed to mention that fact. "Absolutely the most important considerations for a business owner."

Whether she'd backpedaled enough to appease Gabby or Gabby didn't want to bother arguing, she couldn't know. But Gabby merely nodded. "Let's dance, shall we?"

And suddenly an entirely different sort of panic set in. "Dance? Now?"

Gabby gave her a quizzical look. Definitely an upgrade from the irritated one a moment before. "That's why you're here, isn't it?"

"I just didn't expect us to jump right in. You're not going to give me a diagram or something to memorize?"

Gabby bit her lip, barely able to suppress a smile. She'd expected someone older, stodgier. Not hot, though that's exactly what Jude was. And she managed to be stilted and a bit stuck up at the same time. Working with this woman might drive her to drink, but she'd come out with some stories, that was certain. "That's not really my style."

Jude frowned. "What is your style, then?"

She told herself the edge in Jude's voice was nervousness, not disdain. Whether she believed herself was yet to be determined. "The first and most important step is to get you to feel the music."

Jude's lip curled, and it became a lot harder to argue against disdain. "Feel the music? Are you serious?"

Deep breath. Patience. "Yes. Dancing is more about letting your body run the show, not your brain. And your body feels rhythm naturally."

Jude folded her arms, and despite telling herself the movement was off-putting, Gabby's body had some feelings of its own. "You'll have to forgive me. I have a great deal more faith in my brain than the way my body may or may not feel rhythm."

"If I promise you will have steps to memorize, will you let me do it my way?"

Jude seemed to consider her options. Like, really consider them. It wasn't hard to imagine a virtual pro-and-con list tallying in her mind. "For now."

Something told her that was a major concession, coming from the likes of Jude Benoit. "I'll take it." She tipped her head. "For now."

Jude's expression changed. Her features didn't soften, exactly, but Gabby couldn't help but get the feeling she'd just won a battle or, perhaps, scored a point in some imaginary game. Jude's eyes almost playfully gleamed, and had Gabby not found her attractive before, well, that would have done it. "All right, then. Let's get started."

She looked Jude up and down. "Did you want to change?"

Jude glanced down at her outfit, then at her. "Is that necessary?"

"Entirely your preference." Even if Jude in a pair of athletic shorts and a T-shirt might prove less distracting than Jude's current look of gray pants and white oxford with tiny gray dots was shaping up to be.

"I'm comfortable like this."

I bet you are. "Like I said, your call. You will want to get the shoes you're planning to wear and bring them from here on out."

Jude offered the slightest of nods. "Noted."

"Okay. Shall we?"

Jude made a sweeping gesture with her hand. "By all means."

She couldn't tell if Jude was poking fun or if the formality came naturally. She had a feeling it was the latter, which meant her job might have just gotten a whole lot harder. She crossed the studio to where her phone sat on top of the sound system. She scrolled through her tried-and-true playlist before settling on Rosemary Clooney's "Sway."

Just as the sound of the opening horns came through the speakers, she turned to face Jude, only to watch her stiffen all over. Oh, dear. She returned to Jude, extending her hands but letting them hover over Jude's hips rather than settle on them. "May I?"

Jude frowned but nodded.

Gabby started easy, with nothing more than a gentle swing of her hips. She applied subtle pressure, encouraging Jude's to do the same. Not the smoothest movement, but not the worst she'd seen. And Jude did seem to connect with the beat almost immediately—a huge relief. Trying to teach someone who lacked inherent rhythm to dance was a nightmare. "There you go."

"I'm not sure what this is supposed to accomplish." Jude continued to move under Gabby's hands even as she complained.

"It's getting your body to tap into the music so your brain doesn't have to."

Another frown. "Are you sure we shouldn't start with the steps? We don't have a lot of time, and, not to sound arrogant or anything, I can learn and memorize almost anything. You just have to teach me."

Gabby dropped her hands and stood straight. "If that's what you want, why are you even bothering with an instructor? You'd do just as well with a book or a video or some stickers on your floor."

Jude scowled.

Okay, time to try another tack. "What do you do, exactly?"

Jude gave her a quizzical look but didn't seem offended. "I'm a venture capitalist."

Not as helpful as she might have hoped since she wasn't entirely sure what that was. But she wasn't about to admit that fact. "What's the single most important skill in being successful? I assume, of course, you're successful."

The playful rib was definitely the way to go. Jude lifted her chin. "Instinct. Specifically, my ability to read people. It doesn't matter how good the idea or the business is if the person behind it isn't right."

She smiled, grateful for the clue about what exactly Jude did as much as the fact that Jude had played right into her hands. "Not the numbers?"

"Don't get me wrong, the numbers have to be there, but it's more than that."

She opened her mouth, but Jude didn't give her the chance to speak.

"Oh, I see what you did there. Well played."

She smiled again. Jude might turn out to be an obstinate, clumsy pain in her ass, but she had a sense of humor. Or at least the semblance of one. She could work with that, too. "Thank you."

In the time it took them to have that argument, the song ended. She started it again and returned to her position in front of Jude. "Now, where were we?"

CHAPTER THREE

Jude's computer hadn't even finished booting before Muriel appeared in the doorway with a cup of coffee. They'd agreed that sort of thing wasn't part of her executive assistant responsibilities, but she did it anyway. Probably so Jude wouldn't break the espresso machine Muriel had insisted they needed for the office. Whatever the reason, she'd settled on gratitude as the most appropriate response. "Thank you."

Muriel acknowledged the statement with a nod before setting the mug on Jude's desk. "Well?"

"Well, what?"

"The dance lesson. How was it?"

Without further prompting, she mentally summoned the sensation of Gabby's lower back under her hand, Gabby's grip on her shoulder. "Fine."

"Really? That's all you're going to give me?"

She should have known better than to think that would suffice. "It was good. A little unstructured for my taste, but whatever."

Muriel frowned. "Unstructured?"

She waved a hand before she could stop herself. "I figured we'd select a dance, and she would teach me the steps."

"And that's not what happened?"

She could still feel Gabby's hands on her hips, guiding them into a synchronous sway. "She said I needed to feel the music first."

Muriel let out a snort that she barely tried to cover up with a cough. "And how did that go?"

Despite her apprehension, Gabby had managed to make her not feel silly. Well, not too silly. "Like I said, it was fine."

"If you don't like her, tell me now so I can find someone else. You don't have time to waste."

She told Muriel almost everything, certainly more than their professional relationship called for. Of course, she'd known Muriel close to twenty years now, and Muriel had become more of a constant in her life than most of her friends and family. Certainly more than any romantic relationship she'd managed to sustain. But something about this situation made her hesitate. "I like her just fine."

The frown became a look of suspicion. "Did you sleep with her?"

"What? God, no." She'd thought about it, even had a dream about it, but Muriel didn't need to know that.

"But you want to."

Jude scrubbed a hand over her face. "No, I don't."

"Your personal life is your business, but you know you're a terrible liar, right?"

It was true. She had absolutely no poker face. A bit of a liability in her line of work, but she'd learned to work with it instead of against it. "You saw her. She's gorgeous. But she's essentially an employee. I'm not an idiot."

Muriel's lips pursed, making her look about two decades older than her thirty-eight years, which Jude wouldn't hesitate to point out if she continued to carry on like this. "She's not, but maybe it's better if you think of her that way."

"I resent what you're insinuating."

Muriel smirked. "It wouldn't be the first time."

"You say that like I make a habit of sleeping with business associates." Which, technically, she'd done only once.

"I was talking about resenting my insinuations more generally."

The deadpan delivery got Jude to crack a smile even if she didn't want to. "Are you done with the inquisition? Can we get to work now?"

"Honey, if this was an inquisition, I'd have a lot more info, and you'd be a hell of a lot more uncomfortable."

Jude was technically the boss; she didn't doubt it for a second. But Muriel never hesitated to go toe-to-toe. She appreciated that. She also appreciated that Muriel had the idea of dance lessons in the first place. The whole thing might be akin to torture, but that was her problem, not Muriel's. "Fair enough. It was weird, but I think Gabby knows what she's doing, and I'm cautiously optimistic."

"Since I've seen you turn cautiously optimistic into a ten-million-dollar deal, I'll take it." She turned and sashayed from the office without another word.

Jude picked up her Americano and took a sip. In addition to keeping her on her toes, the woman sure as hell knew her way around an espresso machine. Probably time to give her another raise, just to make sure she didn't get ideas of looking for greener pastures or less high-maintenance bosses.

She scribbled a note to that effect on her desk blotter and turned her attention to her email, sparing one more thought for the gorgeous Gabby Viard and the next time she'd have Gabby in her arms.

❖

Gabby dumped the perfectly toasted croutons into a bowl. She squeezed a lemon into the skillet of shrimp and gave it a toss before doing the same with them and carried both to the table. "I love it when we get to eat together."

It was a rarity. She and her housemates—a teacher and an ER nurse—had essentially opposite schedules more of the time than not.

Leah took the bowl of shrimp and added several to the salad in front of her. "Same. Especially when you cook."

Shantal took the croutons and added nearly enough to hide the lettuce. "Especially when you make croutons."

They passed bowls and a bottle of chardonnay until everyone had a full plate and full glass. Gabby lifted hers. "Cheers, girls."

Glasses clinked, and she took a small sip before diving into her dinner. "What do y'all have going on this weekend?"

"I pulled three twelves this week, so I'm blissfully off." Shantal, the nurse, set down her fork long enough to lift her arms and wiggle her butt in a seated happy dance.

"Nice." Leah nodded. "I have to grade papers, but I'm going to put it off until Sunday and hate myself."

Gabby chuckled. "At least you're honest."

"We should go out," Shantal said.

Leah nodded. "We should. How long has it been since we had a girls' night out?"

"Ages." Shantal huffed out a sigh. "Because we're old."

Leah frowned. "We aren't old. We're responsible."

Gabby pointed with her fork. "You're just still scarred from running into a student on Bourbon Street last year."

"That's true. Not my best moment. Anyway, I'm not talking about getting hammered in the Quarter. We should go out for sophisticated cocktails like the high-class dames we are."

It sounded fun, a lot more fun than their last—and last—drunken foray to Bourbon Street. "I wish I could, but I've got to work."

Shantal scowled. "Girl, it's Friday night."

She shrugged. "It's a private lesson."

"Ooh." Leah wiggled her eyebrows suggestively.

Gabby rolled her eyes. "Dance lesson. Don't be twelve."

Shantal shook her head. "No. I'm with Leah. Every time you say that, that Tina Turner song plays in my head. You know, dancer for money."

"Do what you want me to do," Leah said matter-of-factly.

"You two are hopeless."

Leah shrugged. "Hey, I'm not judging. It's a good gig if you can get it."

Shantal made a face. "I wouldn't go that far. I wouldn't want to whip some nasty, smelly dude around the dance floor."

It was Leah's turn to roll her eyes. "You're so biased against men."

"Damn right I am."

As the sole straight member of the household, Leah took a lot of ribbing about both her preference for men and her general taste in them. Since Gabby felt at least a little bad about that, she opted to change the subject. "This client is a woman."

Leah squeezed her eyes closed and raised her hands, both sets of fingers crossed. "Please tell me she's a hot model type and not some sixteen-year-old girl getting ready for her coming-out ball."

"Definitely not sixteen. Older than me, probably, at least by a little." She thought of the way Jude's shoulders filled out her dress shirt and the way her pants hugged her ass. "And she could be a model, but it would be for one of those companies that tailors men's clothes to women's bodies."

Leah whistled, and Shantal's mouth formed a perfect O. Shantal asked, "A butch? You got a butch client?"

She let out a sigh. "She's a rich and uptight butch, but really nice to look at."

Leah and Shantal nodded in unison. "But can she dance?" Leah asked.

"Well, no. That's why she's getting lessons."

Leah gave her an exasperated look. "You know what I mean."

She did. And she remained on the fence with Jude. She was pretty sure Jude had decent rhythm. Whether she ever loosened up enough to move beyond a series of memorized steps was still up in the air. "We'll see."

"If anyone can teach her, it's you." Shantal pointed at Gabby with her fork.

"Agreed. You'll have to give us updates every time you see her." Leah nodded.

"Thank you both for the vote of confidence."

Shantal shrugged. "You taught my dad to cha-cha. In my book, you can do anything."

They finished eating and cleaned the kitchen. Leah and Shantal decided to go out, but to their favorite dive bar for a round of pool instead of somewhere that would require dressing up.

Shantal went to her room to change out of scrubs, returning less than two minutes later in jeans and a tank top. "You ready, princess?"

Leah gave Shantal a withering stare, then picked up her purse. "I was waiting for you, for the record."

Gabby followed them to the front door. "I'll miss y'all. Have a margarita for me, and call if you need a DD."

Leah smiled. "Oh, we will. Have fun with your hottie. I hope she doesn't step on your toes."

"Literally."

Shantal laughed at her own joke, which made Gabby snicker more than the joke itself. She shooed them out the door and headed to her bedroom to change.

She stood in front of her closet, considering her options far more than she would for a typical day in the studio. Would Jude show up in business attire again? Not that it mattered. She didn't dress to impress her students. Even the hot butch ones.

Still. Jude would probably be dancing with a woman in a full-length gown. She should get used to having that fabric swirling around, right? She pulled a flowing wrap skirt from a hanger, pairing it with her favorite sleeveless black leotard. It made her feel good, not because it gave her really nice cleavage. She pulled her hair up in a twist and applied her usual work makeup: mascara and lip gloss. Even if she kind of wanted to impress Jude, she absolutely didn't want to give the impression she was trying to.

At the studio, she flipped on the lights and adjusted the thermostat. She checked her email, adding another handful of names to the beginning ballroom and swing classes she had starting the following week. And then she did what she always did before a class or a private lesson: she cranked some music, did some stretching, and danced.

Chapter Four

Jude walked into the studio, a low-grade headache simmering at the base of her skull. At the wall of sound, she literally stepped back. She closed her eyes for a second and took a deep breath, willing away the throb that threatened to take hold in time with the pulsing bass.

The music stopped abruptly, the quiet almost as jarring. She opened her eyes and stepped the rest of the way inside. The cool air and softer light helped. Another deep breath. There, she was fine.

"Sorry."

She looked through the door leading from the small reception and waiting area into the main studio. Gabby stood in the middle of the dance floor—tight top, flowing skirt, and bright smile. An entirely different sort of throb took hold. "Hi."

"I was warming up and lost track of time. I don't generally greet students with that many decibels."

That sort of thing annoyed her in principle: lateness, lack of preparation. Even in a situation as minor as this, it was a business, and she was a client. But her annoyance had less to do with that and a whole lot more to do with the fact that she couldn't get Gabby out of her head. "It's fine."

Gabby came out to where she'd stopped, just inside the door. "Still. How are you? How are you feeling about lesson number two?"

Nervous. Determined. More excited to touch you than I should be. "I'm trying not to have feelings on the matter."

Gabby gave her a slightly exasperated look. "You know that's the wrong answer, don't you? Dance is all about feeling."

Jude let out a sigh and managed to keep it from being a groan. "So you keep saying."

"I know you're anxious to learn steps, so that's what we'll do today."

Thank God. With something concrete to occupy her brain, maybe she could stop thinking about every perfect curve of Gabby's body. Or the way she smelled like orange blossoms and sunshine. Or the way her smile always seemed to reach her eyes. "Fantastic."

"Is there a prescribed dance or song, or is it, um, your choice?"

The obvious stumble over what to call her made Jude smile. "Majesty's choice."

Gabby nodded. "Majesty. Right. So, Majesty, what's your choice?"

She didn't know enough to have any ideas, which irritated the hell out of her. "I was sort of hoping you'd have suggestions. A waltz, maybe?"

Gabby recovered quickly, but not before Jude noticed the shadow of a scowl at the mention of a waltz. "If that's what you want, that's what we'll work on."

"Do you think that's a bad idea?" Jude cringed. When was the last time she had such uncertainty in her voice? She cleared her throat. "I mean, you're the expert. I'm open to suggestions."

"Are you?" Gabby looked incredulous.

She attributed most of her success to two things: trusting her gut and knowing when to enlist the expertise of others. Well, using those things to take calculated risks. She considered it a more refined approach to venture capitalism than many of her male counterparts embraced. "What do you suggest?"

Gabby hesitated for a moment, and Jude imagined her considering how frank to be with her thoughts. "I've never been to the ball, but I've gone to the parade every year. It's pretty irreverent, right?"

Drag kings, political satire, and over-the-top costumes were the hallmark of Artemis. All with a heavy sprinkling of rainbows and glitter. Anyone who believed gay men had cornered the market on flamboyance clearly had never encountered this Mardi Gras krewe. "That's one way of putting it."

"So, I'm guessing the ball isn't some stuffy, traditional affair."

"You're right. There's a nod to tradition, like having an opening dance, but no one takes herself too seriously."

"Then why are you shaking your head?"

Jude chuckled. She might take things—herself included—too seriously most of the time, but she wasn't incapable of laughing at herself. "Because when I learned I'd have to do this whole first dance thing, I forgot that and got hung up on all the—how shall we say?—negative experiences from my childhood."

If Gabby's playful smile turned her on, this softer, reassuring one had the potential to do more serious damage. "I see."

Jude waved a hand. "Which is of no consequence now. But thank you for reminding me what we're preparing for."

Gabby nodded, taking the hint. "If it saves me from a waltz, you're more than welcome."

Was she imagining it, or did she detect a hint of flirtation in Gabby's voice? Not that it mattered. "Win-win. So, if not a waltz, then what?"

Gabby tipped her head back and forth. "Even if we stick with traditional ballroom, we have so many options. Do you want to be playful or sexy or dramatic? And more importantly, how skilled will your partner be?"

Shit. "About that."

Gabby raised a brow.

"I'm not sure about my partner yet. I still need to secure a date for the night."

"Oh."

"I mean, I'll have a date. But this was sprung on me just last week, so I haven't asked someone yet." Not that her list of options was all that long. But Gabby didn't need to know that.

"You know that's kind of an important part of all this, right?"

She blew out a breath. "I know. I'll get it sorted soon."

"And bring her to at least a few of your lessons?"

Jude tried to imagine any of her friends or professional acquaintances gliding around the dance floor with her and failed. The only woman she could imagine in her arms was Gabby. Something else Gabby definitely didn't need to know. "Absolutely. Soon. I promise."

If Gabby picked up on the fact that maybe Jude was trying too hard, she didn't let on. "Great. So, why don't we play with a few styles and see what feels good to you?"

She was more relieved than the moment called for, but whatever. "Sure."

"Do you know if you want something slow and flowing or higher tempo?"

"Um." Uncertain and indecisive. Great.

"One isn't necessarily easier than the other. Sometimes a faster pace is more forgiving of missteps."

She could appreciate that, even if her frame of reference had nothing to do with dance. "What do you think?"

"We should put on a few songs and see what feels good."

She was pretty sure the only part of this that would feel good would be her hands on Gabby. But since she wouldn't be dancing with Gabby at the ball, that shouldn't factor into her choice. "I'm game."

Gabby walked over to where her phone sat on the stereo. "Okay. We'll start with the more vanilla and work our way up. You give me a yes, a no, or a maybe."

She had a hard time imagining getting excited about any of them, but she didn't want Gabby to think her difficult on top of everything else. "Okay."

❖

Gabby didn't know whether to laugh or cry. She'd spent close to twenty minutes flipping through song options—classical, jazz, modern. Jude managed to look alarmed, irritated, intimidated, and downright pouty. Not that there weren't infinite song choices, but she didn't even seem to be finding traction in a genre. Maybe she should just take charge and pick.

What if... She scrolled through her playlist and tapped her selection. The horns blasted, and she braved a look at Jude. Aha! A smile.

"I think we have a winner."

"Wait. What do you mean? Why do you say that?"

She hit pause. "You smiled. It's literally the first song you smiled over, and I'm pretty sure we've gone through hundreds."

Jude frowned. "Yeah, but I was remembering the way you made me sway my hips and how silly it felt. That's different than thinking it's a good idea."

"Ah, but you did sway. Whether you wanted to or not, you felt this song."

Jude made a face she couldn't quite decipher. But then it was like she caught herself and her features smoothed out. "What sort of dance would go with this song?"

"A cha-cha or a rumba. It could be really fun. And we could keep it fairly simple or spice it up based on how you feel after a couple of weeks." It didn't take much to envision them sweeping around the room, Jude's hands confident on her. Or to imagine them all dressed up, dancing at the ball together, with hundreds of people looking on. She cleared her throat. "Oh, and your partner, of course."

Had she not had to yank herself out of a daydream, she could have taken more delight in watching the thoughts and feelings play across Jude's face. Excited to uncertain, uncertain to irritated, irritated to resigned, resigned to determined—it was almost comical how obviously each one gave way to the next. "All right."

For some reason, she really wanted to see that excited face again, to have Jude enjoy what they were doing and not just tolerate it. She had no doubt she could teach Jude the steps, but could she get her to have fun? "It's a short song, too. Not even three minutes."

Jude smiled. Not excitement, maybe, but genuine humor. "Sold."

"And since I know you've been dying to, let's walk through the steps of the two dance styles and see what feels more natural. Then we can start to drill and memorize."

Jude folded her arms. "Why do I get the feeling you're making fun of me?"

She shook her head. "Not at all. Teasing, maybe. Definitely humoring. But I also get that's how you learn and what'll make you feel comfortable. We want to work with that, not against it."

It must have been a sufficient explanation because Jude gave a decisive nod. "All right."

Progress. Hooray. "Let's start with the cha-cha. It's really just a step, then back, and a one-two-three in place."

Jude's brow furrowed in concentration. Like before, her expression had an almost cartoon-like quality. "Okay."

"Step, back, one-two-three." This time she did the steps in time with the counts. "Now you try."

Jude managed the steps, but her rhythm was off. "Ugh."

"No. You're really close. Think of it as slow, slow, quick, quick, quick. The quicks are almost more shifting your weight than steps."

"Right." Jude did it again.

"Better."

"Don't coddle me. I do not need to be coddled." Jude's emphasis on the "do not" had a vehemence that gave Gabby a hint of what she might be like when angry.

"I'm not coddling, I swear. I am going to encourage, though, and tell you when you're doing something right. This isn't boot camp."

Jude's shoulders dropped. "Sorry. It's just more important that I do it right than I feel good about myself."

She might not have meant anything, but the declaration gave Gabby a pang of sadness. "If I do my job, the two aren't mutually exclusive."

Jude cracked a smile. "Point taken."

"Okay, let me show you the rumba now, since I'd prefer it for this song." She demonstrated a few rounds of the basic box step.

"I like that. It's simpler."

"It is, to learn, but I also think the flow is nicer to watch. Do you want to try it?"

Jude nodded, then stared intently at Gabby's feet.

"It's slow, quick, quick." She did the steps. "Like, a four count but the first step takes up two counts."

"Yep. I get it."

"I'm just going to put the music on low so we can feel the tempo." She adjusted the volume and restarted the song.

"I just want to state, for the record, I never learned the rumba, even in my terrible dance classes."

Gabby couldn't suppress a smile. "That might be good, actually. Clean slate."

Jude returned the smile. "Clean slate."

She positioned herself in front of Jude. "You're the leader in terms of steps and position, but I'll do the actual leading for now. Back leading, if you will."

"Whatever you say."

They walked through the basic box step a few times. Jude wasn't elegant, but she wasn't terrible. The smile was gone, though, replaced by that look of fierce concentration. "What do you think?"

Jude looked up and blinked, as though the question surprised her.

"It seems good. If you think it's what we should do, then I defer to you."

She let herself look Jude up and down. Black pants today, with a periwinkle button-down. "Why do I get the feeling you don't do that very often?"

To her credit, Jude looked slightly offended. "I believe in enlisting experts, but also trusting them. I would be a shit businesswoman if I didn't."

Gabby offered a nod of concession. "Touché."

Jude's smile seemed almost playful. "So, expert, what do you think?"

Just when she thought she was getting a handle on Jude, Jude had to go and turn the tables. Normally, she liked being kept on her toes. But something about Jude made her wary. Maybe it was because she obviously came from money. Or maybe it was her own naggingly persistent attraction to Jude. Not that either of those things should matter. Jude was a student, nothing more. "I think we have our second winner of the day."

"Thank God. Now could you please give me a diagram or something to take home?"

Despite the wariness, she laughed. "I'm going to make you practice first, but I think that could be arranged."

CHAPTER FIVE

Jude took the file from Muriel. "I need a date."

Muriel folded her arms. "I've been telling you that for the last five years."

"To the ball." Whether she needed a date—or dates—otherwise was not up for discussion.

"Oh."

"Yeah. And not just any date. One who can dance with me."

"Mm-hmm." Muriel kept her arms crossed and tipped her head to one side. "Is this a problem you're asking me to solve for you?"

Muriel solved all sorts of problems, including ones not in her job description. Dumping this on her plate was a step too far, but knowing that didn't make it any less tempting. "No. I'm just complaining."

"Well, you stopped complaining about the dance lessons, so I'll let you whine about this."

Jude smiled in spite of herself. "Thank you."

"Who are your prospects?"

She merely shrugged.

"Come on. You know lots of women."

She did. And if she needed a date for a fund-raiser or a business luncheon or even a golf tournament, she'd know who to call. This was different.

"Who did you go with last year?"

Jude pressed her lips together without realizing it, then made a point of relaxing her features. "Annalise Moreau."

"Right, right. Didn't she wind up trying to sabotage the EcoPen deal?"

"Sabotage might be a bit of an overstatement." However, it had taken some scrambling to undo the damage done when Annalise tried to undermine Jude's relationship with the CEO.

Muriel's face indicated she wasn't willing to budge. "Either way, a no."

"Definitely a no."

"Mmm..." Muriel stared at the ceiling. "When was the last time you went on a date that didn't have a business purpose?"

She so didn't want to answer that. "I plead the Fifth."

Muriel returned her gaze to Jude, shaking her head and tutting her disappointment. "We need to get you a life."

"We?" Perhaps she could hide behind indignation.

"I'd say you, but you've established you're a raging incompetent at doing so."

It was hard to be indignant when someone was speaking the truth. Even if Jude didn't like it, she couldn't argue the accuracy of Muriel's words. "Okay, fine. But this ball is in three weeks, and trying to meet someone, click with them, and learn how to dance with them feels like a fool's errand."

Muriel blew out a breath, her way of conceding the point. "I'll concur, but that doesn't solve the problem of you getting a date for the ball."

"Do you want to be my date?" She knew she was pressing her luck, but she had far worse options on the table.

Muriel blinked at her, that slow, intentional blink of disbelief. Jude imagined her cooking up an elaborate put-down, but she simply shook her head again. "No. I do not."

"I hope you know that wasn't me attempting to get out of having to deal with this."

Blink.

"I mean, at least not entirely."

Blink.

"You're smart and funny and attractive, and if we didn't work together and you didn't scare me a little, I'd totally ask you out."

"How is it possible for you to have negative moves? I always thought you had no moves, but it's worse than that."

Jude shrugged. "I hide it well."

"What about your dance instructor?"

"What about her?" Other than the fact that she was gorgeous and funny and did things to Jude's libido that shouldn't be legal.

"Why don't you ask her to be your date?"

"That's a terrible idea." It was, wasn't it?

"You've already admitted you find her attractive. And, obviously, she can dance."

It wasn't hard to imagine picking Gabby up in a limousine, sipping champagne in the back. A late supper after the ball. Bringing Gabby home, walking her to her door. Gabby's hand on her lapel, inviting her in for a nightcap and—

"Look, before you shut me down, hear me out."

She signaled for Muriel to continue. Better to be suspected of arguing than saying where her thoughts had actually gone.

"What if you paid her? Like as a professional dancer to be your partner."

Jude winced. "You don't think that's a little *Pretty Woman*?"

Muriel gave her an exasperated look. "Depends. You going to fall in love with her?"

"What? No. God. Of course not."

"Sleep with her?"

A much more likely proposition, but still so far outside the realm of her reality, even if she wanted it more than she cared to admit. "Absolutely not."

"So, then, a strictly professional arrangement."

Muriel made it sound so simple. Still.

"She's a professional dancer, not an escort. Why are you being such a prude?"

Jude glowered. It was exactly the wrong—or right, depending—thing to say. She'd been raised by a devoutly Catholic mother who cared about propriety even more than appearances. Jude had spent the first half of her life chafing under both and the second half trying to finesse her way out of them without breaking her mother's heart. Not an easy task. "Pulling out the big guns, I see."

"It's a perfectly good idea." Muriel lifted a shoulder. "Besides, I really don't want to be roped into being your date."

She couldn't help but smirk. "Even if I paid you?"

Muriel didn't flinch. "Not even then."

"If I didn't know you loved me, that might hurt my feelings."

That got her a withering stare, but then a smile. "I do love you. I'm also proud of you for using the word *feelings* in a sentence."

The quip was clever, even if the underlying sentiment stung just a hair. "All right, smart aleck. Let's get back to work."

"So, you're going to ask Gabby?"

The plan did have its merits, merits that had nothing to do with wanting Gabby on her arm or wanting to spend time with her. Really, it would be the most efficient thing to do. Not only would she not need to bother finding another date, but she also wouldn't have to coordinate schedules to practice dancing with them. "I'll think about it."

Muriel retreated to the doorway but turned. "Do you want me to ask her for you?"

The idea had a certain logic. Muriel had arranged the lessons in the first place. This would merely be an extension of that task. If she wanted to keep the whole arrangement, as Muriel had said, strictly professional, it might be the best way to handle it. But the idea of her assistant procuring her a date felt just a step too far. Whether too far in the direction of being a sad sack or an asshole, she wasn't sure. But she had no interest in either. "No, thank you."

"But you're going to?"

Damn, the woman was pushy. "I said I'd think about it."

"Oh, to be a fly on the wall for that conversation."

Rather than giving her a chance to reply, Muriel hightailed it back to her office. Jude shook her head but smiled. Who needed a wife or a girlfriend when she could get such loving harassment every day at work?

"Break?" Without waiting for a reply, Gabby paused the music and picked up her water bottle.

Jude nodded and chugged her own water. "You know, I kind of thought I was in good shape."

She chuckled. "That's what everyone says."

Jude scowled.

"I'm not saying you aren't. It's just different muscles. Different kind of stamina."

"You say that to everyone, don't you?"

She didn't even try to hide a smirk. "Maybe."

Jude wiped her brow and smiled. "I appreciate your honesty."

She was appreciating the way Jude's cologne became ever so slightly more pronounced when she sweat, but she knew better than to admit it. "I try."

"I feel like we're making progress, though."

"We are." More quickly than she'd expected, to be honest.

"And you aren't just saying that to stroke my ego?"

She set down her water and gave Jude her full attention. "I don't stroke egos."

She expected a retort, or perhaps a comment about Jude not needing her ego stroked. What she got was a laugh, a real and true belly laugh. The kind that had Jude wiping a tear from her eye.

"You don't believe me?"

"Oh, no." Jude shook her head. "I believe that more than pretty much anything you've told me so far."

If Jude wasn't such a serious, uptight sort of person, she might think Jude was teasing her. Given how much she was both of those things, Gabby didn't know what to make of her remark. Rather than digging, she opted to change the subject. "Any progress on the partner front? We're nearing the halfway point, and it would be helpful for you to start practicing with someone other than me."

Jude's expression turned serious, even more serious than her usual demeanor. "About that."

She didn't like the sound of that—not the words and not Jude's tone. "Yes?"

Jude straightened her shoulders, making her already good posture even more erect. "I wanted to ask if you'd consider being my partner."

The words computed, but nothing else did. "Like, for the ball?"

She caught the start of an eye roll before Jude closed her eyes briefly and cleared her throat. "Yes. I'd pay you, of course. Like an extension of our lessons. And I'd compensate you for the whole evening, not just the actual dance."

It was hard to know whether Jude wanting to hire her was better or worse than Jude asking her out. "Are you that worried about embarrassing yourself or that hard-pressed for a date?"

Jude didn't hesitate. "Both, but also neither. The ball is more of a professional event than a social engagement, at least for me. If

I make a fool of myself, that's what people are going to remember. That wouldn't be good for my business or the causes I'm an advocate for. Dancing with you as my partner is probably my safest bet, not to mention the most efficient."

Had Jude asked her out—or hit on her—she would have declined on principle. And yet, this almost sterile business proposition left a bad taste in her mouth. That made no sense, really, since she'd been hired as a professional dancer before. Only those times had been strictly dancing and not couched in being someone's date. "Who knew you were such a romantic?"

"I know it's a bit unorthodox. I promise my intentions aren't untoward."

Untoward? Who even said untoward? "It's not that." Though, yeah, it was totally that.

"The thing is, it would be awkward if you were only there for the dance, so I'm asking you to be my date for the entire evening. But I also respect your time, as much as your talent. And we don't have enough of a personal relationship that I'd feel comfortable taking advantage of you without offering something in return."

Jude's explanations were making things more awkward rather than less. Should she say something? How did one tell someone to stop talking without being rude, anyway? "I'll think about it."

Jude frowned. "Is that your polite way of saying no but trying to make it seem like less of a turn-down?"

Instead of an eye roll of her own, she pinched the bridge of her nose. "No. One, because that's not how I operate. Two, because you need to finalize your partner sooner rather than later."

"Oh." Jude, to her credit, looked reasonably cowed.

"I'll let you know by our next lesson." Which was all of two days away.

"All right."

For some reason, she expected Jude to press more. Or maybe to backpedal altogether. Was Jude a more patient person than she'd given her credit for, or was this some secret negotiation strategy Jude used to get what she wanted? "Shall we get back to work?"

"You're the boss."

Like the ready agreement, she couldn't help but wonder if some hidden meaning or ulterior motive lurked in Jude's words. It was so unlike her to overthink everything. Of course, working with Jude was shaping up to be unlike any other lessons she'd given.

They made it through the rest of class, even starting on some basic turns. Jude thanked her for taking time on a weekend and headed out without another mention of her invitation. Or offer. Whatever the hell it was.

She headed home for a late lunch before her evening basic ballroom class and talked Leah into doing yoga with her. Though, really, she wanted to process more than she wanted to do sun salutations. So that wouldn't be too obvious, she waited until they were underway before spilling.

"Wait, wait, wait. She what?" Leah dropped out of down-dog and landed on her knees.

Gabby pushed her head a little deeper between her arms before doing the same. "She offered to pay me to go to the Artemis ball with her."

"Like as her…" Leah trailed off but wiggled her eyebrows with more than enough innuendo to finish the question.

"No. Christ. As her dance partner." She hesitated. "And as her date."

"Did you say yes? Please tell me you said yes."

Instead of answering, she transitioned into some cat-cow stretching.

"Gabby."

She might be a grownup, but it was impossible not to respond to Leah's teacher voice. "I said I'd think about it."

"What is there to think about? You're teaching her the dance, so you know that part will go well. Easy money, which is reason enough. And it's the hottest lesbian event of the year."

She gave up on any illusions of yoga and sat cross-legged on her mat. "I know."

"So what's stopping you? Please don't say some sense of propriety. I might not be able to forgive you."

The icky feeling she couldn't shake might be a distant cousin of prudence, but that wasn't it exactly. "The idea of being paid to be someone's date just feels gross."

Leah mirrored her position and propped her elbows on her knees.

She leaned forward. "Is it because you wouldn't go out with her otherwise or you would?"

Gabby blew out a breath. "Yes."

"Hold up. Which?"

"I'm not sure and sort of both."

"Oh."

"Exactly." She'd been turning the proposition over in her head and kept arriving at the same impasse. And she'd promised Jude an answer at their next lesson.

"And it feels like saying yes closes the door to any chance of a real date."

"No. I mean…" What did she mean? Yes, she found Jude attractive. Also slightly maddening. And while she didn't have any sort of formal code against personal involvement with her students, everything about this felt like it was crossing a line. "It just feels messy."

"And you don't like messy."

It wasn't that she didn't like complex and nuanced things. She preferred for everything to be on the table. And she wasn't sure she could put everything on the table when it came to Jude. Well, not *could*. She could do whatever she put her mind to. In the case of Jude, she wasn't sure she wanted to open the door to anything more than the time they spent together in the studio. But since she didn't want to own any of that to herself, much less her friends, she settled for, "Exactly."

"I get it, but I still think you should say yes."

She shrugged. "Well, I have two days to decide. I'll let you know how it turns out."

Leah shook her head. "My life is so boring."

Gabby hoisted herself back to downward-facing dog before looking at Leah. "Boring is underrated."

Leah let out a sigh but joined her. "If you say so."

Chapter Six

Jude walked into the studio, more nervous than the day of her first lesson. Okay, that might be a bit of an overstatement, but not much. After making a complete idiot of herself last time, she honestly had no idea if Gabby would agree to her proposition. If she didn't, not only would Jude feel like more of an idiot, but her most promising option for a date to the ball would be gone, too.

Inside, the air was cool and inviting. A weird thing to say mid-February, but not in Louisiana. She changed her shoes and emptied her pockets of her phone and keys.

Gabby was already in the studio, stretching. Jude couldn't help but appreciate the graceful movements of her limbs—both the view and knowing what those limbs would feel like in her arms. Of course, she'd also been thinking more than a little about how Gabby would feel in her arms not on the dance floor. She shoved those thoughts aside. If Gabby had any idea, she'd nix Jude's request faster than Jude could say *strictly professional.*

Gabby looked up and smiled. "Hey."

Deep breath. You're fine. "Hey."

"You okay? You look really stressed tonight."

Funny how fear of rejection could do that to a person. "All good. Just, um, a hectic day."

Whether Gabby believed that or not, she nodded. "I get the feeling most of your days are like that."

She shrugged. "I like to think I thrive under pressure."

Gabby grinned. "So you've said."

She'd sort of hoped Gabby would bring up the question on the table first, but it didn't look like that would be the case. "Mostly."

"Well, I remain optimistic your ability is going to serve you here, especially as we get closer to the big day."

Despite the churning in her stomach, she smiled. "So you've said."

Gabby tipped her head. "Touché."

"I wanted to—" She'd barely started her apology-slash-explanation when Gabby said, "So I—"

Jude bowed slightly. "Sorry. Go ahead."

Gabby nodded. "I've been thinking about your proposition."

Jude braced herself.

"I'll say yes, but on one condition."

"What's that?" She had a hard time imagining saying no to anything Gabby requested.

"You don't pay me."

She didn't know what she'd expected the condition to be, but it certainly wasn't that. "I wasn't trying to insult you. I hope that isn't how it came across."

"I believe you."

Not a denial, but she'd take it. Gabby's opinion maybe shouldn't matter so much, but it did. "Okay, good."

"But the idea still doesn't sit well with me. Especially since what you're asking for isn't just a dance partner."

"I get that. I just didn't want to be presumptuous or assume you'd be interested or—"

Gabby lifted a hand. "I try not to presume anything, which is why I'm saying yes. Well, conditional yes."

This stipulation would make it a hell of a lot harder to keep her imagination in check, but that seemed like the least of her problems. "I accept this condition. Though I'm hoping you'll let me do something nice to say thank you."

"You don't need to. Going to the ball will be a treat. And dancing with you will be easier than trying to get you comfortable with someone else at this point."

She frowned. "Oh."

"Well, don't look so dejected. It's going to be easier for you, too."

Right. That should make her feel relieved, not disappointed.

"Besides, now that I know it's going to be us, I plan to talk you into a more elaborate number."

"You think so, huh? Why didn't you make that one of the conditions?"

"I didn't need to. I'm very convincing."

Damn it all if Gabby's confidence didn't amp up Jude's attraction even more. "We'll see about that."

Gabby walked—sashayed, really—over to the sound system. A moment later, the opening strains of "Sway" came through the speakers. "Let's get started."

Jude lifted her arms into dance posture. "Yes, ma'am."

Whether she was relieved over having a date to her fancy ball or had gained confidence from knowing who her dance partner would be, Gabby couldn't say. But either way, Jude killed it during their hour and a half together. By the time they wrapped up, Gabby had worked up a sweat of her own, and they'd run through the entire song without breaking stride. A rather uninspired performance, but a complete one. In her book, that counted as a huge step in the right direction, so much so that she called it a few minutes early and talked Jude into a little bit of a cool-down before leaving.

Jude made a face when she pulled out the yoga mats but didn't complain. Not that Gabby put a lot of stock in having the upper hand, but it was fun to have Jude extra compliant. At least for the moment.

"I've been thinking." Jude sat up from a straddle stretch, clearly hiding a wince.

"Have you now?" Something told her that when Jude Benoit started thinking about something, all hell was about to break loose.

"I don't want to be too forward or give the wrong impression, but it would be nice if we went out to dinner, spent some time together outside of class before the ball."

"I don't understand."

"Well, if you aren't there as a paid professional dancer, you're technically going as my date, and it would be strange to do that without ever seeing each other outside of class."

"After all that, are you asking me out?"

"No, no, no." Jude took on a look of equal parts alarm and discomfort. "I just don't want the night of the ball to be awkward. Or for people to ask me something basic about you that I don't know."

She turned her head and narrowed her gaze. "Wait, are you asking me to be your fake girlfriend?"

Jude blanched. "Oh, God. It sounds like that, doesn't it? I'm not. I swear."

The intensity of Jude's reaction made her laugh. "Just a fake friend, then."

Jude didn't seem to find that concept funny. "Can't we just be real friends?"

The earnestness should grate on her, but she found it oddly endearing. "Friends would be nice."

Jude's features relaxed. "Are you free tonight?"

She knew it wasn't a real date, but that didn't stop her pulse from jumping. "I am."

Jude smiled. "Fantastic. I really want to go home and take a shower first, but I'll refrain since…you know."

"Friends." Even if a slightly sweaty Jude made her think of the sorts of friends who came with benefits.

Jude nodded. "Friends."

"There's a great Lebanese place a few doors down. Not the best ambiance, but the falafel is to die for." And hopefully the heavy garlic and fluorescent lighting would keep her body and her brain on the same page.

"Sounds perfect."

"Great. I just need a few minutes to lock everything up."

"Wait. Did you come into the studio just for our lesson today?" Jude sounded incredulous.

She shrugged. "Monday night isn't really prime time for dance lessons."

"So, you're working on your day off? For me?"

The sincerity of the question, paired with the earnestness a moment ago, made her heart rate do weird things. "It's okay. I don't keep regular business hours."

"Still. That seems like a lot of trouble to go to for one lesson. I'm not sure how much I'm paying you, but I should be paying you more."

"Are you so rich you try to give money away, or do you consider yourself that difficult?"

She'd meant her remark in a teasing way, but now Jude looked even more serious. "Neither."

"I was kidding. Relax."

Jude continued to frown. "Sorry."

"Don't apologize. But if we're going to be friends, some ribbing will be involved. I'm not sure I can contain myself."

"Right."

"You don't relax well, do you?"

That got her a rueful chuckle. "What gave you that impression?"

"Lucky guess."

Jude looked down for a moment, then into Gabby's eyes. "I don't mean to be so serious. I'm worse when I'm operating outside my comfort zone."

That, she'd believe. She wished she could see Jude at work—comfortable, confident, and in command. "Well, hopefully hanging out will make you more comfortable, which will make dancing together even easier."

Jude nodded, earnest once again. "I hope so."

"And who knows, we might even enjoy ourselves?"

Jude lifted a shoulder and smiled. "I promise I won't talk about business plans or mergers and acquisitions."

There, that was better. "See, you've got a sense of humor hidden in there after all."

"Right. Sense of humor. That's it. I was definitely joking." The eager nod made it clear it was this that she was joking about.

"You bring more of that to the dance floor, and you might actually have fun."

"Let's not get carried away."

Gabby grinned, determined to do exactly that. "Let me get my things, and I'll meet you out front."

❖

Jude took a sip of her iced tea and told herself to relax. It wasn't a date. She'd said so herself. It was two people getting to know each other under the auspices of friendship. Like someone she'd clicked with at a networking event or an old business-school acquaintance. Only she didn't have sex dreams about people she met at networking events or took Advanced Derivatives with. At least not that she could recall.

But Gabby didn't know about the sex dreams. Or the way Jude's heart rate increased in ways that had nothing to do with a cardio workout each time Gabby stepped into her arms. And she intended to keep it that way. If Gabby had half a clue where her mind was half the time they were dancing together, she'd no doubt back out of being Jude's date. She'd probably drop Jude as a student, too, faster than either one of them could say *two left feet*.

No, this whole situation was hers to handle. It probably had as much to do with her nonexistent love life as any inherent attraction to Gabby. At least that's what she kept telling herself.

"You're walking through the steps in your mind, aren't you? I can tell." Gabby rested her elbows on the table and propped her chin on laced fingers.

"Guilty." Better to be guilty of that than what she'd been thinking.

She was spared any follow-up questions by the arrival of their food. Once it was all in front of them—a plate of hummus, another of baba ghanoush, grape leaves, shawarma, pita—it hit her that perhaps they'd gone overboard with the ordering. But Gabby merely smiled. "Hope you're hungry."

What was it about sharing plates that created a sense of intimacy? Was it eating the same foods? The brush of hands over a bowl of olives? Whatever it was, she lost track of worrying about the dance or trying to impress Gabby and simply enjoyed her company. It was unexpected. It was lovely. And, when push came to shove, it felt a hell of a lot like a date.

Unfortunately, she also managed to lose track of time. When her phone pinged with a seven-thirty alarm, she had to do a double take.

"Let me guess. Running off to a hot date?" Gabby grinned before popping the last grape leaf into her mouth.

"I thought we established I don't have hot dates," Jude replied, surprising herself.

"Right, right. My mistake."

Gabby didn't ask, but she felt the need to explain. "Do you remember Muriel? The woman who set up our lessons."

Gabby smirked. "Oh, I remember. I thought maybe she was Secret Service, and you were going to turn out to be the governor's kid or something. Is your not-a-hot-date with her?"

She hadn't given a lot of thought to that initial meeting, but the description made her smile. "It's with her son, actually. I'm tutoring him in math."

"Oh, that's nice. How old is he?"

"Seventeen." When Gabby gave her a quizzical look, she added, "Muriel had him young."

"Ah. I was about to be very jealous of her gene pool."

"I'm pretty sure hers is stellar, but yeah. He's slogging through AP Calculus with the hope of getting some college credits under his belt, and it's getting the better of him."

"You close multi-million-dollar deals, but you're tutoring a high schooler."

"He's a good kid." She shrugged. "And I like math."

"Be careful. Word might get out that you're charming."

Gabby offered a wink, which only added to her confusion about the exact implications of her teasing. What was she supposed to say to that? "I trust my secret is safe with you."

Not the best comeback, but probably not the worst.

"Depends. Are you going to play hero over the check?"

"Nope."

Gabby nodded. "Good."

"But only because it's already taken care of." It was fun to watch Gabby's eyes narrow for a moment before she laughed. Well, fun since the laugh came so quickly. She'd worried Gabby might be genuinely irritated. "It seemed like the least I could do."

"Mm-hmm. Which was why you had to be sneaky about it."

"I just didn't want it to be a thing. If something is within my control, I want it to go smoothly."

Gabby folded her arms and leaned forward. "And what do you do when things aren't in your control?"

"I trip over my own feet. I thought we'd established that already, too."

Gabby leaned back in her chair and laughed. Again, Jude had to remind herself they weren't on a real date. "Sorry. My bad."

"So, I hate to go, but I really need to. That's the alarm that usually reminds me to leave the office."

"You're usually still in the office at seven thirty at night?"

It was her turn to fold her arms. "Does that surprise you?"

"Not in the least. Well, this was fun." Gabby angled her head slightly. "More fun than I would have expected, if I'm being honest."

"Maybe you'll have to agree to do it again. Now that you've admitted I'm charming." She stood and Gabby followed.

"I could probably be persuaded. Especially since you let me talk you into that spin sequence at the end."

They exited the restaurant. Dusk had given way to darkness. Gabby raised a brow but didn't argue when Jude walked her to her car. "The board of the Artemis krewe is doing a dinner to kick off Mardi Gras week, the night before the ball. It's a fund-raiser to support the parade, but also some of the local LGBTQ resource centers and the Trevor Project."

Gabby smiled. "Oh, that's cool. Great causes, too."

"I'm expected to be there, obviously, but I was wondering if you might want to go with me."

"Two events with the same woman and people might think your fake date is really your girlfriend."

"Why do you keep calling them fake dates?" The question came out much sharper than she'd intended. "I mean—"

"Jude. Teasing."

Jude swallowed. "Sorry."

Gabby looked slightly exasperated, but she smiled. "It's fine. But people probably will assume we're together."

The more time they spent together, the more she wished they were. "I can think of worse things."

"All right, then."

Gabby's answer gave nothing away, driving Jude slightly mad. "So, that's a yes?"

"Yes."

Phew. "Excellent. I'll see you in a couple of days?"

"That you will." Gabby paused briefly, and it was all Jude could do not to kiss her. "Only three lessons to go."

Of course that's where Gabby's thoughts were. "It's hard to believe."

Gabby smirked. "Time flies when you're having fun."

For all that she'd dreaded dancing and dance lessons and the prospect of putting herself on display, the last few weeks actually *had* been fun, occasional bouts of bickering notwithstanding. Yet even those had left her thinking about her life and her choices, about how maybe she could do things differently and find more joy. As much as she harbored a colossal crush on Gabby at this point, it was that feeling, that reflecting, that stood out most of all.

"Um, have a good night." Gabby looked at her expectantly, clearly wondering where her mind had wandered.

"You, too." She offered a smile and a wave, then retreated in the direction of her own car, not wanting to reveal the sentimental trajectory of her thoughts.

CHAPTER SEVEN

The final week of lessons flew by. By the last one, Jude allowed herself to think she'd actually pull it off. She also allowed herself to think that her time with Gabby—the teasing during lessons, another friendly dinner—might be the start of something more. But before she could entertain that possibility, she had to get through Mardi Gras. That included tonight's fund-raiser dinner and the question of whether they were in real date territory.

She pulled up to the address Gabby had given her. The house was cute, a traditional shotgun style that had either been lovingly maintained or thoughtfully restored. She cut the engine and headed up the tidy walk to the porch steps. Before she even reached the top step, the door opened.

Gabby stepped out and quickly closed the door behind her. "Hey."

She stopped short, tripping over her own feet. She'd like to say Gabby startled her, but that would be a lie. It was lust, pure and simple. Gabby wore a form-fitting cocktail dress in a color that reminded her of burnished bronze and heels that made the ones she danced in seem downright utilitarian. She was, in a word, stunning. Jude swallowed. "Hi."

Fortunately, Gabby didn't seem to notice her almost face-plant. Either that or she covered her reaction well. "Can I just say I love that you're always on time? It's such an underrated thing."

Gabby tucked a lock of hair behind her ear in that way she did, and Jude almost drooled. She lifted the bouquet of peonies, suddenly feeling silly for bringing them. "These are for you."

Gabby's eyes lit up before going wary. "Thank you. I…"

She remembered Gabby's comment about having roommates, and it hit her that maybe Gabby didn't want her to meet them. Or, perhaps more likely, the other way around. "Sorry. They're a bit presumptuous. I didn't mean to—"

"They're lovely. I'm being weird because my roommate is babysitting her six-month-old niece, and she just got her to fall asleep after literally hours of crying. I don't want to be the one who wakes her up," Gabby angled her head, "and then leaves."

Jude laughed. Of all the reasons for Gabby not to invite her in, that one hadn't crossed her mind. "I have heard it's best to let sleeping babies lie."

Gabby took the flowers. "Funny. You're funny. Do you mind if I just tiptoe in to put these in water?"

Even if part of her wanted to see Gabby's space, get a feel for her life outside the studio, she wasn't about to chance waking a baby—or seem overly curious. "Of course. Take your time."

Gabby disappeared but returned in what felt like a matter of seconds. "Thanks."

"You look fantastic, by the way. I meant to say that before. Assuming, of course, it's okay to mention it." She lifted her shoulder in what she hoped was a lighthearted, good-natured sort of shrug.

Gabby smiled. "Compliments among friends are always welcome. And while we're at it, you're looking even sharper than usual."

She was probably just being playful, but Jude's shoulders straightened, and a flush warmed her cheeks. "I thought you might tease me about having a dress version of my uniform."

It was Gabby's turn to lift a shoulder. "It might be a uniform, but it suits you."

"Well, thank you." She gestured in the direction of her car. "Shall we?"

Gabby smirked. "We shall."

She let Gabby lead the way down the sidewalk but snagged the passenger door before Gabby had a chance. That earned her a bland look. "Force of habit. Humor me."

Gabby's eyes danced. "Oh, I'll humor you all right."

She held the door while Gabby slid into the car, then skirted the hood to her side. Gabby's comment played in her mind. What the hell was that supposed to mean? And more importantly, what was she supposed to do with it?

"This is a dinner dinner, right? Not some passed-hors d'oeuvres situation that's going to leave me hankering for the Popeye's drive-through?"

For some reason, that remark made her relax. "Real dinner, I promise. I've been to the restaurant catering it and was more than impressed."

Gabby nodded, ostensibly satisfied. "So, are you nervous?"

She stopped for a red light and turned her attention to Gabby. "Why would I be nervous?"

"You were just so freaked out by the ball, I wondered if it was a general social-anxiety thing."

"I love that you don't sugarcoat things."

Gabby shrugged. "Life's too short."

If only it were that simple. "Well, I also appreciate your concern, but no. I can work a room in my sleep. It's the dancing that gives me nightmares."

"Ah. That's good."

"Don't get me wrong. It doesn't come naturally. But it's a skill I've practiced and honed enough that I can do it well. It's exhausting, but I can fake it."

Another red light and another glance at Gabby. This time, she resembled a scientist studying an interesting specimen. "Maybe you're not faking. Maybe you're just an introvert."

"Tomato, to-mah-to, no?" In her book, they amounted to pretty much the same thing.

"Being an introvert means you might be perfectly good at it, but it takes energy rather than gives you energy. That's completely different from faking it."

She would have thought Gabby was teasing her—again—but her expression remained serious. "It's nice of you to stroke my ego, especially off the dance floor."

Gabby huffed out a sigh. "I'm not stroking your ego. I…"

She returned her attention to the road, waiting for Gabby to continue rather than being brave enough to finish her sentence.

"I think you might be better at things, and probably have more fun, if you relaxed a little."

Jude laughed.

"You don't agree?"

She schooled her expression and cleared her throat, not wanting to get on Gabby's bad side before their date even started. "It isn't that I don't agree or don't believe you. I just don't work that way. I never have."

"Not even as a kid?"

She let out a sigh of her own. Her childhood had been almost obscenely privileged. It had also been rigid. And instead of rebelling against that rigidity, she had learned to operate within it. Aside from her sexuality, at least. No one could change that, no matter how much her mother wished for it. "It's not that I never relax. Rest and relaxation is essential for health and well-being. I'm just not one of those let-loose types."

She pulled up to the Pontchartrain Hotel, behind another car being valeted. Gabby continued to give her that curious look, but some other emotion lurked there, one she couldn't quite place. "I want to poke fun at you, but I think I feel sorry for you more than anything else."

She smiled. "How about neither? I do all right. And I'm less of a workaholic than I used to be."

Gabby shook her head. "If you say so."

The car in front of them pulled away, and Jude slid into the spot. A second valet was already heading for Gabby's door, saving her from having to argue or placate or anything else. "I do."

Gabby sipped a glass of champagne and studied the crowd. The banquet room had more personality than one at a chain hotel might and looked to be near capacity with a hundred or so guests milling around. Based on age and attire, she guessed it was a mixture of old money and new, along with people who were part of the krewe and people like her, just along for the ride. But with only a few exceptions, they were women. Suits and ties as much as dresses, but all women. Knowing she had at least one thing in common with the majority of them proved oddly reassuring.

Even as Jude's words in the car lingered in her mind.

Jude's matter-of-fact delivery made her almost sad. Like, for all her success and being good at practically everything—save dancing, obviously—she simply couldn't master letting go. Of course, it didn't seem to bother Jude. Or, if it did, she regarded it as something innate, as fixed as how tall she was.

Speaking of tall, Jude strode toward her with purpose. "Sorry. There's always the chance of a little shop talk at functions like this, but I wasn't expecting to be pulled into a full business meeting."

She appreciated the apology almost as much as she appreciated the way Jude filled out that designer suit. "You do what you need to do. I'm perfectly content to people-watch."

Jude gave her an incredulous look. "I wouldn't have pegged you for that."

"Really? Why not? People are fascinating."

"I figured you for the chat-up-anyone type."

Jude's smile, paired with the suit and maybe the champagne, gave Gabby a flash of doing a whole lot more than chatting her up. "I enjoy that, but sometimes it's fun just to watch."

"Look at us, having something in common." Jude snagged a glass of champagne from a passing waiter and raised it.

She tapped her glass to Jude's. "So, do you know most of these people?"

"Maybe a quarter of them. A few from business deals and a few from nonprofit circles." Jude nodded in the direction of an older couple. "Mabel and Juanita took me under their wing when I first started showing up for the gay chamber events, got me connected. They're talking with Helen, who's one of my investors. I worked with her for five years before we realized we were both family."

"Are all your friends a decade or two older than you?"

Jude laughed. "Not all, but I'm definitely guilty of being an old soul."

"That's nothing to be guilty about." If anything, it proved oddly endearing.

In the remaining twenty minutes of the cocktail hour, no fewer than a dozen people came up to Jude—mostly older, but some closer to their age. Whether a business associate or friendly acquaintance, every single one had words of congratulations and praise for Jude's being named Majesty. It was almost like Jude had celebrity status, at least in these circles.

Jude was gracious and funny, self-deprecating in a way that came across as charming more than awkward. She introduced Gabby as a friend, though Gabby was pretty sure most people assumed their relationship was more than platonic. Not in a skeevy way, though. No, it felt more like that sort of casual speculation that came with someone who kept their personal life private.

Dinner was announced, and of course they were seated at the head table, with the deputy mayor and the provost of Loyola and her wife, the dean of Tulane Law. Had Gabby been prone to insecurity, the present company might have done the trick. Fortunately, the final couple were part of the Artemis board, an artist and a community organizer who felt much more her speed.

Jude had assured her the food would be decent, but the meal was exquisite. And the conversation proved more engaging than she'd anticipated. Who knew college bigwigs could be so funny?

As the waitstaff began to circulate with coffee and dessert, she excused herself. In the ladies' room, women gathered at the mirror chatting. She used the restroom, then joined the klatch, focusing on washing her hands more than the conversation.

"I was wondering how long it would be before someone landed Jude Benoit."

Gabby just barely resisted an eye roll, though it would be hard to say whether she was more irritated on Jude's behalf or her own. She looked up, making eye contact in the mirror with a woman she'd not met. "No one has landed anyone. We're just friends."

Barbara, the deputy mayor, finished applying fresh lipstick and caught Gabby's gaze in the mirror. "Honey, friends don't look at friends the way Jude was looking at you."

The comment caught her off guard. She'd noticed Jude staring at her now and again, but she'd chalked it up to her intense personality more than anything else. Even tonight, on what was ostensibly a real date, Jude seemed to oscillate between the kind of attentiveness that came with attraction and an almost inscrutable way of seeming elsewhere.

Barbara slipped her lipstick back into her purse, then put a hand on Gabby's arm. Friendly, if a bit more familiar than the circumstances warranted. "I hope you don't think I meant anything bad by that. Jude has a reputation of being an all-work-and-no-play sort. It's nice to think she's letting loose."

Gabby laughed in spite of herself. "I'm not sure I'd go that far."

"Well, it is Jude Benoit we're talking about. Letting loose is relative." Barbara gave her a wink and went on her way.

She lingered in the bathroom for a moment. Did she want to be the reason Jude loosened up? And, maybe more importantly, did Jude actually want that?

CHAPTER EIGHT

When the program ended, it seemed like half the room flocked to their table. Gabby sipped her coffee and watched Jude effortlessly talk to no fewer than a dozen people. She smiled and laughed; she shook hands and gave hugs. And even without trying to eavesdrop, she heard Jude recall names, ask specific questions about people's lives, and seem genuinely interested in the answers.

If she hadn't been attracted to Jude before tonight, she would be now. Only, she had been before. Tonight merely amplified that fact, liking Jude as a person on top of the physical attraction. Less stubborn, more at ease, and with a quieter sort of confidence than she would have given Jude credit for.

Despite all her teasing about fake dates, she was very much enjoying this real one.

But what would happen after tomorrow night, when their professional relationship ended? Would Jude still want to see her? Or would she get swallowed up by work in ways Gabby had only begun to glimpse? Was all the getting-to-know-you genuine or just cover for the fact that she'd asked her dance instructor to be her date?

"Don't tell me I've worn you out. I didn't think that was possible." Jude's comment came with a playful smile that sent Gabby's thoughts in an entirely different direction.

"Oh, no. My mind must have wandered while you were doing all your mingling." She stuck out a hand and wiggled her fingers.

Jude laughed. "I'm sorry about that. Thank you for being so patient."

She resisted a joke about it being part of the job, not wanting to own that's where her thoughts had been. "I was enjoying watching. You're good at this."

Jude gave an offhanded shrug. "Practice."

She grinned. "Well, you know my feelings about that."

"Indeed I do." Jude looked around the room before returning her gaze to Gabby. "Hey, if you really aren't too beat, would you like to grab a drink? The views from the bar on the roof are spectacular."

Definitely not what she was expecting. "I'd love that."

Jude angled her head in a way that was hard to read as anything but flirtatious. "Then let's."

The bar, Hot Tin, had a swanky vintage feel, complete with low light and intimate seating areas. More crowded than she might have expected for a Thursday night, but it was carnival season.

"Do you want to go check out the view while I order drinks?"

Smooth. "Sure."

"They do a traditional hurricane that will blow your socks off, but I have a feeling they can make just about anything."

She wasn't a big rum drinker, but if they were known for it, she should at least give it a try. "That sounds good."

Jude headed to the bar, and she stepped out onto the patio. The night was chilly by New Orleans standards, and the space was otherwise deserted. She strolled to the railing and soaked in the view. The downtown skyline shimmered, complete with the Superdome lit up purple.

"It's great, isn't it?" Jude appeared at her side and handed her a glass.

"I'm not sure I've ever seen the city like this before."

"I don't think many have. Not a lot of tall buildings out this way."

She appreciated the comment, that it didn't make her wonder seem unsophisticated. "Cheers to seeing things in new ways, then."

They enjoyed the view for a few minutes, then headed inside, claiming a cozy little love seat that left no space between them. Much like their dinners together, conversation flowed freely. Unlike those times, she couldn't take her eyes off Jude's face, her mouth, the way her tie fell perfectly between her breasts. She'd crossed the line from appreciating into wanting and saw no use in pretending otherwise.

"One more?" Jude gave Gabby an almost hopeful look.

She shook her head. "We shouldn't if we're going to drive."

Jude lifted a shoulder. "We wouldn't have to drive if we stayed."

She'd have expected Jude to offer a cab or, more likely, a fancy car service. The suggestion they not leave at all caught her by surprise. "This isn't the Quarter. I'm guessing the bar will close at some point."

Jude angled her head slightly. "I meant the hotel."

She'd mostly known that's what Jude was talking about, but she wanted to hear her say it. It wasn't the poshest hotel in the city, but it was up there. At least by her standards. The idea of dropping however much on a room just to have another drink was kind of nuts. Of course, that wasn't really what they were talking about. "Friendly slumber party?"

Jude blushed. "I—"

"Kidding. You're skittish tonight."

"Am I? Sorry. I don't mean to be."

"It's okay. Now that I know why, it makes sense."

Jude's eyes grew large. "Not that I—"

Instead of letting her finish, Gabby closed the short distance between them and pressed her lips to Jude's. Not a serious kiss, just one meant to quiet her. Brief, but it still managed to send sparks zipping through her. "Jude. Relax."

Jude blew out a breath. "Right. I swear I'm not always an oaf with women."

She lifted a brow. "Just on the dance floor?"

That comment made Jude laugh, and she seemed to relax. "Yes. Exactly."

They could continue this dance for a while, probably, but if they were heading in the same direction, she saw no need to draw it out. "How about we skip the next round and you see if a room's available?"

Jude opened her mouth, then closed it. Like maybe she wanted to ask if Gabby was sure but then thought better of it. "That sounds like a fantastic idea."

❖

Jude slid the key card into the lock and took a steadying breath. Sure, this wasn't her usual MO. But it wasn't the first time she'd spent the night with a woman in a hotel room, either. She was just out of practice. It was definitely that and not some undercurrent of significance that she was spending the night with Gabby.

The light flashed green and the lock clicked. She opened the door, holding it so Gabby could go in first.

"So chivalrous." Gabby tossed a playful glance over her shoulder.

She was obviously being playful, but Jude took the comment to heart. "Do you want chivalry?"

Gabby turned fully, folding her arms and jutting her hip. "Do I seem like the kind of woman who needs it?"

Jude took a moment to appreciate the perfection standing before her. Despite the quiver in her chest telling her this was a much bigger deal than she wanted it to be, her confidence grew. "You don't need it. But needing it and wanting it every now and then aren't the same thing."

Gabby lifted her chin slightly and smiled. "Smooth."

"I'm not trying to be." She really wasn't.

"It's not a bad thing. I just wasn't expecting it."

She dropped the key card on the dresser and set her wallet next to it. "No? What were you expecting?"

"I'm pretty sure that's a trick question."

"Why? Because you expected me to be as bumbling and awkward as I am attempting a reverse-spin combination?"

Gabby laughed. God, she had a sexy laugh. "See? Trick question. If I say yes, I'm insulting you. If I say no, you're probably going to assume something worse."

Was Gabby nervous? Fascinating. "Okay. How about you tell me what you want, then, instead of what you were expecting?"

Gabby's shoulders rose, then fell. "I want you. This. Tonight. I'm still not convinced it's a good idea, but I want it."

"That's pretty general, but I'll take it."

A more subtle shrug this time. "I prefer to think of it as spontaneous. If you don't get bogged down in wanting things to go a certain way, it's easier to avoid disappointment."

Gabby's tone was casual, but like before, something about the comment struck her. For all her talk of relaxing and letting go, part of Gabby's free spirit was self-protection. She might not want to admit it, or even see it that way, but it resonated deeply with Jude. Of course, little dampened the mood more than a heart-to-heart about fears and disappointment, so she filed it away for another time. "You'll have to give me feedback, then, so I know if I'm doing it right."

That got her another laugh. "We both know I'm not shy when it comes to that."

For some reason, having Gabby put her in the driver's seat made her feel bold. Not boardroom confident, maybe, but a hell of a lot more than she was on the dance floor. She lifted her chin. "I hope I don't regret asking for it."

Gabby smirked. "You'll be just fine."

If a small part of her wanted to toss Gabby onto the bed and devour her, the larger part had more restraint. After all, they'd hardly even kissed. Even without all the nerves, she wanted to give them a moment to settle into each other, into what they were about to do.

She slipped off her jacket and draped it over a chair, then crossed the room to where Gabby stood. She took a moment to appreciate just how gorgeous Gabby looked in her dress, since hopefully she wouldn't be wearing it for long. Gabby gazed at her with a mixture of amusement and desire. It was all the invitation she needed.

Unlike the kiss in the bar, Jude controlled the pace of this one. She started slow, wanting to savor the taste and texture of Gabby's mouth. So much better than she'd imagined and yet not nearly enough.

She angled her head to take them deeper. Gabby gripped her arm and followed her lead. Jude put one hand on the back of Gabby's neck, the other around her waist, pulling her close. The position was just similar enough to their dance posture that it hit her how many times she'd wanted to do this during lessons and rehearsals. Had Gabby wanted that, too?

Either way, Gabby was definitely on board now. Her chest pressed into Jude's suggestively, and her tongue teased and tormented. And the little noises? God, they were enough to unravel her.

She eased the zipper down the back of Gabby's dress, allowing her fingers to dip below the loosened fabric and skim along Gabby's shoulder blade. Rather than satisfy her need to feel Gabby's skin, the touch only intensified it. She pushed the fabric from Gabby's shoulders. The dress slinked down Gabby's torso but caught on the luscious curve of her hips.

"Here, let me get that." She tugged gently on the fabric, and it slid to the ground, pooling at Gabby's feet. She took Gabby's hands in hers and stepped back to appreciate the view.

Gabby smirked. "You're wearing a hell of a lot more clothes than I am."

Jude dropped Gabby's hands and held her arms wide. "Well, we don't want that."

"Yeah." Gabby reached out and loosened her tie. "Fair's fair."

Gabby's fingers moved as skillfully as the rest of her, making quick work of Jude's tie, cuff links, and shirt. Watching her was hypnotic, interspersed with small jolts of electricity every time skin grazed skin. "You're good at this," she managed to say.

"Lots of costume changes," Gabby said with a wink.

"I appreciate that answer, even if it's only partially true."

"Mostly." Gabby tipped her head playfully, then pointed at Jude's undershirt. "And I appreciate that. Very old school."

"It's nice to know some of my old-fashioned sensibilities appeal."

"How about classic? It has a much nicer ring."

Jude smiled. "I can get behind that."

"Oh, good." Gabby reached for Jude's belt next, threatening to short-circuit her brain. "I'm hoping you'll do some very not old-fashioned things to me in that big, beautiful bed."

In part because she wanted to keep Gabby on her toes and in part because she didn't think she could tolerate another minute of not pressing her body to Gabby's, Jude wrapped her arms around her and, with a single step, sent them both tumbling to the bed. Despite her reputation of not being the most graceful, she managed to turn so she was flat, and Gabby landed half next to and half on top of her.

"Again, smooth." Gabby's eyes danced with humor.

As good as it looked on her, Jude wanted to replace amusement with something else entirely. She brought her hand to the back of Gabby's neck and pulled her in for a kiss. And when Gabby's lips parted and invited her in, she didn't even try to resist.

When she finally eased away—as much to catch her breath as make sure they were on the same page—Gabby's eyes had gone dark with desire. *There. That was better.*

Without asking if it was okay, she reached behind Gabby and flicked her bra open. She half expected another jab, but Gabby's smile was much more *yes, please* than gentle tease. She slid the bra away and allowed herself a moment to simply enjoy the perfection of Gabby's full breasts and dark nipples.

She rolled so that their positions were reversed, with Gabby on her back and Jude braced over her. She took one, then the other of Gabby's nipples into her mouth, homing in on every arch of Gabby's back, every sigh. Without stopping, she ran her hand up and down Gabby's torso, over her belly, and across her thighs. Gabby's sighs turned into whimpers. She opened her legs and thrust her hips slightly, the sexiest form of consent Jude's imagination could conjure.

It would have been easy enough to shove Gabby's barely existent panties to the side, but she didn't want to. She wanted to feel every inch of Gabby, without even a stitch of fabric between them. She sat up just enough to work them down Gabby's legs, returning before Gabby could utter a word of protest. "Now, where was I?"

She'd planned to go slow, to give them both a chance to settle into what they were doing. But Gabby was hot and wet, and Jude's plan, along with most of her self-control, evaporated. She traced her fingers along either side of Gabby's clit, then squarely over her hard center. Gabby gasped and arched—graceful, sensual, perfect.

She continued to stroke, and Gabby continued to move under her, grasping her shoulder with one hand and scratching lightly on the back of her neck with the other. Gabby seemed to melt into her and guide her all at once. Just like on the dance floor.

"More. Please."

Gabby's whispered demand sent her to a plane she wasn't sure existed. She slid one and then a second finger into Gabby and realized, no, this was the plane of pleasure she wasn't sure existed. "Fuck."

Before she could apologize for the expletive, Gabby smiled against her neck. "Yes, please."

What was it about a woman saying *please* in bed that sent her into orbit? Rather than wasting time trying to figure it out, she obliged. Slowly at first, so she could bask in the way Gabby rose to meet her, pulled her fingers in.

But Gabby had other ideas. She moved against Jude with some inexplicable mix of intention and abandon. She locked eyes with Jude and, without words, made her desires perfectly clear.

Time seemed to spin out and stop at the same time. She lost

herself in the way Gabby said her name, the way she said yes, over and over. When Gabby arched against her and paused, Jude held her breath. When Gabby's body sagged, muscles trembling, Jude quivered.

After a minute, Gabby let out a sigh and opened her eyes. "That was amazing."

She said it so casually, seemed so relaxed, it was all Jude could do not to laugh. "I'm pretty sure you're the amazing one."

Gabby rolled onto her side and poked a finger lightly to Jude's chest. "We can both be amazing. That's the beauty of it."

Jude flopped onto her back. "No argument here."

"Good. I'd hate for you to be contrary before I go down on you."

Jude made to sit up. "You don't have to—"

Once again, Gabby pressed a finger to the center of her chest. "Let me."

Jude allowed her head to fall back as Gabby moved along her. She settled herself between Jude's legs and looked up at her with a knowing smile. The combination alone was nearly enough to send her tumbling into orgasm, but she managed to hold back. She swallowed, reminded herself to breathe, and tried to imprint every detail of the moment into her memory.

"Mmm. That's better."

Gabby's mouth was just like the rest of her—firm yet soft, confident, sure. It took mere seconds for Jude to lose all grip on rational thought or the ability to formulate words. Fortunately, Gabby didn't seem to need them. She coaxed Jude closer and closer to the precipice, only to pull her back from the edge and do it all over again. And just when Jude hit the point of thinking she couldn't take much more, that she'd have to beg, Gabby guided her there and over.

Most of the time, her orgasms were quick, a release of pent-up pressure that proved satisfying, if not inspiring. This was different. It reminded her of the crescendo of a song, the dramatic finale at the end of their dance. A perfect culmination that left her breathless and a bit in awe.

Gabby crawled up the bed and kissed her. "That was fantastic."

Jude nodded and tried to formulate words while Gabby settled in next to her. "I think that's what I'm supposed to say."

Gabby lifted her head from Jude's shoulder and smirked. "We can be of the same mind, you know."

Jude kissed her and went for a smirk of her own. "I've heard that before."

"Whoever said it sounds really smart. You should listen to her."

She chuckled. "I probably should."

Gabby settled back in next to her. "Thank you for asking me on a real date."

She kissed the top of Gabby's head and let out a contented sigh, unsure of when she'd had a more perfect night. "Thank you for saying yes."

CHAPTER NINE

Gabby woke with that unsettling sensation of not knowing where she was. She took in the crisp hotel linens and artful decor. With it, the details of what she'd been doing in those sheets a few hours before hit her. Right.

She reached across the bed in search of Jude but found the spot next to her empty and cool. Alone or alone alone? She sat up to find all signs of Jude gone—even the coat she'd tossed on the chair when they'd come in.

She shouldn't feel disappointed, but she did. Silly really. It was a Friday morning, and Jude likely had to work. Still, a note would have been nice.

As she tried to make peace with not getting even that, she spotted a folded piece of paper on the dresser. Happy she no longer needed to, she climbed out of bed and padded over. When she picked it up, three folded twenties fell to the floor.

> *Sorry to sneak out, but you're cute when you're asleep. Room paid up and checkout extended till noon. Have a lazy morning if you can. Money is for an Uber, or buy yourself a little something pretty. After last night, you earned it.—J*

Happiness gave way to a sinking feeling, which quickly turned into a churn that threatened to have her running for the bathroom. Of all the insulting, demeaning, and otherwise offensive things Jude coulld have come up with, leaving money took top prize. Well, money paired with the you-earned-it comment. What the actual fuck?

She read the note again, balled it into a tight wad, and threw it in the garbage. A second later, she fished it out so she could tear it into tiny pieces, then returned it to the trash can. She scanned the room. She didn't usually have the urge to throw things, but this morning wasn't shaping up to be usual. Knowing the damage would be billed to Jude made her feel petty instead of vindictive.

She let out a groan and stalked around the room, gathering her discarded clothes, before realizing she needed to pee. In the bathroom, the gorgeous marble shower reminded her how much she'd been looking forward to using it. But all she could think about now was escape.

After pulling on her clothes from the night before, she picked up her purse and checked her phone. A teasing text from Shantal appeared on her home screen, but not a word from Jude. Another string of expletives escaped, this time out loud. She ignored the text, at least for now, and ordered a rideshare. She had half a mind to take the money so she could throw it in Jude's face, but she tucked it with the twenty Jude had left for the housekeeping staff instead.

On the way home, she drafted and deleted a dozen scathing messages to Jude. No, this was a conversation to have in person. And since the last thing she wanted was Jude showing up at her house to pick her up for the ball, it was going to have to happen immediately. Well, after a shower at least. It wasn't her style to show up at someone's workplace, but Jude hadn't left her much choice.

By the time she was in the elevator up to Jude's office, the heat of her initial anger had faded. The indignation remained, though. And, perhaps worst of all, the humiliation. If it hadn't been for that, she might have gone back the way she'd come and settled for the silent treatment.

When the elevator door opened, she got off and looked around. To her left, an accounting firm. No, thank you. To her right, logos for an attorney's office and Benoit Capital. Bingo.

She wasn't sure what she expected, but the casual elegance of Jude's reception area wasn't it.

"May I help you?" The greeting came from a good-looking nonbinary person in a tweed blazer.

Her initial surprise at not seeing Muriel behind the desk gave way to an extra layer of indignation. Of course Jude would have two assistants. Or maybe she went through assistants that quickly and Muriel was long gone. "I'm looking for Jude Benoit."

"Well, you're in the right place. Do you have an appointment?"

"No, but Jude is a"—what?—"a friend." The word left a bad taste in her mouth, but it was more likely to get her access to Jude than the truth.

"I'll see if she's free. Can I get your name?" The friendliness of the question and the bright smile told her Jude didn't often have angry women storming into her office.

"Gabriella Viard." She lifted her chin, slightly annoyed with herself for using her formal name. "And thank you."

They picked up the phone, and she resisted the urge to pace around like a caged tiger. Instead, she took a seat in one of the wing chairs in the waiting area and tried to ignore the way the leather felt like butter.

"Jude will be right out."

Before she could offer to show herself back, a frosted-glass door opened, and Jude appeared. "Gabby."

The bright smile and warmth in Jude's voice made it clear she was happy to see her. And oblivious to the fact that Gabby was upset. "We need to talk."

The universal meaning of the phrase landed, and Jude frowned. "Okay. Um, come on back to my office."

Part of her wished she were the sort of woman to cause a scene, to embarrass Jude in front of her employee. She wasn't though, not even a little. She followed Jude into a spacious office that had far more personality than she wanted to give Jude credit for.

"This is a pleasant surprise."

For some reason, the cluelessness made her anger surge. "I'm sure the help doesn't make a habit of showing up at your office very often. You probably prefer to keep it all separate."

"What?" Jude looked genuinely confused.

"That's what I am, isn't it? I mean, that's why you left money on the dresser. A tip for good service."

She had the pleasure of watching Jude blanch. "That's not—"

"Isn't it? All that talk about being friends or, God forbid, dating for real. It was all bullshit."

"That's not true."

"Oh, but it is. I'm not sure if you did it on purpose or if you wanted to mean it in the moment, but I never stopped being someone you hired. Which, honestly, I might not have minded so much if we hadn't gone to bed together."

Jude's mouth opened and closed a few times. She had a feeling it wasn't very often Jude Benoit was rendered speechless. It was damning, but satisfying in a way.

"I'll see myself out."

"Gabby, wait."

She paused, more reflex than intention.

"It felt rude to just go and leave you stranded. I was trying to be nice."

Somehow, clumsily condescending grated on her even more than straight-up jerk would have. "Nice is how you should treat the server at a restaurant, so you've just proved my point."

"I didn't mean—"

"I don't care what you did or didn't mean, Jude. I just know how you made me feel. And I feel shitty."

She'd planned to storm out, but regret more than indignation moved her feet out of Jude's office. She was so focused on getting out that she almost plowed into someone in the short hall. She looked up to apologize and found herself face-to-face with Muriel.

"Please tell me you're here for a rehearsal. I'm dying to watch."

Not twenty-four hours ago, the comment would have made her laugh. Now, it made her feel like a fool. An angry fool, but a fool nonetheless. "You might not want to waste your time talking to me and start finding your boss a new partner."

A weak comeback, to be sure, but she wasn't keeping score. Without waiting to see if Muriel had a reply, she kept walking—out of the office, out of the building, and as far out of Jude's life as possible.

❖

Muriel let out a long-suffering sigh. "What did you do?"

Jude scowled. "Why do you assume I did something wrong?"

Muriel folded her arms and stood there, not speaking.

"I took Gabby to the Artemis banquet last night, and we slept together." Literally one of the best nights of her life. Like, still had her body humming if she let herself think about it. And she'd managed to fuck it all up.

"And? Were you that terrible in bed, or did you stick your foot in your mouth afterward?"

Funny, for as awful as those two things sounded, she'd take either over what had happened. "Neither."

"So, again, what did you do?"

"Well, I'm pretty sure sleeping together in the first place wasn't the best idea." Though she couldn't bring herself to regret it. Well, at least that part of it.

"Yeah, but Gabby isn't the sort of woman who does anything she doesn't want to. I may have only met her once, but I got that vibe loud and clear."

Jude blew out a breath. "I left, okay? I left this morning before she woke up."

"Jesus Christ, Jude. Did you not even leave a note?"

"Ha." She thought she'd done so much better than that.

"Is that a yes or a no? I don't know how to interpret this version of self-loathing."

Another breath, but this one came out as a growl. "I had an early meeting and tried to be thoughtful but managed to make her feel like a hooker."

Muriel was generally unflappable, yet her eyes got huge. "Oh, my God. It is like *Pretty Woman*."

Their conversation from a couple of weeks ago came crashing back. "It's nothing like *Pretty Woman*."

"I'll be the judge of that. Tell me everything."

She did. Arranging late checkout, paying for the room, leaving money for Gabby to take an Uber or whatever home. And the note, the one she'd meant to be lighthearted but turned out to be so very wrong. The entire time, Muriel just stood there, shaking her head.

After she'd finished, Muriel made a face that seemed to hold as much pity as it did judgment. "The cab fare did it. That's totally insulting."

Jude stuck out her hands in exasperation. Why was she the only one who got it? "But she rode with me. It would have been rude to leave her stranded there."

"One, you implied she doesn't have the means to get her own

ride home. That's a condescending, rich-person, dick move. Two, you made it seem like spending the night with you was something she felt pressured to do and not something she chose based on her own free will and desire. And three, you never talk about someone earning anything after sleeping with you. If I have to explain that one to you, you deserve everything Gabby laid on you and more."

Ugh. "I get it, loud and clear. You have to know I didn't mean it that way. I was talking about the dinner and the mingling and stuff."

Muriel rolled her eyes. "Of course I do. You have a heart of gold. You're an idiot when it comes to women, but your intentions are always good."

At this point, the remark was a small consolation, but she'd take what she could get. Even with the "idiot" comment. "Thank you."

"You in love with her?"

"Can we not go there, please? Today has already sucked enough."

"You know saying that answers the question, right?"

Sigh. *Yeah.* "I still don't want to talk about it."

Muriel tipped her head back and forth. "Okay. Let's talk about the ball instead. What are you going to do?"

She scrubbed a hand over her face. The ball was at once the biggest and the least of her problems. "I don't know. Do you know how to rumba?"

Muriel didn't answer right away, and Jude imagined her debating whether to go with the sarcastic retort or the gentle letdown. But then she angled her head slightly. "As a matter of fact, I do."

"Are you saying that to rub it in or because you would consider saving my ass?" Because, with Muriel, it could go either way. Not with stuff that really mattered, but this was a gray area.

Muriel pressed a hand to her chest. "That hurts, Jude."

For the life of her, she couldn't tell if Muriel was teasing her or genuinely hurt. And since she seemed to have completely lost the ability to say the right thing to a woman, it was anyone's guess. "I'm sorry. I didn't—"

"I'm kidding. Well, mostly kidding. You know I've got your back."

A tiny amount of the pressure in her chest eased. "Yeah, but you also believe in making me suffer when I deserve it."

That got her a smile. "True. Honestly, though. Aren't you even going to try to make things right with Gabby?"

It was clear Muriel was no longer talking about the ball or her dance partner. She considered Muriel's earlier question, the one about whether she was in love with Gabby. And though she wasn't quite ready to own all the ramifications of the answer being yes, it didn't make it any less so. "I'm not sure I can, but I plan to try."

"And admit this is about Gabby and not about some silly dance routine."

God, the woman was relentless. "You realize I should say no on principle."

"But I just offered to be your backup date, so you owe me."

Touché. "I owe you a lot more than confessing my feelings for another woman."

"Yeah, but that's what I want."

In spite of the colossal mess she'd made of things, Jude smiled. "Fine. I'm in love with her."

"It's so romantic."

She shook her head. "It's only romantic if it works."

"Oh, it's going to work." Muriel smirked. "Haven't you seen the end of *Pretty Woman*?"

She found about a thousand flaws with that argument, ranging from real life not working like the movies to the fact that Gabby wasn't a sex worker to begin with. But, in spite of all that, she really wanted to be optimistic, and she could use all the help she could get. "So, what do I do?"

"Well, you're going to start with flowers."

Chapter Ten

Shantal closed the door and came into the living room bearing a vase overflowing with flowers. "Tulips this time."

Gabby closed her eyes for a second and let out a sigh. She hadn't even arrived home before the first delivery. Roses first, followed by sunflowers, then gerbera daisies. And now tulips. Each bouquet included a card that read simply: *I was an ass and I'm sorry.*

"This is some pretty next-level groveling." Shantal set the vase on the coffee table, since all the other tables already had an arrangement. "What are you going to do?"

Her initial plan had been to ignore. It worked with the first delivery and even the second. But now that they were on number four and Jude's apologies continued, her resolve had begun to waver. "I don't know."

"If a guy pulled this on a straight girl, she'd be engaged to him by now."

She shook her head. "Don't be mean. Straight girls have standards, too."

"Okay, fine. If some hot dyke sent me flowers every hour on the hour to apologize for something, I'd sure as hell have kissed and made up by now, too."

She sniffed. "Have a little self-respect."

Shantal flopped onto the sofa. "You're so fucking stubborn. I know what she said was awful, but she seems to feel pretty bad about it."

"I'm sure she does." That wasn't the problem. "But that doesn't change the way she sees me, sees our relationship."

"Yeah, but maybe she doesn't view you that way, and she was just an idiot who stuck her foot in her mouth and can't get out of her own way."

The thought had occurred to her, but she hadn't let it take hold. That would make her go soft, and she wasn't ready to do that. And, to be honest, she wasn't sure she wanted to be ready. "And what if she's just groveling so I don't leave her high and dry?"

Shantal winced. "Yeah. There's that. Are you going to?"

She hadn't decided about that, either. On one hand, she had no desire to see Jude. On the other, agreeing to be Jude's partner had nothing to do with them dating or sleeping together or anything else. Sure, there'd been the premise of friendship, but at the time, saying yes had been a professional decision. It made her job easier and might garner her some free publicity. Backing out would be unprofessional. Regardless of her feelings about Jude, she had very strong feelings about being unprofessional.

"Aren't you going to read the card?"

She shrugged. "They've all said the same thing."

Shantal plucked the envelope from the plastic clip nestled among the flowers and slipped out the card. "You might want to read this one."

Shantal handed it to her and she skimmed the words, then read them again. And again after that.

For the record, I'm not apologizing so you'll dance with me.

"Well?"

"What if she's just saying that so I won't think that's what she's doing?"

Shantal let out a low whistle. "Damn, woman. You're tough."

She was. She'd let her guard down, and somewhere along the way she'd developed feelings for Jude. Not platonic feelings, either. And that made everything about the current situation a thousand times worse.

"You wanna talk about it?"

She let out a sniff. "Not really."

"You want a drink?"

Kind of. "I've got a class this afternoon."

Shantal frowned. "That's too bad."

She hefted herself from the sofa. "No. It's exactly what I need to clear my head and not think about this for more than five minutes."

"You like her, don't you?"

Ugh.

"You don't have to tell me, but I can see it on your face."

"Nothing about her is my type. You realize that, right?" Telling herself that had done little to change things.

Shantal grinned. "Are you trying to convince me or yourself?"

"Shut up." The comment only made Shantal laugh, which in turn made her laugh.

"How far gone are you?"

"Too far, girl. Way too fucking far." Even as she said that, it hit her that she was making too much of it. She didn't get wound up over relationships. They either were or they weren't; she enjoyed them or she walked away. She just needed to figure out which side of the coin Jude was going to land on. Feeling slightly better, she headed to her room to dress for work. She'd get to the studio early and dance away her frustration and see what was left after that.

By the time she emerged, Shantal had moved to the kitchen and was chopping onions and a bell pepper. "I'm making gumbo, if you want some when you get home."

She closed her eyes and let out a happy sigh. "Yes, please and thank you."

Shantal smirked. "Good to know this Jude mess hasn't messed with your appetite."

"Nothing does that." She gave Shantal a hug from behind. "Thank you for listening to me whine."

"You didn't whine. You processed your feelings. It's a thing."

"Ha-ha." Before she could formulate more of a comeback, the doorbell rang.

Shantal glanced at her watch. "Either she's picking up the pace or this one's early."

"It could be anyone, you know." She knew it wasn't.

"Mm-hmm."

Gabby headed to the front door. The guy standing on the other side wore the uniform of a delivery person but held no bouquet of flowers. "Gabriella Viard?"

Why did she have the feeling she was being served? "That's me."

He handed her an envelope. "Have a nice day."

The only thing on the front of the envelope was her first name, written by hand. "Um, thanks. You, too."

She closed the door and turned to find Shantal hovering in the doorway to the kitchen. "Where are the flowers? You didn't refuse them, did you?"

"No flowers. Just this." She held up the card.

Shantal hurried over. "Is that her handwriting? Did she hire a courier to deliver a handwritten note? That's pretty damn romantic."

Logic told her it had to be, though she realized now she'd never seen Jude's handwriting. "I don't know but probably?"

"Well, open it already."

"Oh, my God. You're so impatient."

Shantal shrugged and offered another grin in lieu of an apology. Gabby took a deep breath and slipped the very nice, very expensive piece of stationery from the envelope.

Dear Gabby,

I'm resisting showing up on your doorstep, but only because it seems creepy and aggressive given the circumstances. If you've gotten the flowers, you already know I'm sorry. But I'll say it again because it bears repeating. I'm sorry. I could swear up and down my intentions were good, but if my actions hurt you, it doesn't matter. I hope you'll give me the chance to apologize in person, to find a way to make it up to you. I don't expect to see you tonight, but I'm hopeful you'll consider seeing me after that. I care about you, but perhaps more importantly, I have the deepest respect for who you are and what you do. Thank you for bringing me out of my shell. And, again, I'm sorry.

Jude

She read the note a second time and then a third, at which point Shantal started shifting dramatically from foot to foot like a five-year-old needing to pee. She handed Shantal the paper, watching as she read.

"Damn. That's good."

"It is, isn't it?"

Shantal folded her arms. "You're going to give her another chance, aren't you? You have to."

She didn't have to, but she wanted to. "Maybe. Probably."

"Are you going tonight?"

She let out a sigh. "Yeah."

"Are you going to tell her, or are you going to make her sweat?"

While the latter was tempting, it wasn't her style. She picked up her phone and dashed off a text, hitting send before she could second-guess herself.

I'll see you tonight, but I'll meet you there. We'll see about the rest after.

Jude paced the length of her office while Muriel perched on the corner of her desk. They'd spent the better part of an hour attempting to rumba together with less-than-ideal results. Any illusions she had about being the one leading Gabby were long gone. Muriel, bless her, was proving more patient and more gracious than Jude probably deserved, but even that was wearing thin.

And then Gabby's text came through, throwing everything back into disarray. "Do you think she means it, or is she just saying she'll show up so she can *not* be there and stick it to me extra?"

Muriel made a face. "Hard to say."

Jude stopped long enough to give her an exasperated look. "Not helpful."

She resumed pacing, and Muriel drummed her fingers on the desk. "What exactly did she say again?"

Jude stopped once more. She pulled out her phone and read the text.

"And what did you say after?"

She blew out a breath. "I said, 'I'm profoundly grateful, but I hope you know I care about you more than the ball.'"

Muriel's expression confirmed it wasn't the greatest reply in the world but not the worst. "And she didn't answer you after that?"

She shook her head. "But she does teach a class this afternoon."

"Mm-hmm, mm-hmm. I'm going to say there's an eighty-five percent chance she shows up."

"Eighty-five? Where'd you get that number?"

Muriel shrugged. "I think it's likely, but ninety made it seem too much like a sure thing."

Jude frowned. "I hope you have a more thorough system for managing our investment portfolio."

"Are you complaining?"

"I really have a knack for saying all the wrong things to women, don't I?"

"Not always." Muriel smiled and stood. "I'll be dressed and ready to go at seven. I expect a limo."

"Wait, you're still coming?"

"We can't have you without a partner, even if the chances of it happening are slim. Besides, maybe I want to go."

She wasn't sure how she'd managed to luck out with Muriel, but she promised herself to be better at showing her appreciation, and not just with salary. "You are a goddess."

"I know." Muriel winked. "I also know you're going to give me the rest of the afternoon as personal time so I can shop for a dress that's not a decade old and get my hair done."

"Absolutely. That's a great idea." Jude nodded with more enthusiasm than was probably appropriate. "Not that you won't look fabulous no matter what. I just think you deserve whatever you want for covering my ass."

"Thank you." Muriel made to leave, but Jude called her back. "Yes?"

"Is it insulting if I tell you to expense everything?"

That got a chuckle. "Not at all."

She appreciated the answer, even if it left her slightly confused. "And why is that?"

Muriel rolled her eyes. "Because we aren't sleeping together."

"Oh. Right." God, she was bad at this.

Muriel went on her way, leaving Jude to slosh around in her own thoughts. What a roller coaster the last twenty-four hours had been. But even as she thought that, it hit her that she was the source of the turmoil. It didn't sit well, saying the wrong things and generally being so bad at something. It made her want to swear off relationships and focus on things she did well.

Yet even as those thoughts played in her mind on repeat, Gabby's words crept through. Gabby telling her to relax, to let go. Gabby insisting that doing things clumsily with heart often worked better than unfeeling precision. She'd meant it about dancing, of course, but something told her that Gabby's philosophy on life wasn't so very different. Jude had been suspicious at first, but Gabby's persistence had worked. She'd finally managed to shut off her brain enough to feel the music and trust her body to know what to do.

Last night had been like that, too. Once Gabby had made it clear she wanted Jude as much as Jude wanted her, she stopped overthinking. And the result had been, well, mind-blowing.

And then she'd gone and fucked it all up with trying to cover logistics instead of imagining how Gabby might feel and what she might want or need after waking up alone. What a fool.

Well, she'd learned her lesson. Hopefully, Gabby would give her another chance. And hopefully, with technically two dates now instead of one, she'd manage to pull off this damn dance, one way or the other.

CHAPTER ELEVEN

Jude sat in the back of the limo, her leg bouncing spastically. Muriel reached across the seat and squeezed her knee, not at all gently. "Ow."

"You have to stop that. You're driving me crazy."

She resisted the urge to resume fidgeting. "Should I have a drink? Maybe I should have a drink."

Muriel let out one of her long-suffering sighs. "You don't need one. You're fine. You handle multi-million-dollar acquisitions without batting an eye."

"This is different." She didn't even try to keep the whine out of her voice.

"You're being a baby. Toughen up, buttercup."

She attempted and failed to hold back a smile. "I'm overlooking your insubordination only because I know I'm being ridiculous."

Muriel angled her head slightly. "And this is different from how we do things every day how?"

She reached over and gave Muriel's hand a squeeze. "Thank you for coming."

Muriel shrugged. "We can't have you looking like a fool. It would be bad for business."

She knew it was more than that. Muriel did, too. But their dynamic didn't include getting sentimental about things. Fortunately, the limo pulled under the portico of the banquet hall, saving either of them from having to go there.

They'd no sooner checked their coats than Muriel's gaze shifted from Jude's face to something over her shoulder. "Oh, thank God."

Jude turned, and, as much as it was clichéd to say her heart stopped, she'd have sworn it did, only to restart and race like an engine revved too high. "Gabby."

Gabby gave her a quizzical look. "Why do you look surprised? I said I would be here."

"I was worried you'd think better of it and change your mind."

Gabby's eyes narrowed.

"Not because you would generally go back on your word, but because I might deserve that."

"Ah." Her features relaxed. "Well, I don't do vindictive, even if I might be tempted."

Jude nodded. "I appreciate that."

She returned her attention to Muriel. Even with paying for the gown and the trip to the salon, even with the fact they'd essentially planned this ahead of time, switching dates at this point felt like a jerk move. "I…"

When she didn't continue, Muriel angled her head. "No longer require my services."

The choice of words made Jude feel like the biggest possible asshole. It also gave her a flash of what her life might be like without Muriel in it. "No. I mean, I…You went to all this trouble. For me. I…"

Muriel pressed her lips together. For a split second, Jude thought she might be near tears. But then she laughed. Like, really and truly laughed. Given her track record lately, Jude wasn't sure if it was a good sign or a bad one. "And I'm thrilled to be off the hook."

"Oh."

Muriel's eyes grew huge. "Wait. Did you think I'd be disappointed?"

"Well."

More laughter. The kind that had Muriel doubled over and tears in her eyes. "You're something, Benoit. You know that?"

Again, she couldn't tell what Muriel actually meant. "So, we're good?"

Muriel righted herself. She took a deep breath and clapped a hand on Jude's shoulder. "I'm glad you're better with money than you are with feelings."

"Is that a compliment? I'm not sure that's a compliment."

Muriel shook her head. "I'll see you later, Boss." She offered

Gabby a look that had to be femme code for something. "She's all yours."

Jude returned her attention to Gabby. "Hi."

"Hi."

"I'm really glad you're here." She hesitated a moment before adding, "For a lot of reasons."

Gabby's expression remained passive. "We should probably talk about those reasons, but for the moment, we should focus on the dance."

She nodded more vigorously than was probably necessary. "Yes. I don't want to say I'm freaking out, but I'm definitely freaking out."

Gabby offered a smile, though it was hard to tell what feelings might be lurking behind it. "You got this."

More nodding. "I know."

"Know, but also feel. Remember?"

Right. She mustered a smile of her own. "Yes."

Gabby tipped her head to the main ballroom. "Shall we?"

The cocktail hour passed in a blur. The emcee came on to thank everyone for coming and pump up the parade the next day. She bantered with the crowd a bit, joking about the open bar and reminding folks that no one wanted to be riding a float with a hangover. And then she announced the court, culminating with Jude as Majesty.

She took Gabby's hand. The lights in the room dimmed, and they moved into position. Gabby's hand on her shoulder, her hand on Gabby's waist, Gabby's gaze steady on hers. The familiarity of their stance anchored her in the moment but also threw her back to the hours in the studio. She could do this.

Gabby smiled. "Relax, breathe. Feel the music, and don't forget to have fun."

She took a deep breath. The opening beats of the song pulsed through the room. And just like the last few times they rehearsed, she managed to do exactly that.

❖

The music ended, and Gabby let her body arch back and drape over Jude's extended arm. Applause and a few cheers filled the air. Jude blinked at her, clearly more in disbelief than victory. She smiled. "You did it."

Jude shook her head. "*We* did it."

Jude's features transformed, and the combination of joy and relief on her face melted her. Not that she wasn't already pretty melty over Jude. "Yes, *we*. Though you definitely worked harder for this."

"I'm just going to bask for a second." Jude closed her eyes.

"You deserve it." Seconds ticked by. "That said, are you going to help me up before the clapping stops and our exit gets a hell of a lot more awkward?"

Jude shook her head again.

"You should trust me on this one. There's nothing worse than—"

Jude's mouth covered hers, squelching any further protest. And then she didn't want to protest anymore. All she wanted to do was sink into that kiss and the feeling of Jude's arms around her.

It might have started as one of those make-a-point kind of kisses, but it morphed into something a whole lot hotter. The applause intensified, along with more cheers and a few whistles. Jude finally pulled away, and she opened her eyes. They remained in the middle of the dance floor, bathed in the spotlight. Was it the brightness that had her vision blurring? Or was it the kiss?

"Now I'll help you up," Jude said with a grin.

Jude levered her to her feet with at least as much finesse as they'd managed in practice, maybe more. Despite her early protests, Jude didn't hesitate to take a bow. Gabby did the same, and they made their way to the head table while the DJ announced the dance floor officially open. Dozens of gowned and tuxedoed women flooded the space, and the party began in earnest.

Just like at the dinner, Jude became the center of attention. Friends and colleagues and strangers made their way over to say nice things. She was pretty sure she even saw a couple of women slip Jude their number, which she found equal parts funny and insulting.

The night passed in a whir of dinner and drinks and dancing. A few people she knew were there, and she caught up with them, skirting questions about whether she was Jude's dance instructor or her girlfriend. She caught Jude watching her more than once, though she couldn't quite tell what was happening behind those intense green eyes.

When the party started to wind down, Jude snagged the chair

next to her and fixed her with an earnest look. "I know better than to presume you want to go home with me, but I do have a limo, and I'd love to give you a ride home so we have a few minutes of quiet to talk."

"Limo, huh?"

"I reserved it when I thought we were coming together, and then it was too late to cancel?" Jude offered a shrug.

"What about your backup date?" She couldn't really blame Jude for asking Muriel to come along, but she felt a lingering weirdness about it.

"She apparently bumped into an old flame. She texted me an hour ago telling me my services, ride or otherwise, were no longer needed."

She laughed, both at the choice of phrase and the idea of the seemingly strait-laced Muriel going home with someone. "Well, then."

"So, is that a yes?"

"Yes."

A few minutes later, she found herself in the back of the plushest limo she'd ever seen. Not that she'd had a lot of rides in limos.

Jude settled in, only to sit forward again. "Would you like something to drink? Champagne? Water?"

She didn't normally find nervousness endearing, but she appreciated it in the moment. "I'm good, thanks."

Jude sat back, then turned in the seat to face her. "I hope you didn't show up tonight because you felt sorry for me."

A smile tugged at the corners of her mouth. "Maybe a little."

"I mean, to be fair, it would have been a disaster without you. Poor Muriel was a good sport about it, but apparently you only let me think I'm leading."

"Well…" She didn't want Jude to take any teasing the wrong way.

Jude raised both hands in a show of concession. "I have no illusions."

"I hope you know I would have shown up no matter what. We had a professional arrangement, and I wouldn't have left you in the lurch because I was mad at you."

Jude's hands dropped, along with her gaze. "Does that mean you're still mad at me?"

She took a deep breath. "You do grovel exceptionally well."

Jude looked up, expression hopeful. "It's the least I can do for being an exceptional ass."

"It is."

"So, you forgive me?"

She wanted to explain to Jude why she reacted the way she did, why she was so sensitive to the kinds of things Jude's actions implied. But tonight wasn't that night. "I do."

Jude blew out a breath and her shoulders relaxed. "Thank you."

"As for the rest of it—"

"I realize now it was presumptuous of me to kiss you out there. I'm sorry for that." Jude shook her head, her expression grave.

"You don't need to apologize."

"Still. My brain really wasn't working at that point."

She couldn't help but laugh. "You know, you might do better if you listened to your brain a little less."

Jude winced slightly. "And my heart a little more?"

She wouldn't have used the word *heart*, not after the day they'd had. But that's what she'd meant, what she'd been trying to convince Jude of all along. "Something like that."

"Well, in that case, you should probably know that I've fallen in love with you."

Her heart tripped in her chest even as the rest of her hesitated, searching Jude's face for a meaning other than the obvious one. "You have?"

"I know it's kind of fast, but you make me feel things I'd forgotten how to feel. I love spending time with you, but it's more than that. It's like—I know this is going to sound cheesy—but it's like I like myself better when I'm with you."

"I love you, too."

"And I know it's a lot to spring on you after—wait. What?"

She took a deep breath. Not what she'd planned to say tonight, but nothing with Jude seemed to go how she thought it would. "I said I love you, too."

Jude blinked. Much like when they finished their dance, her eyes revealed as much disbelief as anything else. "Really?"

"It came as a surprise to me, too, but there it is." She might not have expected it, but she wasn't the sort of person to deny it.

Jude smiled. "Wow."

She nodded. "Yeah."

"So, now what?"

It was nice that, after everything, Jude would defer to her. "Well, maybe we start with telling the driver to take us both to your place."

"Oh, I like the sound of that." Without hesitating, Jude pressed the button that lowered the glass separating the front seat and relayed the change of plans. She settled back and took Gabby's hand, placing a kiss on each of her knuckles. "Thank you for giving me another chance."

She wouldn't have classified it as that, but it essentially was. "Things rarely go smoothly the first time through."

Jude nodded. "A wise woman told me that once."

She remembered the conversation, from one of their first lessons, and smiled. "You should probably listen to her."

"I plan to."

"Jude?"

"Yeah?"

"You should kiss me now."

Jude's gaze raked over her, like she was trying to take in every inch of her. And then she did.

Just As You Are

Angie Williams

CHAPTER ONE

Dylan checked the address in her email once more. She hated first dates. She probably wouldn't even bother if her best friend hadn't pushed her to try a dating app. Maybe this time would be different? The last first date she'd had was with her ex-girlfriend Michelle.

Now, two years later, Dylan found herself sitting in her car on a warm Northern California evening, trying to dredge up enough courage to put herself out there again. She hoped this time would be different. She wasn't exactly sure what she expected to happen, but whatever her future held, she would have to take the first step. Dylan startled when the phone in her pocket buzzed.

"Why are you calling me? I'm on a date, Val."

"Are you on a date, or are you sitting in your car, staring at the poor woman's front door?"

She sighed. Sometimes Dylan wished Val didn't know her so well. "I was just about to get out of the car before my meddling best friend interrupted me."

Val laughed. "Sure you were. Take a deep breath."

"I don't need—"

"Do it, Dyl. Close your eyes. Take a deep breath, and envision yourself being your charming self on this date."

"I don't want to do your therapist mumbo jumbo right now, Val."

"Close your eyes, take a deep breath, and envision yourself being your charming self on this date."

"Christ." Dylan leaned her head against the back of the seat and did as she was told. "I really hate it when you do this."

"You know it helps, so stop complaining."

Dylan let out a slow breath and pictured herself sitting at a table with her date. Carrie was laughing at something she had said, which made her feel good. The tension in her shoulders slowly relaxed. Most of the communication between them had been through email and texts since Carrie had reached out to her through the dating app they both used. It was challenging to get a sense of someone through written communication, but she could tell she was smart, funny, and a genuinely good person. The few photos Carrie had shared on her dating profile had piqued Dylan's interest right away. Average height with brown, wavy hair and green eyes. Things had gradually become more and more flirty as Dylan had let her guard down.

"Feeling any better?"

She hated to admit that Val was right, but the exercise had helped. "Yeah, a little. Thanks, man."

"You're welcome. Now repeat after me. Carrie isn't Michelle."

"Val—"

"Come on, Dyl. Humor me. Carrie isn't Michelle."

Dylan sighed. "Carrie isn't Michelle."

"She isn't going to make me feel like shit just because I don't fit her definition of who a butch lesbian should be."

"Jesus. That's kind of harsh."

"Harsh but accurate. Come on. I'm enough for Carrie, and she's not going to want me to be anything other than who I am."

"That's a lot to repeat."

The sound of Val's quiet laughter lifted Dylan's spirits. "You're going to be okay, man. It's going to be great."

The light on Carrie's front porch came on, and Dylan glanced at the clock on her dash. "Shit. If I don't go, I'm going to be late."

"You got this."

"I got this. Thanks, Val."

"Good luck."

Dylan tucked the phone back into her pocket, picked up the bouquet from the passenger seat, and headed toward the door. The brick path that led up to Carrie's porch was bordered with flowers, and Dylan smiled at the little feminine touches. She'd always been more masculine herself but was drawn to feminine women. Not delicate ones necessarily. She appreciated a woman who was very much in touch with her femininity but wasn't the damsel-in-distress type.

When she finally reached the door, she hesitated. She'd enjoyed getting to know Carrie so much, and this next step was difficult. What if Carrie was disappointed? She was confident in almost every other area of her life, but this was her weakness. Having a father and then a girlfriend who only ever told her she wasn't enough had left her damaged and insecure. She worried she wasn't the person she advertised herself to be because she wasn't good at things they had decided she should be good at. What if Carrie felt the same way? What if Carrie—

"Hey," Carrie said. Dylan looked into Carrie's eyes for the first time and found only warmth.

"Hey, I…these are for you."

Carrie smiled and reached for the flowers Dylan offered. "Thank you. They're beautiful. Sorry I startled you. I saw you on my security camera and was beginning to wonder if you had second thoughts."

"No. Sorry. No second thoughts."

"Good. Come on in." Carrie stepped back to allow Dylan into her home.

"Thanks. You look beautiful, by the way." Dylan's heart beat faster as they stepped into the light of the hall and she was able to see her more clearly. Carrie was stunning in a simple floral dress, light makeup, and no shoes. She slid her hands into her pockets to control the urge to touch her. It was strange to get to know someone online before actually meeting them in person. An established comfort comes from chatting with someone for hours, but it's still like you're complete strangers when you're finally together.

Carrie pulled Dylan down to place a soft kiss on her cheek. "Thank you again for these incredible flowers, and you look very handsome." Dylan touched her cheek where she'd been kissed and smiled. So far, so good.

"I was worried the suit jacket and tie would be too much, but my best friend talked me into it." Val had convinced her if she wore jeans underneath, she would be dressed down enough to not look like she was trying too hard but dressed up enough to look like she cared about how she looked.

"Your best friend has good taste. Let's go into the kitchen so I can put these flowers in a vase."

Dylan followed her through an arch into her open-concept home.

The vaulted ceilings made it seem much larger than it probably was, but the custom trim made it feel welcoming. "I love your house. Have you lived here long?" Dylan sat in a chair and watched as Carrie busied herself with the flowers. Her hands were small and looked delicate but strong. She assumed they'd have to be since Carrie had told her she played guitar in a band.

"I've been here, gosh, three years now. I bought it from my grandma when she moved into a retirement community with some of her friends. My grandparents took good care of it, but it hadn't been updated in about two decades. I pretty much had to start from scratch, but I'm proud of the progress so far."

"Mind if I..."

"Nope. Snoop away," Carrie said with a wink.

Dylan noticed a wall displaying what must have been at least fifteen guitars of all shapes and sizes. Some of them looked like styles she'd seen before, and some were quite beautiful. "These are gorgeous. How long have you been playing?"

Carrie pulled out a stepladder to retrieve a vase from a tall shelf in the kitchen. "Can I get that for you?" Dylan walked toward her, but she waved her off. "I've got it. Thanks. Ladders are a short girl's best friend." Carrie then poured water into the vase and began arranging the flowers. "I started playing when I was six. My dad played, and it was something we always did together. Something we still do, in fact. Do you play?"

"A little. I'm sure I'm not as good as you, but I can carry a tune. Maybe you and I can play together sometime?"

"I'd love that," Carrie said. "I think that'll do." She set the bouquet on the table and stood back to get a better look. "They're beautiful, Dylan. Absolutely perfect."

Dylan's chest swelled with pride. "I worried you might be disappointed they weren't roses, but even though I don't know you very well, you seemed like a wildflower-bouquet kind of girl to me."

"Sounds like you know me pretty well already. Ready to go?" Carrie slipped on a pair of high heels and picked up her purse from the hall table. "Oh, will this dress be okay for where we're going? You said Ca'Bianca, right?"

"You look absolutely beautiful. It's perfect." Dylan waited for Carrie to lock up, then offered her arm. When they reached the passenger-side door, she held it open and waited for Carrie to settle into her seat before jogging around to climb in herself.

"I know the freeway is the fastest way to get there, but since it's almost sunset and we have a little time until our reservation, would you mind if we took the scenic route?"

"I'd love that."

Dylan loved Northern California with its vineyards surrounded by modest mountain ranges. This time of year, the vines provided a carpet of green bordered by gently rolling hills of brown, with the occasional grouping of evergreens. She would never grow tired of this view. "I don't know if I've ever asked you where you're from. We've talked about so much, but that never came up."

"I grew up in Arizona, but I've been in California for ten years. I moved out here to help my grandma when my grandpa passed away."

At a fork in the road, Dylan took a left, which would put the view of the sun setting over the vineyards on Carrie's side of the car. "Beautiful, isn't it?"

Carrie sighed and snuggled into the seat, obviously enjoying the scenery. "It's gorgeous."

"Mind if we stop and watch the sunset? We're only a couple of minutes from the main event." Dylan drove a few feet farther until she found a space large enough to pull off the road and parked. "Should we get out?" she asked.

"Do you mind?"

"Not at all." Dylan came around to help Carrie from the car. The ground was a little uneven, so she wrapped her arm around her shoulders and guided them toward a large tree that had fallen over and provided the perfect place to sit. The summer's warmth had given way to cool evenings, so she removed her jacket and slipped it around Carrie's shoulders.

"Thanks," Carrie said as she gingerly sat on the log and rested her head on Dylan's shoulder.

"I wish we'd thought to bring your guitar. The only thing that could make this better would be a song." She was eager to hear Carrie play. They'd talked a little about her career as a musician, but Carrie had seemed hesitant to share too much. Dylan assumed she must be great since she did it for a living, but she couldn't wait to hear for herself. "Maybe next time we'll have a picnic, and you can bring it?"

Carrie smiled. "Maybe. That would be nice. We should bring two, so we can play together." Dylan's heart skipped when she pictured their next date. She was sure she'd absolutely embarrass herself struggling to keep up with a professional, but the thought of playing together made her smile.

They sat silently as the last of the day's light dimmed and left them in darkness under a blanket of stars. The warmth of Carrie's body as she snuggled close made Dylan smile. "This is really nice," Dylan said. Carrie kissed her gently on the lips and sighed. The last thing Dylan wanted to do was interrupt the perfect moment, but she knew they should leave for the restaurant or their table would be given away. "Ready to go?" she asked.

"I suppose." Carrie stood and held out a hand to help Dylan to her feet. "I'm having a really great time, Dylan. I've never had much luck with dating apps, but they just might have gotten this one right."

"I'd give this date five stars, no doubt," Dylan said.

"Five stars. Goodness. That's high praise. I'm reserving my final review for the end, but it's looking pretty spectacular so far."

"You're a tough critic."

Carrie laughed and climbed back into the car when Dylan held the door for her. "Not tough. I just want you to earn those stars."

"Challenge accepted." Dylan checked the time on her watch and calculated that they'd be a few minutes late to dinner. If this had been a date with her ex-girlfriend, Michelle, the tardiness would have inevitably led to an argument, where she would have certainly made Dylan feel like a complete failure for their delay.

But Carrie wasn't Michelle, and after a deep breath to calm her anxiety, Dylan jogged around the car and pulled back onto the road. The twists and turns were trickier in the dark, but Dylan did her best to drive safely without making them even later than they were. She'd always been a reasonably good—Bang!

Dylan held the steering wheel steady as the car fought for control. "What the hell?"

"I think you blew a tire."

"Fuck."

"It's no big deal. Pull over right here in this clearing. Grip the wheel. If there's sand, you can easily lose control."

Dylan steered onto the shoulder and brought them safely to a stop far enough away from the road to not need to worry about passing traffic. "Well, fuck. Excuse my language."

Carrie giggled. "Yeah. You don't need to worry about that with me. Good job handling the car. Some people completely freak out, and it will always win that battle."

The compliment was nice, but Dylan didn't know if Carrie was sincere or mocking her for not initially knowing it was a blown tire. She decided to not borrow trouble and give Carrie the benefit of the doubt. She hadn't done anything to indicate she was that kind of person, so Dylan had no reason to assume she meant it that way. With an exasperated breath, she pulled her phone from her pocket and searched through her contacts.

"Who are you calling?" Carrie asked.

"Roadside assistance. I'm really sorry about dinner. By the time they get out here, help with the tire, and we're back on our way, our reservations will be long gone. I promise I'll make it up to you."

Carrie bit her bottom lip and looked like she was doing her best not to say something.

"What?" Dylan asked. She braced herself for the judgment that was sure to come. Her chest tightened as she heard Michelle's voice in her mind, mocking her for not being the butch she outwardly projected herself to be. What a joke. She'd never be able to live up to the expectations she was sure Carrie also had for her.

"It's just...I was wondering why we don't change the tire ourselves. You have a spare, right? We could be back on the road in a few minutes if we work together. If we called the restaurant, we might even get them to hold our table."

Something inside Dylan broke. Maybe it was her patience, or perhaps it was her heart. She wasn't sure which was worse. Though Dylan was usually never quick to anger, the pity in Carrie's voice was the last straw.

"Because, Carrie, I pay roadside assistance for a reason. It's their job to do this stuff, so I don't have to. If a fancy dinner's that important to you, why don't I just give you the cash? You can take someone a little more capable next time."

Anger flashed in Carrie's eyes, and Dylan knew she'd struck a nerve. "A little more capable of what, Dylan? Manners? That's something you seem to be in short supply of. I'm happy I saw this side of you before things went any further. What a fucking disappointment." Carrie pulled her phone from her pocket. "There, my Uber driver will be here in..." she glanced at her phone, "five minutes, and then I'll be out of your hair forever."

Carrie's words were like a slap across her face. She hadn't done anything to deserve Dylan's wrath. She'd been nothing but sweet and kind and nothing like Michelle. Dylan had fucked up royally and wasn't sure how to fix it. "Carrie, I—"

"I don't want to hear it, Dylan. You have issues that have nothing to do with me, and it's not my job to fix you. I really liked you. Things could have been so good between us, but I won't tolerate disrespect. Not now and not ever." A woman in a Prius pulled up, and Carrie opened the door. "Are you going to be able to get home okay?"

Dylan stared silently as the world around her closed in. She took a deep breath and held up her phone. "Yeah, thanks. I'll call roadside assistance. Carrie, I'm really so—"

"Bye, Dylan. Take care of yourself." Carrie slid into the car's back seat and was gone before Dylan could completely process what had happened.

Chapter Two

The sound of pots clanging in the kitchen woke Carrie from a deep sleep. She'd had a little wine the night before to cool her frustration with the way the date ended and fell asleep on her couch. She needed a dog. If she had one, maybe she wouldn't feel this need to find someone else to be with. Surely a dog would be just as good as a girlfriend, and maybe better in some ways. She sighed and forced herself to investigate the noises.

"Jesus Christ," her best friend, Stacy, said when she plopped into a chair at the table. "What the hell happened to you?"

"I'm fine. Just a bad night."

Stacy turned off the burner and sat in a chair next to her at the table. "Carrie, sweetie, she didn't hurt you, did she?"

"No, no, no. Nothing like that. She was perfectly chivalrous. Well, in the beginning, at least."

Stacy stood and walked back to the stove to continue cooking breakfast. "Want to talk about it?"

"Do I have to?"

"It's the least you can do since I came over here to make you breakfast. Your text last night worried me."

"You asked me to tell you when I was home safe, and I texted so you wouldn't worry."

"You texted one word. *Home.* And then you wouldn't answer your phone when I called. Don't you think that's a little concerning after you were so excited to go out with this woman?"

"I'll talk if there's bacon." Carrie knew she sounded pathetic but honestly didn't care. She deserved to wallow in her sorrow for at least a few hours. She'd hoped Dylan would be different. They'd spent so much time talking and establishing the groundwork before they ever met in person, but it still wasn't enough.

Stacy pulled the tray of bacon from the oven and added a few pieces to Carrie's plate with some eggs and toast. "Here you go. Now start from the beginning. What happened?"

Carrie picked up a piece of bacon from her plate and savored the salty crunch while she tried to gather her thoughts about the night before.

"On the way to din—"

"From the beginning. Bacon, remember? You promised."

They'd been roommates for years, but Stacy had moved out when she and her girlfriend, Erica, found a place together on Carrie's block. The happy couple enjoyed their own space, but when Stacy's girlfriend, a Navy lieutenant commander, was deployed with her ship, Stacy often found herself back at Carrie's house for the company.

"Erica needs to come home so you have someone else to harass." Carrie dipped the corner of her toast in the egg yolk and swirled it around. "Fine. From the beginning." She described the events of the night before in as much detail as she could remember. Thinking back on the sweet little things Dylan did and said at the beginning of the date only made her feel even worse about the way it ended. What the hell had happened? She hadn't picked up on anything that would have prepared her for the meltdown over the flat tire.

"Doesn't she know what you do for a living?" Stacy asked. "It's never cool to be an asshole like that, but why in the world would someone not assume the girl who owns her own auto-repair shop would want to fix the tire herself?"

"Yeah, about that…"

"Carrie, why didn't you tell her?"

"You're going to think I'm dumb." Carrie covered her face to hide the blush warming her cheeks. She hadn't planned to not tell Dylan that she was a mechanic with her own shop, but when she'd mentioned her weekend gig as a musician in one of their early phone conversations, Dylan was so excited Carrie wanted to bask in the coolness.

Stacy pulled Carrie's hand from her face and held it. "Come on, Care. Wouldn't your professions be one of the first things you talked about? You're a badass mechanic with a successful small business you've always been so proud of."

"I know. I'm super proud of it, but when I told her I was in a band, she was just so excited. Her excitement tapped into my childhood dreams of being Taylor Swift, and I wanted to ride that wave for a bit. I'd planned to tell her at dinner, but we never got that far."

"So, you lied to her?"

"No. I never lied to her." Carrie pulled her hand from Stacy's and took a sip of her juice. "I told her I was in a local band. She's a big music fan, so we geeked out over that, and the garage day-job just never came up."

"It still doesn't explain why she freaked out about the tire thing."

Carrie picked up their empty plates and carried them to the sink. She thought there was more to Dylan's reaction but couldn't put her finger on it exactly. She seemed very defensive for some reason, which was the part Carrie couldn't explain. "Whatever set her off, it's over now." She placed the dishes in the dishwasher and turned to lean against the counter. "I think I'm going to get a dog."

Stacy rolled her eyes. "A dog is a great idea, but it's no substitute for a girlfriend. Not long term anyway. Maybe you should call her? You were so excited about this girl that I hate to see you write her off after one bad reaction."

"Don't you think I should take it as a warning? If she reacted that way after a flat tire, how's she going to react when something big happens? I don't need someone like that in my life."

Stacy's phone beeped, indicating she had a message. She smiled when she saw who it was. "I'm going to head home. Erica texted that they're pulling into port in thirty minutes, and she's going to call me once they're released."

"I don't know how you can stand being away from her so much."

A sad smile crossed Stacy's face, quickly replaced with the look of someone who was completely in love. "It's hard. I won't pretend like it's not, but I'm so proud of her, and she makes up for it when we're together. Besides, this won't be forever. She has a year left on her enlistment, and then we're going to settle down and make some babies."

"Really?" Carrie wasn't surprised about the settling down part, but this baby thing was new. "I didn't think you wanted kids."

Stacy winked at Carrie and stuffed her phone into her pocket. "I didn't think I did either. It's different when you find the one you want to spend the rest of your life with. Kids always seemed like they'd be too much trouble, but now I don't know. When I dream about our future, I picture her wrestling with our kids in the yard. I think about us reading them bedtime stories, and videotaping ballet recitals, and all the things I never thought I'd want. With her, I want that. I want that for you, too, Carrie. Not the kid part, if that's not something you'd enjoy, but I'd love for you to find someone that makes you dream about a future with them in it."

Carrie sighed and wrapped her arms around Stacy. "I want that, too. I really do. I thought for a minute that person might be Dylan, but I just don't know. I'm almost afraid to even go there."

"Call her. Talk to her about what happened and give her a chance. It would really suck if she was just having an off night and that one thing ruined something that could have been great."

Carrie walked Stacy to the door. "Thanks for breakfast and for listening to me."

"Call her." Stacy's phone beeped once again. "That's Erica. I have to go. I love you, Care."

"I love you, too. I'll think about calling her."

"Promise?"

"Promise," Carrie said. Stacy's phone rang, and she answered it with a final wave good-bye. Carrie watched her walk toward her house with an extra lightness in her step. She desperately wanted to have what Stacy and Erica had, but she refused to excuse bad behavior just because she was lonely. She had to admit that Stacy was probably right about not condemning Dylan so quickly. Carrie wasn't sure she was ready to call her quite yet, but she could at least accept the idea that she might possibly, maybe, think about giving her the benefit of the doubt.

Carrie crawled back onto the couch where she'd slept the night before and closed her eyes. Maybe a little more sleep would help her puzzle out what to do next. As she started to drift back into sleep, she felt a faint buzz. She reached down between the couch cushions and pulled out her phone, where it must have fallen while she slept the night before. It buzzed again. Carrie sat up and swiped the phone to check the messages. Two were from her mom, asking if she was going to her cousin's wedding, one was from her friend Brian asking if she could squeeze his car in for an appointment, and six were from Dylan.

> *Dylan Fleming: Hey, Carrie. I just wanted to make sure you made it home okay.*
> *Dylan Fleming: I'm so sorry about last night.*
> *Dylan Fleming: I'm a total asshole. Please forgive me.*
> *Dylan Fleming: You have every right to ignore me. I don't blame you.*
> *Dylan Fleming: Please give me a chance to apologize in person and explain.*
> *Dylan Fleming: I won't keep harassing you. I'm incredibly sorry. I like you so much. There's no excuse for the way I behaved.*

The last message had come through only a couple of minutes before. Carrie stared at her phone and tried to decide what to do. She thought of Stacy's advice and the promise she'd just made. With a sigh, she messaged Dylan back.

> *Me: I made it home fine. Thank you for checking.*
> *Me: Did you get your car home okay?*
> *Dylan Fleming: Hey! I did. Roadside showed up about 20 minutes after you left and fixed it.*
> *Dylan Fleming: I'm really sorry about how the night ended.*
> *Me: Me, too.*
> *Dylan Fleming: Do you think I could maybe see you today so we can talk?*
> *Dylan Fleming: I promise not to be an asshole.*
> *Me: lol*
> *Me: ...*
> *Dylan Fleming: Pretty please?*
> *Me: I have to go into work for a few hours. Want to pick me up from there, and we can grab some dinner.*
> *Dylan Fleming: Yes! Please. Yes. Should I make reservations somewhere?*
> *Me: No. Let's keep this super casual.*

Dylan Fleming: Perfect. Where should I pick you up?
Me: 2950 South 3rd Street. 5 pm?
Dylan Fleming: Great. 5 pm it is.
Dylan Fleming: Thanks, Carrie.
Me: I'll see you at 5.

Carrie placed her phone on the coffee table and buried her head in the cushions. She wasn't a hundred percent sure she was making the right decision, but she didn't want to look back and regret not at least hearing her out. Things between them had been so promising before that moment, she had to at least give her a chance.

CHAPTER THREE

Dylan tapped nervously on her steering wheel as she followed the instructions from her navigation. The address Carrie had given her was in an unfamiliar part of town. It wasn't far from where Carrie lived, but since she'd picked her up for their date at night, she hadn't paid much attention to the business district she'd passed on her way. To be honest, Dylan hadn't realized Carrie had a job other than as a musician. It made sense. Not many were able to make a living as a full-time performer.

Strip malls and fast-food places gave way to quaint craftsman-style shops with striped awnings that enticed passersby with the promise of fudge and antique clocks. Dylan's navigation system told her she'd arrived at her destination, so she pulled into a small parking lot and found a space in what she had hoped was an out-of-the-way corner of the lot. She blew out a deep breath and checked her reflection one last time before stepping from the car.

She wound her way through the parked cars to the front of the business. Bold letters in a Victorian-era font read "Grice Automotive" across a large picture window. Carrie's name was Grice. Was this her father's business?

A young man with sandy hair sat at the counter, taking notes from a phone call. When he finished, he stood and shook hands with Dylan. "Welcome to Grice Automotive. How can I help you?"

"Hi. I'm looking for Carrie. Is she around?"

"You must be Dylan."

The sly smile on the man's face made Dylan a little self-conscious. "Sounds like my reputation precedes me."

"Sorry. I'm Carrie's brother, Brandon. You're just as cute as she said you were."

Dylan's cheeks warmed. "I...thanks."

Brandon smiled and shook Dylan's hand a little too firmly. "Looks won't help you if you're ever a dick to my sister again."

"Got it."

"Good. Come back with me. Carrie's just finishing up." Brandon led Dylan through a door and into a large garage with several cars on lifts and both men and women in coveralls, covered in grease, working on them. They walked up to a classic Mercedes convertible with someone's legs sticking out from underneath it. "Carrie?" Brandon asked, gently kicking her boot with his own.

"I told you to leave me alone until I finished this, Brandon," a clearly annoyed Carrie replied.

Dylan tried to swallow past the lump in her throat. This wasn't at all what she'd expected, and her feelings of panic and attraction warred with each other as she did her best to sort them out in her head.

"Dylan's here. You told me to tell you when she got here."

"Shit." Carrie slid out from under the car. "I told you to tell me a half hour before she was supposed to arrive so I could make myself presentable, Brandon."

"We got busy. I'm going back to the desk." Brandon turned back toward Dylan. "It was nice to meet you, Dylan. Don't forget what I said."

Carrie rolled her eyes. "Sorry if he gave you grief, and I'm so sorry I look like a mess."

"No, you look...sexy as hell." Dylan's attraction to Carrie at that moment surprised her. Not that she'd never been attracted to strong, capable women before, but something about seeing this very feminine woman in a traditionally masculine role made her catch her breath. "I had no idea you were a mechanic."

"This is my shop."

"What shop?"

Carrie waved the wrench in her hand around to indicate the room they were standing in. "This is my auto-repair shop. Grice Automotive."

"Seriously?" The word was out before Dylan could pull it back. "Sorry. I didn't mean..."

"Why is that so hard to believe?"

"It's not, I just…you seem like such a girl. This isn't at all what I expected."

"You know what, Dylan. I'm starting to feel like this is a huge waste of our time. Why don't—"

"No, please. I'm sorry. I was just surprised. That's all."

Carrie set the tool back into its drawer and wiped her hands on a clean rag. "You're coming across as a total chauvinist, which I have to say is not only a turn-off, it's disappointing."

Dylan rubbed her face with her hands and took a deep breath. "You're right, and I am sorry. Is there somewhere we can talk?"

Carrie checked her watch, then looked at the car she'd been working on. "Steph?" she called out over the sounds of pneumatic tools and people talking.

"Yep," a woman answered, walking toward Carrie from the car she'd apparently been working on that day.

"Can you ask Greg to finish this? It just needs the filter and new oil. He can tell Brandon when he's done, and he'll let the owner know it's ready."

"Sure thing, Carrie. Who's your friend?" Steph looked at Dylan like she wanted to get to know her a lot better.

Carrie rolled her eyes. "Keep it in your pants, Steph."

Dylan gave a little wave. "Dylan."

"Hey, Dylan. I'll let Greg know, Carrie. Have a nice night." Steph winked at her and walked away.

"See ya, Steph." Carrie indicated Dylan should follow her as she made her way toward a door on the room's far side. "I need to take a quick shower, and then we can grab something to eat. The remotes are on the side table if you want to watch something while you wait."

The room was set up like a small apartment, with a bathroom on one end and a sitting area on the other. The couch looked inviting, so Dylan relaxed and scrolled through the channels while Carrie showered. A half hour later, Carrie came back in wearing a red-and-white gingham shirt with well-worn jeans and boots. She looked fresh and beautiful, and Dylan had to force herself not to stare.

"Ready to eat?" Carrie asked.

"Sure thing. Where would you like to go?"

"Are you up for a short walk? There's plenty of great places up the street."

"Sounds perfect." Dylan held the door for Carrie as they walked out of the garage and into the evening's fading light. "It's a beautiful night."

"What's your deal, Dylan?"

"My deal?"

"Yeah. One minute you seem like you're the sweetest person ever, and the next, you're acting like an insecure asshole. What gives? Which one are you?"

Dylan pushed her hands into her pockets and shrugged. "I guess I'm not sure anymore."

"Well, I need you to figure it out before this can ever go any further. I can't deal with the constant hot and cold. If I didn't like who I thought you were before the whole tire thing, I wouldn't give you the time of day. What changed? What triggered you and made you become this different person?"

"Tacos?"

"What?"

Dylan pointed toward a taco truck parked on the side of the road surrounded by several picnic tables. "Want to get some tacos, and then I'll do my best to explain myself?"

Carrie nodded and followed Dylan to the window where they could order. Once they had their food, they found a table as far away from the other patrons as possible and started to eat. The night was quiet except for the faint sound of cars as they drove by. Dylan needed to gather her thoughts and try to figure out the best way to explain her behavior without making herself sound even worse. Carrie looked at her expectantly, but she appreciated that she was giving her time to think.

"I know there's no excuse for the way I've acted. It's cold comfort, but this isn't normally how I am."

"So why now? What did I do that set you off like this?"

Dylan blew out a breath and put down her taco, too distracted to try to eat and talk at the same time. "It wasn't anything you did. I know this sounds pathetic, but you got caught in the crossfires of my broken heart and stupid insecurities."

"What insecurities? When we talked before the date, you seemed so confident and sure of yourself. Where did that person go?"

Laughter from another table pulled their attention from each other for a minute. Dylan appreciated the time it gave her to organize her thoughts. Turning back to Carrie, she cleared her throat and started from the beginning.

"I'm almost afraid to tell you, because the more I think about it, the more pathetic it sounds."

Carrie reached across the table and gave Dylan's hand a gentle squeeze. "Just be honest with me, Dylan. That's all I'm asking. I had so much fun getting to know you and was excited to spend time together. I at least deserve an explanation."

"You're right. You deserve so much more than that. I've been excited, too, which is why I could kick my own ass for being such an asshole."

"Talk to me, Dylan. Stop beating yourself up and just talk to me."

Carrie's open expression helped Dylan relax. What was the worst that could happen? She could call her a pathetic loser and say Michelle was right all along, but Dylan somehow doubted that would be the case. If Dylan was honest, she should have been clued in by several signs from the very beginning as to the person Michelle was. She just didn't want to believe it. Carrie wasn't Michelle and had never done anything to make Dylan think she would treat her the same way. She just had to give her a chance to prove it.

"I wasn't always this insecure. Once, I had all the confidence in the world. I wish you could have known me then."

"What happened to that person?"

"A series of unfortunate events that started when I was right out of college and got a job with a start-up in San Francisco, a tech company called Aerial Command. We wrote software for drone units to be used for search and rescue, bridge inspections, forest-fire prevention, and all kinds of things. It was a great idea, and we had some big backers in the beginning."

"That sounds amazing," Carrie said. "It never occurred to me that you could use drones for that type of thing, but it makes total sense."

"It's a natural progression for that technology, but we were a little ahead of the market. I'll get to that part in a minute. When things were at their peak, I had to attend this fund-raiser party at one of our investors' houses. It was a swanky, suit-and-tie type of deal. Not something I particularly like doing, but I wasn't given a choice. We had to keep the investors happy, and this investor liked to show off, so I went. I planned to get in, show my face, chat a few people up, and escape as soon as possible, but then I saw Michelle."

"Ahh…Michelle's the bitch in this story?"

"Yeah, well, she's the bitch in most people's stories, but at the time I only saw—"

"Boobs?" Carrie said with a wink.

"Um, yeah, pretty much, boobs. It's probably idiotic to tell you this story if I want to convince you that I'm worthy of a second chance. It doesn't exactly make me sound like a superstar or anything."

Carrie popped a tortilla chip into her mouth and waved her hand. "No, no. We've all had bitches in our past. If this one broke the sweet Dylan I caught a glimpse of before, I want to know why."

The casualness of their conversation helped Dylan relax. Before their first date, she had felt at ease in their relationship. Hopefully, some of that comfort was returning.

"Okay, so Michelle and I became an item. She was all about the swanky parties and loved to parade me around in my monkey suit every chance she had. It was exhausting. When we were at a party, she would be all over me, bragging about Aerial Command and my position there, openly flirting with me in front of women she thought might be interested in me to make them jealous. It was ridiculous, but some part of me enjoyed the idea that this beautiful woman wanted me. She made me feel special, which I never really had growing up. I found my confidence in college, and getting my dream job right out of the gate had me convinced I could take on the world. Having a gorgeous woman parade me around and show me off to other people was the icing on the cake." She paused. "I'm not doing a good job of convincing you I'm not an asshole, am I?"

"I'm reserving judgment for now. Want another beer?" Carrie stood and dug in her pockets for money.

"The answer to that question will always be yes. Just so we're on the same page."

Carrie laughed and bought two more beers from the truck. "Okay, so she paraded you around like a prize pony, and the attention felt good."

"Exactly. It felt great until she started to control every aspect of my life. She told me what to wear, what to eat, and criticized the things I said to people. I was a nervous wreck. I was never enough. She wanted me to be this idea she had of the perfect person, and I just couldn't live up to those expectations."

Carrie reached across the table and squeezed Dylan's arm. "I'm sorry she did that to you. For what it's worth, the Dylan I got to know before our first date seemed perfect."

The words were a welcome balm for Dylan's weary soul. She hadn't talked about Michelle with anyone other than her best friend, Val. It was just too embarrassing to admit that she'd allowed someone to take complete control of her life so easily and let that person strip her of her hard-earned sense of self-worth. She desperately wanted it back and knew only she could rediscover it for herself, but having someone she'd come to respect in a very short time tell her she was enough meant a great deal.

"I appreciate you saying that." Dylan took another sip of her beer and cleared her throat. "I was miserable but couldn't see a way out of the situation. I completely realize now, looking at it from a different perspective, I could have just left. I understand that I allowed her to take control of my life, but at the time I couldn't see that."

Carrie shook her head. "I hate this chick, and I've never even met her."

"You'd hate her even more in real life. I'm not proud of my association with her." Dylan rubbed her eyes and blew out a breath. She'd spent so much time trying to forget about Michelle that talking about her now was exhausting, though therapeutic.

Sessions with her therapist hadn't felt as cleansing as telling Carrie. Since Carrie was also a lesbian, maybe Dylan felt she could relate to her problems on a level her straight male therapist never could.

"The last few months we were together were the worst. We lived together, and I worked from home, so I couldn't escape her constant criticism. She once told me she wanted a new faucet in the bathroom, so I called a plumber to replace it. After he left, she berated me for half an hour because I had to call someone else to do a job any other self-respecting butch woman would have finished in thirty minutes. If I dared shed a tear while watching a movie, she would laugh at me and call me a pussy. She constantly judged everything I did against some idea she had about who she thought I should be. By the time I started to wake up to the reality of my situation, a couple of huge backers of Aerial Command had become impatient with the market and bailed, which caused us to pack up our toys and go our separate ways. I got another job almost immediately, making practically the same amount of money, but the new company wasn't as flashy as Aerial Command, so Michelle completely lost interest."

Dylan couldn't bear to share the rest of the story at that moment, but getting the bulk of it off her chest was such a relief. Carrie had every right to run from her as fast as she could and never look back, but Dylan held her breath and waited for a response, hoping she'd given her enough reason to want to grant her another chance.

"Dylan?" Carrie pulled Dylan's hand from where it tightly gripped her bottle of beer and cradled it in her delicate but slightly callused ones. "Are you going to ask me out on another date?"

Hope was the first emotion that flooded Dylan. Hope followed closely by relief. That was enough for now. She could work with hope and relief.

"Carrie, want to go out with me Saturday night?"

"I would love to."

CHAPTER FOUR

Carrie slipped on her dress and checked her watch to see how much time she had to apply makeup before Dylan arrived. She'd told her they would be going to a nice dinner, but Carrie couldn't help but be a little weary after their last attempt at a similar date. With any luck the evening would go smoothly, but she wasn't holding her breath.

She hated having doubts about Dylan. The time they'd spent getting to know each other had possibly set a higher expectation than the real-life Dylan could achieve. Learning more about what happened with her ex-girlfriend helped explain her reaction, but Carrie couldn't bring herself to let her guard down. She'd promised to give Dylan a second chance, and she'd try her best to do just that, but she refused to settle for a relationship with someone who didn't treat her with respect.

The doorbell rang just as Carrie slipped on her heels. She picked up her purse and opened the door to find Dylan looking as handsome as ever in khaki pants, a plaid shirt, and a tie.

"You look...wow," Dylan said.

The seemingly sincere compliment warmed Carrie's cheeks, and she couldn't help but smile. "Thanks. I was thinking the same thing about you. You clean up quite nicely."

"Thank you. Your chariot awaits." Dylan gently placed a hand on Carrie's elbow to guide her down the front steps. She appreciated the gesture since her heels were a little higher than she typically wore.

"I hope you don't mind, but I made reservations at El Coqui this time."

"I love El Coqui. Puerto Rican food is one of my favorites."

Dylan smiled and helped her into the passenger seat of the car. "Perfect. Me, too."

Carrie nervously smoothed any wrinkles from her dress as she waited for Dylan to get situated in the driver's seat. Tension sparked between them, and Carrie wished she knew what to say to put them both at ease. "Have—"

"I—"

"Sorry. You go," Dylan said.

"No, please. You go first."

The traffic was light as Dylan pulled onto the freeway. "I was just going to say that I stopped by the gas station and checked the tire pressure before I picked you up, so with any luck, I'll be able to get us all the way to the restaurant tonight."

Carrie appreciated that Dylan seemed to have a sense of humor about what had happened on their last date. She hoped that was a sign the night would be a good one. "Good thinking. I'd hate to miss out on Puerto Rican food."

When they arrived, the hostess sat them in the back corner. It was the darkest part of the large room, but candles at each table gave the space a romantic feel. "I've never sat back here. I think I've only ever sat up by the big window in the front."

"My best friend since grade school, Val, is one of the owners," Dylan said.

"Really? You're a good person to know."

A waitress arrived to take their drink orders and hand them the menu. Carrie knew she wanted what she always ordered, but she took the time to peruse the menu and read every item description in case something else caught her eye. "I thought you grew up in the Midwest or something?" she asked.

"Yeah. Michigan. My friend Val joined the Army after high school, and I went off to college. We lost touch for a few years, but we were both visiting our families and ran into each other at the store one Christmas. Her enlistment was ending, and she was looking for a place to land. I invited her to come out to San Francisco with me, and since she didn't have any other plans, she packed her bags and moved out west."

Carrie whistled. "Man, that's brave. I can't imagine moving across the country on a whim like that."

"Her family is very conservative, so she'd never felt comfortable coming out. Between the Army and her family's beliefs, I can't blame her for being cautious. I knew, of course, and San Francisco seemed like the perfect place for a young lesbian ready to sow her wild oats, so to speak."

The waitress returned with their drinks and took the food orders. Dylan poured her beer into a chilled glass and held it up to propose a toast. "To mulligans." Carrie hesitated but tapped her glass. She understood what Dylan was trying to say and couldn't blame her for wanting to pretend their first date had never happened, but she wasn't ready to completely forget just yet.

"Is Val the chef or just the owner?" Carrie took a sip of her wine and hoped Dylan would take the hint and return to their previous conversation. She enjoyed learning about Dylan's life and didn't want to deal with what this date was or wasn't at the moment.

"Her wife, Isabella, is the chef. Val is an owner and more of a silent partner. She's very involved, but Bella is the real soul here."

"Isabella is a beautiful name," Carrie said.

"You'll love her." Dylan smiled and stood to hug a stunning butch woman in black slacks and shirt that embraced every curve of her slim body. Carrie hadn't seen Dylan be so open and relaxed before, and she liked the lightness it brought out in her. She hadn't realized this quality was missing from Dylan until now.

"Carrie Grice, I'd like to introduce you to my best friend, Valentina Delgado."

Val turned Carrie's offered hand and placed a gentle kiss on her knuckles. "*Eres una mujer hermosa.*"

"*Eres una coqueta,*" Carrie replied with a wink.

"Oh, Dylan. I like this girl already."

Dylan playfully removed Carrie's hand from Val's grasp. "You have your own beautiful woman. I'm still trying to impress this one, so please don't ruin it for me."

"She's afraid of the competition," Val said to Carrie.

"Yeah, yeah. Where's Bella? Does she know you're out here flirting with my date?"

The banter between them was sweet. Carrie enjoyed this side of Dylan. She was more like the person Carrie thought she was before the flat-tire incident.

"Bella is in the kitchen, but she said to make you promise to save her a dance. That will give Carrie a chance to dance with someone who knows what she's doing. You've come on the best night, Carrie. It's salsa night."

Panic set in when Carrie realized what they were saying. "Oh, no. I don't know how to salsa. I'll watch."

"It would break my heart not to dance at least once with you."

"Okay, that's enough," Dylan said. "Tell Bella I'll give her a rest from your ego and save her a dance. She'll enjoy not having her toes stepped on for once."

Val laughed and squeezed Dylan's shoulder. "I'll see you both later. Enjoy your meal. It's on the house."

"No…" Dylan tried to refuse, but Val walked away before she could stop her. "She never lets me pay. It used to irritate Michelle because she thought Val treated us like we needed a handout."

"Why would she think that? Val's your best friend. I'd never let my best friend pay for a meal at my restaurant."

"I agree. Michelle was weird. I think it was just one more thing she could use to make me feel inadequate, which was a hobby of hers."

"I like her less and less the more I learn about her."

"Me, too."

Something about the way Dylan talked about Michelle set off warning bells in Carrie's mind. Not that she thought Dylan wanted Michelle, but the wounds might still be too fresh for Carrie to risk getting involved. After all, it was the reason Dylan had given her to explain why she'd freaked out over the tire. Not that she was in love with Michelle, but the damage she had done was still there.

The food arrived, and they both moaned at their first bites. "It's nice to be able to meet your friends. Thanks for bringing me here tonight."

"Sorry Val is so forward." Dylan rolled her eyes. "She thinks she's quite the Casanova."

"It's fine. She seems harmless and adorable. It didn't bother me at all," Carrie said.

Dylan had to cover her mouth so she didn't spit out her beer. "Please let me tell her you said she's adorable."

"Why is adorable bad?" Carrie asked.

"No reason. Adorable is great. I think Val was trying for sexy, but

I think adorable is more appropriate." Dylan pushed the picadillo onto her fork with her fried green plantain and took a bite. "Val's never had any trouble getting a woman's attention. Even Michelle had a crush on her."

"You don't think I have a crush on Val just because I said she's adorable, do you?"

Dylan stared at her plate as she pushed her fork around her food. Part of Carrie worried she might be getting into a situation where she would ultimately get her heart broken. It would probably be smart to walk away. But the disappointment she felt over that thought, before they'd even had a chance to explore the attraction they felt for each other, left her confused. "Can I be frank with you?"

The room's noise seemed to drift away as Dylan set down her fork and gave Carrie her total attention. "Please."

Carrie took a sip of her wine and cleared her throat. "I'm still trying to figure you out. One minute you're so confident and sexy, and the next, you act like you're never going to get past this thing you had with Michelle. I don't know what to think."

Dylan pushed her plate aside and took Carrie's hand. "I'm sorry. You're right. I'm still trying to get my footing. I know you don't owe me anything, but if you can be patient with me, I promise to get my head on straight. Please don't give up on me yet."

Warm fingers gently caressed Carrie's hand as she thought about what Dylan was asking. She hadn't done anything terrible. Carrie knew in her heart that Dylan was a sincere, good person. Maybe she wasn't the only one fumbling her way through this. Was she nitpicking everything Dylan did or said to sabotage any possibility of giving her a chance? In theory, Carrie wanted nothing more than to be in a relationship, but she couldn't deny that the idea of being vulnerable with Dylan still had her on edge.

"I'm sorry, too. Maybe I'm letting things get to me that really shouldn't."

Dylan turned her hand over and placed a soft kiss on her palm. "I feel like I keep saying this, but should we start over? I mean, really start over this time? Clean slate? I like you, Carrie. And I don't feel like I'm trying to change who I am to impress you. It's more like I'm trying to show you the real me, and I keep tripping over myself. I can do better."

The idea of starting fresh was very appealing. She could see the potential and knew if they could get past this awkwardness that had settled between them, they had a chance at something special. Exactly what that was, she wasn't sure, but she was excited to find out. "Clean slate it is."

The sound of chairs scraping across the floor drew their attention away from each other. Within minutes, as if by magic, the center of the room became a dance floor. The waitress came by to clear their plates, and two men were right behind her to take their table away. The sudden dimming of the lights startled Carrie, and she reached out to take Dylan's hand. Carrie strained to identify sounds from one end of the room, and then she recognized the gentle beat of a drum, followed by hoots and hollers from the crowd. The anticipation of what was to come had Carrie on the edge of her seat. The noise died down as the lilt of a woman's voice cut through the darkness. She was softly singing something in Spanish that gradually gained tempo and volume as she progressed toward the room's center. Carrie turned to Dylan, but the darkness hid her from view. She threaded their fingers together, the connection comforting.

The voice quieted, and brass instruments cut through the silent room like a bolt of lightning. Drums once again set the rhythm as a light illuminated one of the most beautiful women Carrie had ever seen. She held a microphone as she gently swayed to the music. When the woman began to sing, Carrie was utterly transfixed. She wasn't exactly sure if what was happening was real or a dream. The quiet scrape of a chair told her Dylan was scooting closer. Carrie felt her warmth surround her like a blanket as Dylan wrapped an arm around her and leaned in to translate the lyrics in a whisper.

Puerto Rico was my home,
California's where I am.
No matter how far I go,
My heart belongs to my noble land.

Carrie closed her eyes and allowed herself to soak in the moment. She didn't need Dylan to translate the words, but the effect was intoxicating. The music, the beautiful woman's voice, and Dylan's comfort surrounded her, whispered in her ear. It was all so surreal she wanted it to never end. When the song was over, the crowd went wild with applause. Dylan pulled back and moved her chair to its original position. Carrie immediately missed the intimacy of being in her arms.

"Buenas noches, mi familia." The energy in the room was contagious as Carrie clapped at the woman's greeting. "My name is Isabella Delgado, and we're going to have a wonderful time tonight." The crowd was almost in a frenzy at that point. "As always, this first dance belongs to my wife, mi corazón, Valentina. Are you ready, mi amor?" Val appeared from the crowd and took Bella in her arms.

The music began again, and a man from the band stepped up to the microphone to sing as Val and Bella danced the salsa like they'd done it their whole lives. After a few minutes, couples from the crowd joined them on the dance floor. Carrie had seen people dance the salsa before, but never like this. It was beautiful, and she couldn't pull her eyes away from the way the couples seemed to be in perfect sync with each other. They moved with an energy that existed only for them.

Dylan stood and held out her hand in invitation. "May I have this dance?"

Carrie looked up and smiled but shook her head. She had no idea how to salsa. Dylan squatted down next to her chair, and Carrie leaned down so they could talk over the noise of the music.

"I can't do this dance," Carrie said.

"I can teach you. Don't listen to Val. I'm a good teacher."

"I don't want to embarrass myself."

Dylan looked around the room, pointed to a less crowded corner, and gave Carrie a pleading look that she found impossible to refuse. She stood, and Dylan led her across the floor, through the crowd of dancers, to the area she had indicated. There, Dylan placed one hand in the small of Carrie's back and held the other up for her to take. When she did, Dylan began to lead them around to the beat of the music. She knew she was stumbling through the moves, but Dylan's confidence and strong frame made her feel like she was gliding across the floor.

When the music stopped, Isabella took the microphone back from her bandmate. "*Gracias*, everyone. Let's slow things down a little while we warm up the floor." She turned to her band, and the musicians nodded back before playing a beautiful ballad.

Carrie walked toward their chairs, but Dylan stopped her. "One more?" Carrie hesitated, but she finally nodded and allowed Dylan to lead her around once again. The tension between them seemed to melt as she rested her head on Dylan's broad shoulders and relaxed into the rhythm of the music. This was what she wanted. She could get lost in this feeling, and that was just fine with her. She'd worry about what came next tomorrow. Tonight, she just wanted Dylan to hold her tight.

The song ended, and a faster one began. Dylan looked at Carrie for permission, and when she nodded, they danced for two more. Carrie was exhausted and regretted wearing the shoes she'd chosen, but when the music slowed once again, Val appeared and asked her to dance. She looked at Dylan, who nodded before walking away to find Bella. Val was a wonderful dancer, and Carrie enjoyed the chat they had while they danced. When the music stopped, she looked for Dylan.

"Hey." A warm hand slid into hers as Dylan pulled her close. "Want to get out of here?"

"Yeah. Let's go." Carrie picked up her purse and allowed Dylan to guide her through the mass of people and out a side entrance. A slight chill in the air caused Carrie to shiver.

"Here." Dylan removed her tie and stuffed it into her pocket before unbuttoning her shirt and wrapping it around Carrie's shoulders. The undershirt Dylan was wearing hugged her like a glove and sent Carrie's heart into overdrive. "Sorry we had to park so far from the restaurant. They need more garages down here."

"I should have thought to bring something warmer. I forget how quickly the nights can cool off once summer is over. This helps, though." She tugged on the shirt Dylan had given her. "Thank you."

"No problem."

Carrie slipped her arm into Dylan's as they walked the few blocks to their car. "I had a nice time tonight. Thanks for taking me."

"You bet. Thank you for dancing with me."

"Do you think Val will be upset we left without saying good-bye?" Carrie asked.

They reached the car, and Dylan held the door open for her. "She'll be fine. Besides, she would have tried to dance with you again, and I kind of like to have you to myself. Does that make me sound like a jerk?"

"Not at all. I like it, too."

Dylan's smile pulled one more brick from the wall Carrie realized she'd been building after the night of their first date. She either needed to truly let that first night go or call things off between them, and the thought of doing the latter broke her heart. She wasn't ready to completely open herself up to Dylan, but she committed right then to giving what was happening between them an honest chance.

CHAPTER FIVE

Dylan grumbled and pulled the blanket over her head in an attempt to drown out the sound of her alarm. She'd stayed up way too late the night before to easily drag herself out of bed to meet Val for their morning run. She checked her phone, hoping by some miracle that Val had canceled. When she found only a text from her best friend that said "No excuses," she groaned and tossed the phone back onto her nightstand.

After pulling on a pair of running shorts, shoes, and a hat, she walked out her front door to find Val stretching on her front steps. "You're late."

"How did I let you talk me into this again?" Dylan lifted her arms over her head and began her stretching routine. "You know I hate running."

"Because I like having you in my life, and that sedentary job you have isn't going to keep your heart strong. Of course, if you spend more time with Carrie, you might not need any other form of exercise." Val suggestively wiggled her eyebrows.

"Shut up. Are we going to jog, or did you want to talk more about feelings?"

Val laughed and started to run at a casual pace with Dylan right beside her. "You aren't usually so touchy about talking to me about what's going on in your head. What's up?"

Dylan sped up, and Val kept pace alongside her. "I don't know."

"Do you like her? You seemed into her last night. I haven't seen you that excited—"

"Since Michelle?"

Val shook her head. "No, man. You were never like that with Michelle. You were always a lost little puppy when Michelle was around. She called, and you came running, eager to do anything for her hard-earned approval. From what I saw last night, Carrie isn't like that. She's not looking to control you or make you someone you aren't. She wants you to be who you are."

"And you learned all this just from last night? You're an amazing judge of someone's feelings." Dylan coughed in an attempt to catch her breath.

In unspoken agreement, they slowed their pace to a fast walk. Dylan and Val had run track in high school, but while Val had kept up her physical fitness routine in the Army, Dylan hadn't. After putting her off for the last few years, Dylan finally agreed to start jogging with her three mornings a week. It was part of her effort to leave her past hurts and frustrations behind and live a better, happier life. So far, it had mostly been only painful, but the time spent with her best friend was invaluable.

"I'm not just guessing here, Dyl. We talked."

"Who talked?"

"Carrie and I talked. Last night when we were dancing."

"You danced with her one time. You got all of that from one dance?"

"Let's stretch again, and then we'll start a slow jog to Montego Street. Deal?"

Dylan stopped and used the short wall they were standing next to as leverage so she could stretch out her calves. "What did she say to you?"

"Carrie?" Val crossed her legs and leaned over to touch her toes. Dylan had always admired her flexibility. No matter how much she stretched, she'd never been able to fold her body into the shapes that Val could.

"Of course Carrie. What else did she say to you?"

"Not much. We only danced once, and it's not like it's easy to do much talking when you're dancing. She basically said she liked you and wanted to get to know you better, but she was still a little hesitant."

"She told you a lot for just one dance."

Val shrugged and started to jog again. "Let's go."

Dylan caught up and ran alongside her. "I really like her, Val."

"It's clear you're into her. You seemed pretty hot and heavy on the floor, too. Where did you guys sneak off to?"

Dylan cleared her throat. "What do you mean? Nowhere."

Val gently shoved Dylan's arm. "Well, you just disappeared. I figured you must have found somewhere a little more private." She wiggled her eyebrows again.

"Did you not just hear me say I'm really into this girl?"

Val looked at Dylan with a confused expression. "What's up with you?"

"What if I fuck it up? What if I'm not enough for her?"

"What if, what if, what if..." Val shook her head, turned a corner, and dug in to keep the pace up a street with a steep incline. "You can't worry about *what if*, Dyl. You like her, and she likes you. She seems like a sweet girl. She's already made it very clear to you that she isn't looking for something you can't be. You're going to have to toughen up and trust that she knows what she wants."

Val was right. The only way forward was for Dylan to cut the ropes holding her to her past and Michelle. If she didn't, she'd never be able to move on and find any peace in her life, even without Carrie and a potential relationship with her. Dylan needed to do it for herself and get out of her own way.

They crested the hill and stopped in front of Val's house, a block away from Dylan's. "Fuck me." Dylan collapsed on the lawn and spread out her arms and legs like she was making a snow angel in the grass. "You're going to kill me one day."

Val chuckled and pushed Dylan's knee toward her chest to help her stretch. "Or maybe I'm going to save your life when you're old, and you still have a strong body and a healthy heart. Carrie will appreciate it when you're around to play with your grandkids."

"Whoa. You skipped a few steps there. Easy with the grandkids talk." Dylan lifted her other leg so Val could help her stretch it, too.

"Why do you two have to do these very sexual things with each other on our front lawn? The neighbors already think we're weirdos."

Dylan looked back to see Val's wife on their porch. "Hey, Bella. Your wife can't keep her hands off me."

Val rolled her eyes and slapped Dylan's ass as she stood and reached out a hand to help her to her feet. "You wish, pervert. Want some breakfast?"

"There's no reality where I'd turn down a Bella breakfast. It's the only reason I run with you in the mornings."

"Yeah, yeah." Val playfully pushed Dylan toward the front door of her house. Dylan loved the time she spent with her friends. She smiled as she realized the only thing missing was Carrie. She took a moment to picture Carrie with them, and it filled her with a kind of hope she'd never felt before. It might not be cool to call someone the next morning after taking them out the night before. She was sure she'd heard some rule about not seeming too eager, but she didn't care. After breakfast, she would go home and do a little research on where to take Carrie on another date, and then she'd give her a call. You didn't always get a second chance in life, and Dylan refused to let this one pass her by.

Chapter Six

A line of people stretched around the building and well down the block, waiting to enter the car show. Carrie took her place behind the last person in line and checked her watch. She and Dylan had agreed to meet a half hour before the doors opened, but she'd decided to arrive a little earlier. She was surprised when Dylan had invited her to the car show as their second date. Dylan had likely never gone or even thought about going to a car show before, but she seemed excited when she'd invited Carrie. That reaction earned her points in Carrie's mind. Her mother had always told her she'd know when someone truly liked her because they would do things they never imagined doing to make her happy. So far, Dylan was proving to be willing to put herself out there, even if that made her vulnerable.

"Hey, you." Carrie waved as Dylan approached from the front of the building.

"Hey. I got here early to get us a slightly better position in line." Dylan held up two tickets. "I did a little research last night and read the line started early, so I arrived an hour ago. I wasn't the first one here, but only a few people were ahead of me."

The excitement in Dylan's voice made Carrie's heart skip. "I appreciate you inviting me, Dylan. I know it's not normally your thing."

Dylan offered her hand, and Carrie took it. "It's only not my thing because I've never been. You never know. Car shows may become my new favorite activity. Of course, I may drive you crazy with questions."

"Oh, really?" Carrie threaded their fingers together and luxuriated in the warmth of Dylan's much larger hands.

"I don't know if I mentioned this before, but I ask a million questions, especially when I'm learning about something new."

When they reached the entrance, Dylan held the door for her. Carrie held on tight as Dylan confidently navigated them through the press of people and into the large area where the show was being held. As a petite woman, Carrie appreciated having someone larger to help guide her through a crowd. Dylan had a good five inches on her in height, with broad shoulders and a muscular build. Carrie had been fantasizing about touching her since they danced the other night. Being with her now was sending the butterflies in her stomach into overdrive.

"Where should we start?" Dylan asked.

"Hmm?" Carrie had completely lost track of what they were doing as she ogled her date. "What was that?"

Dylan gave her a knowing smile. "I was asking where you'd like to start."

"Oh, um, let's just start from the left and make our way around."

"That works for me."

As they walked, looking at the different cars on display, Carrie was impressed with Dylan's questions. They were thoughtful, not the types she would have expected from someone who didn't know much about cars. "Are you sure you haven't been to one of these before?"

Dylan turned away in an apparent attempt to hide her blush. "Would I sound completely dorky if I said I spent the evening doing research?"

"What kind of research? Like about cars?"

"Well, yeah, about cars, but specifically the cars that I read we would see at the show. It's fascinating. I always thought of a car as something that got you from here to there, but they're so much more than that. Did you know that a Formula 1 car can drive upside down in a tunnel going 120 miles per hour?"

Carrie had thought she'd had a crush on Dylan before, but hearing her excitement about something Carrie loved so much was making her a little weak in the knees. "I have heard that. Something about the g-force?"

"Exactly. They can produce around 3.5Gs, which gives them

enough aerodynamic downforce to drive upside down in a tunnel. Isn't that amazing?"

"And you just learned this last night?"

Dylan shrugged. "Technically last night and this morning. I'm working on very little sleep at this point."

Carrie swallowed past the lump in her throat. She'd never had anyone she dated put so much effort into showing interest in something so important to her. She felt exhilarated and scared all at the same time. She slipped her hand into Dylan's and pulled her toward a small room that contained extra equipment for the show. With more force than she intended, Carrie closed the door behind them, sealing them off from the rest of the attendees.

"Why are we here?" Dylan asked.

"Sorry, it's stupid, but I just had this sudden urge to be alone with you."

"Did I do—"

"You didn't do anything wrong. I just didn't want to give everyone a front-row seat to us making out." Carrie saw realization cross Dylan's face and laughed.

"You want to make out with me? Here?"

Carrie gently guided Dylan to sit in a chair, then straddled her lap. She pushed Dylan's bangs from her face and gave her a soft kiss on the lips. "Is that okay with you?"

"Uh, yeah, that'll be just fine."

That was all the permission Carrie needed. Without wasting another minute, she leaned down and tugged Dylan's bottom lip with her teeth. She could feel Dylan's rapid breath as she became more and more excited, which drove Carrie's need even more. She wanted this woman. She wanted her in ways they really shouldn't attempt when anyone could find them at any moment. The room was hot, as much from the enclosed space as the heat they were generating between them. Beads of sweat dripped between Carrie's breasts, and the tickle only served to increase her need.

The zipper of Dylan's jeans pushed against Carrie's center as her hips rocked back and forth. Dylan pulled Carrie's shirt from her pants and smoothed her warm hands against her back. Carrie struggled to think, to remember where they were and why they shouldn't just have sex in this room right now. Why she shouldn't be doing this with someone she still had very conflicted feelings about. What was wrong with her?

"God, Dylan, I've wanted you since we danced the other night. I can't get you out of my mind. The feel of your hands on me. The taste of your mouth—"

Dylan kissed her. The hands resting against her back pulled her forward, rubbing her clit even harder against the stiff material of her jeans. Fuck. She had to stop this. They still had so much to discuss and work out between them, but it all felt so good. With every bit of will power she had left, she pulled out of the searing kiss, her nipples so tight they were painful. The image of Dylan taking each one into her mouth and gently sucking it to ease the pain crossed Carrie's hormone-addled mind.

"I'm so sorry," Carrie said, gasping to catch her breath.

"No. I'm...what was that?"

Carrie rested her head in the crook of Dylan's neck and gently placed a kiss on her overheated skin. "I just..." She took a deep breath and did her best to kick-start her brain into articulating her feelings. "First of all, I'm insanely attracted to you."

"Thanks." Dylan's shy smile was adorable, and Carrie gave her a quick kiss to show her approval.

"Second, you've put so much thought into this entire date. And the last date, for that matter. You're so thoughtful and kind, and sweet. I don't understand how someone like Michelle could ever take advantage of you. You researched car stuff so you'd be able to talk to me about something I love, for Christ's sake. Who does that?"

"Did I mention I learned that the man who invented cruise control was blind?"

Carrie couldn't hold back the laughter. "Where are we going with this, Dylan?"

"With what? Us? I like to think we're moving forward. I like you so much, Carrie. I know I still have stuff to work on, but I'm getting there."

"I know that, I really do. It's why I'm still here—"

The door opened, and two men entered the room. Carrie scrambled off Dylan's lap as quickly as she could and gave them a sheepish look as she and Dylan jogged past them and out into the crowd of people.

Once they were far enough away, they both bent over laughing. "Did you see the look on the tall guy's face?" Dylan asked.

Carrie wiped tears from her eyes and tried to catch her breath. "I'm just glad we stopped before our clothes started to come off."

Dylan draped an arm around Carrie's shoulders and pulled her close as they picked up their walk around the show where they'd left off. "It's just a good thing you have more control than I do. If you'd been relying on me to slow things down, those guys would have seen a lot more than they did, and I'd rather they not get a glimpse of parts of you I've been fantasizing about."

"Really?" Carrie knew Dylan was attracted to her, but the thought of her actually fantasizing about her gave her goose bumps.

Dylan gave Carrie a look that could only be described as incredulous. "You're kidding, right? In what galaxy would I not have a hard time keeping my brain focused on anything other than what your lips would feel like pressed against mine? I feel a little guilty that our first kiss wasn't somewhere more romantic. I came up with all kinds of scenarios in my head, and not one of them involved the storage room at a car show."

"No?" Carrie laughed and wrapped an arm around Dylan, looping a finger in her belt loop. "Well, I don't regret it one bit."

"Oh, me neither. In fact, I'm happy to find another completely inappropriate place here to start again."

"First, let's walk around, and you can impress me with your geeky car facts," Carrie said.

"Geeky?"

"Geeky is adorable."

Dylan rolled her eyes. "Here you go with the adorable thing again. You know I don't usually consider adorable as something I should strive for."

Carrie pulled Dylan down to kiss her cheek. "You know many lesbians find adorable women irresistible, right?"

Dylan blushed. "I didn't know that, but now that I do, adorable doesn't seem so bad after all."

Two hours later, Carrie could tell Dylan was nearing exhaustion.

She tended to get caught up in the excitement and could spend an entire day there without stopping for a break, but the crowds and onslaught of information were taxing for someone who wasn't as familiar with auto shows as she was. "Ready to go? I could use some food and a cold drink."

The expression of relief on Dylan's face made Carrie smile. "I'm ready if you are. I don't think we've seen everything here, so if you want—"

"I'm good. I'm pretty tired. Where would you like to have lunch?"

"There's a great pizza place just a couple of blocks from here, if that sounds good to you."

"Perfect."

They exited the building and walked hand in hand toward their destination. In fact, they'd been holding hands most of the day. Carrie tried not to read too much into it, but the fact that it seemed to come so naturally had to be a good sign.

Once they were seated in their booth and had ordered a pizza to share, Carrie excused herself to use the restroom. Before returning to the table, she texted her best friend, Stacy, an update she'd promised to send.

Me: Everything is perfect.

Stacy Rawlings: How did she handle being around all the car stuff?

Me: Great. She was totally cool about it and seemed genuinely interested.

Me: She asked lots of questions. I can't wait to chat about it.

Stacy Rawlings: That seems like a good sign.

Me: An excellent sign. And we held hands the whole time.

Stacy Rawlings: How are her hands?

Me: Weird question.

Me: Wonderful.

Me: Big, strong, warm. Perfect.

Stacy Rawlings: <swoon>

Me: We might have made out in a storeroom, too.

Stacy Rawlings: What!? Call me when you're home. I want all the deets.

Me: lol Maybe some of the deets.
Stacy Rawlings: We'll see. ;)
Me: I'll call later. Love you.
Stacy Rawlings: Love you, too.

Carrie tucked her phone into her pocket and walked back to the table. The pizza had just arrived, and the waitress was placing them each a slice on a plate.

"Everything okay?" Dylan picked up her pizza and took a bite.

"Perfect. I had to text Stacy to let her know everything was all right. She's a worrywart and likes me to check in when I'm out with someone new."

Dylan was silent until she finished her slice. "She's still worried about me." It was a statement, not a question. "I'm not really new at this point, am I?"

Carrie set down her pizza and took a sip of her beer. She'd walked right into this one. "No, not really. She just wants to make sure I'm safe. She's just looking out for me."

"This wouldn't have anything to do with our first date and me being an asshole, would it? She's probably not a huge fan."

The look of shame on Dylan's face broke Carrie's heart. She didn't deserve to continue to beat herself up over one mistake. She'd had a bad night. Everyone had bad nights, and it wasn't right that she continued to agonize over a poor reaction during a stressful situation. Carrie wasn't sure how to explain that the bigger issue was that Dylan was still struggling with damage from her ex-girlfriend. How could Carrie say that to her without upsetting her more? How could she tell her she felt this incredible attraction to her but struggled to trust that she was ready to be in a relationship?

"Can I ask you a question?"

Dylan looked suspicious but nodded. "Sure."

"Are you over Michelle?"

"Michelle?"

Carrie could see that the question had caught Dylan off guard. The last thing she wanted to do was upset her, especially after they'd had such a nice day together, but they'd never be able to move forward without having this discussion. Dylan deserved to know about, and have the opportunity to address, any hesitations Carrie might have. "I guess my real question is, are you sure you're in a space where you're honestly ready to start a new relationship?"

"Did I do something to make you doubt that I'm ready?"

The last thing Carrie wanted to do was introduce even more self-doubt into Dylan's mind, but they needed to address this subject. "You haven't. I can tell Michelle really did a number on you, and sometimes I worry that you might not be as ready to move on as you think."

Dylan pushed her plate forward and sat back in the booth. She looked exhausted, and Carrie wanted nothing more than to wrap her arms around her and tell her everything would be okay.

"What can I do to convince you I'm ready? I like you, Carrie, and I don't want Michelle to take yet one more thing away from me. I promise that I'm completely over her. I know I have some scars that are still healing, but the feelings I have for you…I never felt this way about Michelle. Ever. When I'm with you, I feel like I can do anything, like I'm enough, and that's such a gift. You're a gift, and I hope you give me the chance to prove to you that I'm worth the risk."

Carrie slid out of her side of the booth and gestured for Dylan to scoot over so she could sit next to her. Once they were side by side, Carrie wrapped herself around Dylan's arm and rested her head on her shoulder. "I think you're a gift, too. I want things between us to work, Dylan, but I'm scared this thing with Michelle still has you in pieces. How can we go forward if you're stuck in the past?"

"I understand. I'm so sorry I haven't been great at proving to you that I've moved on. It was just such a huge thing, and this is technically the first time I've been with a woman since my relationship ended. I don't blame you at all for questioning whether I have my shit together. I'd probably do the same thing in your position."

"Where do we go from here?"

Dylan wrapped an arm around Carrie and pulled her tightly against her. "Now I find my balls, so to speak, and show you the confident person I used to be. I can be that person again, not just for you, but for myself. I have to find her before I lose myself completely. I can't believe I'm suggesting this, but what do you think about slowing things down a little? I'd still like to hang out and get to know each other but pause on taking things further. Give me a little time to work on some of the things you've brought up, and then if you still don't think I can be the person you need, I'll understand."

"It feels good to be in your arms," Carrie said.

"We belong together, Carrie Grice. I feel it in my soul."

Carrie wiped a tear from her cheek. "I think so, too. I support whatever you need, Dylan. Whatever I can do to help you, just ask."

Dylan dropped money on the table for the bill and held out her hand to help Carrie from the booth. "Let's start with ice cream. Sound like a plan?"

"All good plans start with ice cream. That's just a fact."

The sun blanketed them in warmth when they stepped back onto the street. As they made their way toward an ice cream shop, Carrie smiled at the hopeful feeling in her heart. The fact that Dylan was willing to work on the things that were holding her back meant everything to her. She cared enough about Carrie to try to be the best person she could be, and that went a long way toward making Carrie feel good about where their relationship was heading.

CHAPTER SEVEN

Dylan checked her hair in the rearview mirror one last time before getting out of her car and walking up to knock on the door. When Carrie had texted and asked if they could hang out, she regretted canceling her appointment with the barber the day before. They'd texted each other every day for the last several weeks and talked on the phone every night before bed, but hadn't gone on an actual date since the car show.

The few times they were able to get together for coffee had been outstanding. Each one ended in a short make-out session in one of their cars afterward. Dylan had started seeing her therapist again, and they'd made considerable progress in reaching the root of her insecurities. She still had work to do, but she was feeling stronger than ever. Even her morning jogs with Val had become easier, and the time she had to talk to her best friend was helpful. Things were looking up, and Carrie's suggestion that they get together couldn't have come at a better time.

Before she reached the top step of the porch, the door opened, and Carrie ushered her in. "Hey," Dylan said as she took in the sundress Carrie was wearing. The white cloth against her olive skin was striking and left Dylan a little breathless. "You look amazing."

Carrie took the bottle of whiskey Dylan held and pulled her into the kitchen. "So do you. I missed you."

"I missed you, too. I'm glad you invited me over." Dylan sat on a stool at the kitchen counter. "Dinner smells amazing."

"I made mushroom risotto and a salad. Does that work for you?"

The large open kitchen was beautiful. Dylan wasn't much of a cook, but an image of herself and Carrie making a meal together flashed through her mind. The domestic scene brought a smile to her face. "Yeah, risotto and salad are perfect. Can I help you with anything?"

Carrie pulled two bowls from a cabinet near the sink and two small plates for salad. "Would you like to dish us each a bowl of risotto, and I'll get the salad ready?"

She knew she was smiling again but couldn't stop herself.

"What?" Carrie asked.

"Nothing." Dylan ladled risotto into the bowls and sprinkled a little extra Parmesan on top of each one. "Should we have wine with dinner and graduate to whiskey for dessert?"

"I like how you think. Croutons on your salad?" Carrie held up a bag Dylan recognized from her favorite bakery.

"Yes, please. Montez Street Bakers make the best." Dylan tucked the bottle of wine under her arm and picked up a bowl in each hand. She watched Carrie sprinkle croutons on the salads and then followed her into the dining room. "Your house is great. I know I saw it a little before our first date, but I didn't notice this beautiful dining room before. It seems like a big house for just one person."

Carrie handed her a wine opener while she gathered wineglasses from the hutch near the table. "It is. My grandparents had four kids, but they were spaced out enough that only three were home at one time. They needed the four bedrooms until my Uncle Roy moved out. Once they were down to only two kids, she turned the extra room into an office. She was an accountant."

"That's impressive." Dylan poured them each a glass of wine. "She sounds like a cool lady. I could never be an accountant."

"Me, either. She was also a pilot," Carrie said.

"No way."

Carrie swelled with pride. "Yep. She made postal flights during World War II. The local man who did it left for the war, and she already had her pilot's license, so she flew them while he was gone. She loved it, but of course, he wanted his job when he came home from the war. They expected her to go home, raise kids, and cater to her husband."

Dylan rolled her eyes. "Ugh. I'm so glad things aren't like that now."

"Me, too. Don't get me wrong. I want to settle down, have kids, do the whole domestic thing, but I want a partner interested in sharing those duties with me, who doesn't expect me to be the little wife and stay home raising their children without any help. I don't judge women who choose to do that. It's just not for me. I want a true partner."

Dylan nodded. "I want the same. My mom was a housewife, and she loved it, but my dad was completely helpless when it came to cooking, cleaning, kids, anything other than his profession, and after a while, it all wore her down to the point that she became bitter. I think if he'd even given her one night a week to hang out with her friends or just take a hot bath and read a book, she would have been a completely different person. I've never wanted that—either side of that equation. I've always thought I'd find an equal partner to share my life with." She chose to leave out the part where her mom eventually became an alcoholic and her father finally left her for another woman. Dylan's childhood had always been a source of embarrassment. She was confident Carrie wouldn't judge her or think less of her, but some things she just didn't want to discuss until they'd gotten to know each other a little more.

"This is amazing, by the way," Dylan said, hoping to lead the subject away from her messed-up family. "I haven't had risotto in years, but this is reminding me how much I love it."

Carrie graciously accepted the redirection. "It's easier than people would lead you to believe. It's all about patience, but if you can allow it time, it's well worth the effort."

Dylan looked at her almost-empty bowl. She hoped Carrie might be talking about more than just the meal she'd made. "This seems like a good opportunity to thank you for your patience with me. You've given me more than I probably deserve."

Carrie pushed away her empty dish and took a sip of wine, a cautiously measured response. "If I didn't think you were deserving, I would have moved on. I'm not the type of person to put effort into someone I can't see being with in the future. I'm in my mid-thirties. That's not old by any means, but I'm also past the age where I want to waste my time. I believe in you, Dylan. I like you a lot."

Dylan's eyes started to burn, and she quickly took another sip of wine before tears could fall. She cleared her throat and pulled Carrie's hand into hers from where it rested on the table. "I'm very grateful, because frankly, the thought of no longer having you in my life breaks my heart."

"Do you mind if I ask how your therapy's been? I only ask because you've been fairly open about it so far, but don't feel like you have to talk about it if you aren't comfortable."

"Not at all." Dylan poured the last of the wine into Carrie's glass and stood. "Let's put this stuff away and sit by the fire. Do you mind? I might need whiskey if we're going to talk about feelings."

Carrie laughed and helped Dylan gather the dishes from the table. It didn't escape Dylan's notice that she and Carrie had become more comfortable with each other in the short time since they'd started hanging out. Probably more so than she'd been with Michelle in their entire relationship. This was all Dylan had ever wanted in her life. She would do whatever it took to get to a place where she could be the best version of herself, not only for Carrie but for her own happiness.

They worked together to put everything away and soon sat on the couch in front of a crackling fire. Dylan sipped her whiskey and luxuriated in its smoothness. She closed her eyes and rested her head back against the cushions, allowing the sting to travel down her throat on its way to help her sort through the jumble of emotions she was experiencing. Finally, she looked up to find Carrie patiently watching her. My God, she was beautiful.

"You don't have to talk to me about this if it's too much right now. It's not why I invited you over for dinner."

Dylan took Carrie's hand from the back of the couch and threaded their fingers together. The warmth of Carrie's touch was like a balm to her soul and gave her the courage she needed to speak. "I want to talk to you, which is strange, because I'm not usually comfortable discussing my feelings with anyone other than Val."

Carrie squeezed her hand. "Thanks for trusting me."

"Therapy is...good. We've talked a lot about why I allowed Michelle to control me and make me feel like I wasn't good enough. I told you a little about my dad earlier. He wasn't a terrible dad, but I was never quite what he had in mind when he learned he would have a baby girl. I think he felt like if I was going to dress like a boy and act like a boy, I should do everything he would expect his son to do. That just wasn't me. I was a total computer nerd who played video games. I wasn't into fixing cars or hunting or any of the things my dad tried to convince me I should do if I were butch. I was really into remote-control stuff, which eventually led to drones and programming the systems that control them. He never got it and wasn't afraid to let me know what a disappointment I was."

Dylan had never been one to open up about her childhood or discuss any of the things that made her vulnerable, but between her therapy sessions and the comfort she felt with Carrie, sharing this part of herself felt good.

To Carrie's credit, she silently held Dylan's hand, giving her full attention to what she was saying. The support she felt was like a warm blanket, and she knew then what a blessing it was to have Carrie in her life.

"Do you have siblings?" Carrie asked.

"Nope. Just me. My dad and I are okay now, I guess. My parents divorced when I was in high school, and he married a woman about half his age. They have a couple of kids of their own. I'm not part of that family. He calls me on my birthday and at Christmas every year. We do all right."

"You told me once that you had all kinds of confidence in college. How did you get to that point?"

Dylan rubbed her thumb back and forth across the palm of Carrie's hand, and the motion helped ground her. This was a lot of feelings to visit, but it was necessary if she wanted Carrie to understand her fully.

"Confidence, arrogance, call it whatever you want. It's not always easy to tell the difference when you're that age." Dylan rolled her eyes, which made Carrie laugh. "Let's call it confidence, though."

"Deal. Confidence it is." Carrie sipped her wine, then pulled Dylan's head into her lap and started playing with her hair. This had to be a good sign. Maybe there was something to this sharing feelings thing after all?

"I got a full-ride scholarship to UC Berkeley for aerospace engineering."

Carrie's fingers stilled, and she gripped Dylan's hair slightly. "Are you serious? You're a freaking rocket scientist?"

Dylan chuckled. "Technically, yes. Top of my class. Hence the arrogance."

"I guess so. Not to be an asshole, but you're telling me you're an aerospace engineer, and you didn't know how to change a tire?"

It wasn't meant as a jibe, but it landed like a blow just the same. "Jesus, Carrie. One skill doesn't necessarily translate to the other."

"Oh, God. I'm so sorry." Carrie placed a hand over her mouth as if just realizing what she'd said. "I didn't mean it like that, Dylan. It just came out."

Dylan started to get up, but Carrie pulled her close. "I'm so sorry, baby. That was insensitive. Please forgive me."

It *was* kind of funny that a rocket scientist didn't know how to change a tire. If Dylan pushed her bruised ego aside, she could see the humor in that scenario. "I'm sure I could have figured it out. But my gut reaction to situations like that is to just call for help. My dad planted that seed. He convinced me that I couldn't do things, but then I went to Berkeley, where underclassmen idolized me. I had more girls wanting my attention than I could have ever dreamed of, and by my junior year I already had big companies recruiting me. I was living a life I'd never dreamed possible, and that's exactly why I fell into Michelle's trap. I was ripe for the picking, as some people would say. She's beautiful, smart, and knew what to say to stroke my ego enough for me to follow her wherever she decided to lead me. I was a complete jackass." Dylan's shame about being duped by someone she should have known was terrible from the start left a heaviness in her heart she wished she could ignore.

"I don't think that makes you a jackass. You were finally getting the positive attention you'd never received but always craved as a kid. You gravitated toward people who gave that to you because you needed to feel like you were important to someone. Like you were enough. That hardly makes you a jackass. It makes you human."

Dylan appreciated the sentiment more than she could ever hope to express in words. Beating herself up over who she'd become during that time in her life had only held her back from moving past it. Dylan settled back onto Carrie's lap so she could play with her hair some more. "So how are you feeling now? Has the therapist helped you wade through those feelings?"

"He's helped a lot. I'm beginning to like myself again, which feels good. I realize I don't have to fit into some mold and live up to someone else's expectations to be the person I know I am. Took me a little while, but I'm getting there."

Carrie took a drink of her wine, then cleared her throat. The warmth from the fire was like a blanket around them, and Dylan released a contented sigh. "This is nice," Dylan said.

"Dyl?"

"Yes?"

"Can I share the things that I'm looking for in a woman? The traits I'm attracted to?"

Dylan sat up and gave Carrie her full attention. "Please. I'd love to know."

Carrie smiled. "I'm not sharing this as a laundry list of things I want you to do or be. These are things you already do, and they're among the many reasons I'm so attracted to you. These aren't qualities only a butch lesbian can possess, but I have to admit, add these characteristics to a strong, incredibly hot stud like you, and I'm a goner."

"I think you're pretty spectacular, too." Dylan's cheeks warmed with what had to be a blush.

"I love that you hold the door open for me. Always. The gesture makes me feel special. I realize it's a courtesy that comes naturally to you, rather than a game you're playing to earn points. Chivalry is just what you do."

"To be honest, it makes me feel good, too. Any small thing I can do to take care of you, to show you how much you mean to me, is another chance for me to remind you of my feelings. Without words."

Carrie took Dylan's hand and ran a delicate finger along the lines on her palm. "I love how strong you are. I know I'm the mechanic and in no way a delicate little flower, but I'm so attracted to your strength and the confidence with which you carry yourself. Even when you're feeling insecure, you still give off this confidence that I find incredibly sexy. When you took me dancing, I was scared to death because I'd never danced the salsa before. I thought trying it would be a complete disaster and would only embarrass me. But it wasn't. I realize now I've never actually had a dance partner who truly led me around the floor like you did. You were in complete control, but you weren't controlling. It was like my feet weren't touching the ground. You were taking me on a journey, and all I had to do was enjoy it. I can only describe the experience as amazing."

Dylan turned to sit against the couch's other arm, inviting Carrie to cuddle into her arms instead. She let out a contented sigh when Dylan wrapped her arms around her and held her tight.

"I love how delicate but capable you are," Dylan said. "Once I got over my issues, I realized what a turn-on it is to be with such an incredibly beautiful, exquisite, feminine woman who also happens to be strong, smart, and confident. You being those things doesn't make me any less of what I am. I've never met anyone like you, Carrie. I'm sorry I was such an ass in the beginning. Sorry I'm…broken."

Carrie sat up and spoke directly to Dylan. "Everyone is broken in one way or another, Dylan. You've recognized your weaknesses, and you're willing to do the work to, if not exactly fix them, at least learn how to not allow them to control your life. I don't expect you to be perfect. I'm not perfect. I can sometimes be a little defensive about people underestimating me. I'm a femme woman who owns an automotive repair shop. I've been underestimated most of my life. I don't always react the way I would like to when I feel challenged by someone, but I try. I've gotten better about it over the years. Those situations will always come up unless misogyny somehow miraculously becomes a thing of the past."

"As if." Dylan rolled her eyes.

"Exactly. I deal with it, though. I just let my work speak for me. People will respect me or they won't. It's not my job to change their mind."

Dylan pulled her back into her arms. "You're a good influence on me, Carrie Grice. I'm incredibly lucky you came into my life."

Carrie squeezed Dylan's arms tighter around her. "Yeah. Me, too."

Something in the way Carrie spoke made Dylan pause, but she tried to push those feelings away and focus on the fact that they were together. In each other's arms. God, Carrie felt so good there. Dylan let her hand rest on Carrie's flat stomach as they both silently watched the flames dance around the logs in the fireplace. She hadn't felt this close to someone in a very long time, and she was almost afraid to move, worried it might break them from the moment.

The soft fingers of Carrie's small hands moved down to slide beneath the hem of Dylan's shirt. The move was subtle, but Dylan's heart rate immediately went into overdrive at the possibility of what it meant. Carrie gently grazed her fingers over the warm skin of her stomach. She wanted this woman more than she'd ever wanted anyone in her life, but she was also afraid to move too fast and rush Carrie into something she might not be ready to do. Dylan lowered her head and kissed the side of Carrie's neck, right below her ear. Carrie's rapid pulse thrummed against her lips.

"Dylan?" Carrie's soft voice broke through the silence.

"Hmm?"

"Will you make love to me?"

Dylan swallowed past the lump in her throat and forced herself to take a deep breath instead of screaming "Yes!" at the top of her lungs. "I'd love to." *Deep breath. Keep breathing. Keep it together.*

Carrie stood and held out a hand to help Dylan to her feet. "Let's go to the bedroom. I want to be able to take our time, and we'll be more comfortable there."

"You lead the way." Dylan tried to tamp down her excitement and play it cool, but thoughts of what was about to happen crowded out her ability to hide her emotions.

"You're shaking," Carrie said when they reached her bedroom door.

"I'm...excited."

Carrie began to unbutton Dylan's shirt. "Me, too. This feels different somehow. More important."

"I agree. I feel it, too. I just hope I—"

"Dylan?"

"Yeah?" Dylan's heart felt like it would explode out of her chest as Carrie placed kisses along her bared collarbone.

"Will you lead me through this dance as well?"

Dylan wasn't a religious person, but at that moment, she said a silent thank you to the universe for bringing this woman into her life. "It would be my honor."

CHAPTER EIGHT

The lights were off as Carrie led Dylan into her bedroom for the first time. She'd made sure things were tidy earlier in the day, in hopes the evening might end here. She wasn't one to have casual sex, not because she had a problem with it, but because it had simply never been her thing. Too much emotion was tied up in physical intimacy for her to let her guard down enough to let it go that far. She'd had one-night stands, and while they satisfied her physically, they always left her a bit hollow inside. Leading Dylan into her room, she knew that whatever happened next would be on an entirely different level than any sex she'd ever experienced before. She had no idea how this woman she hadn't met all that long ago, who had come into her life with more than one obstacle to overcome, had wound herself around her heart quite so tightly.

She felt the weight of the evening, of Dylan especially, laying her heart bare and allowing Carrie to know her in a way she suspected not many others did. Such a gesture of trust wasn't lost on Carrie, and she wanted to connect with Dylan in a way that was intimate and wholly mutual. She was falling for this woman, and for once in her life, she was ready to see where these emotions took them. She wanted to see where her heart led her, no matter the outcome.

Once they reached the bed, Dylan gently guided her to sit on the edge. Dylan's shirt was half unbuttoned from what they'd done in the hall, and the sight of her partially open flannel shirt with a tight tank underneath was enough to make Carrie weak. "Let me help you—"

"Uh-uh. This is my show to direct, remember? You need to have patience, my beautiful girl."

Carrie gasped as Dylan slowly thumbed open the remaining buttons and slid her shirt from her shoulders, dropping it on the floor next to the bed. "Do you have a dim light I can turn on so I can see? I don't want to miss a moment of being with you for the first time."

"The dresser. Over there by the door. You'll see a few candles and a box of matches."

Dylan leaned down and gently kissed Carrie's lips before going to light the candles. Carrie kicked off her slippers and twisted to reach the zipper on the back of her dress to lower it, but Dylan guided her hands away. "Hey, sweetie. I'm going to have to keep a close eye on you. You asked me to take charge, and that's exactly what I plan to do. We have a long night ahead of us. Let me take care of you. Agreed?"

Carrie was pretty sure she'd just melted into a puddle and would slide off the edge of the bed at any moment. She'd suspected Dylan would be good at this, but dear God, this was more than she'd ever hoped for. "Yes, ma'am."

Dylan smiled, then pulled off her boots and dropped them onto the floor next to her shirt. "You don't have to call me that. This time. Not that I'm against it, because believe me, I'm a fan, but this time I don't want anything other than to please you." Carrie couldn't tear her eyes away from Dylan's toned body and the muscular arms that were now exposed. Dylan Fleming was an incredibly hot woman, and Carrie suddenly felt a little shy about exposing her own body. She'd never been ashamed of her physical shape. She worked out, ate well, had a very manual job, but Dylan…They'd messed around so Carrie definitely knew she had a hard physique under all that flannel, but she'd had no idea how attractive Dylan would be.

All she could do was silently watch as Dylan pressed her lips against Carrie's and gently pushed her back to lie flat against the bed. Having this strong, confident woman above her, kissing her like she'd never in her life been kissed before, intoxicated her. Just as Carrie was beginning to struggle to catch her breath from excitement, Dylan broke the contact and made her way down the length of Carrie, planting kisses as she went. The bed shifted as Dylan slid off and knelt on the floor in front of her legs, which were still draped over the side. Carrie started to rise so she could see what was happening, but Dylan stopped her with a gentle hand. "Relax, baby. I'm going to take care of you. Let me make you feel good."

This was everything and almost too much. Carrie's breathing was so rapid, she was beginning to feel light-headed. "Dyl, baby, I—"

"Shhh…" Dylan slipped her hands under Carrie's hemline and rubbed her calves as she pressed against the front of Carrie's legs. "It's okay, Care. Just breathe, baby. Everything's okay. If you need me to stop, don't hesitate—"

"No," Carrie said with more vehemence than she intended. "No, please. I'm fine. Just excited. Please don't stop. I feel like such a fool. I promise I've had sex before."

Dylan chuckled. "I have no doubt. You're an incredibly gorgeous woman. I'm sure you've had to fight them off with a stick."

"I don't know about a stick, but—oh." Dylan slid her hands higher to caress the tops of her thighs. She couldn't decide if she wanted to snap her legs tight because the sensations were too much or spread her legs farther apart to encourage Dylan to take her faster.

"Spread your legs for me, sweetheart. May I lift your dress so I can see your beautiful body?"

Carrie nodded and spread her legs a little farther apart. The room wasn't exactly cold, but when Dylan lifted her dress and exposed her from the waist down, Carrie felt a mild chill, or maybe it was only a thrill of excitement. She wasn't exactly sure of anything right then other than the anticipation of what was to come, pushing her close to what felt like insanity.

"My God, Carrie. You're breathtaking."

Carrie held her breath as Dylan took her time, running her fingers across every inch of exposed skin on her legs. All she could do was clutch her dress and hope she didn't embarrass herself. She'd never felt so bare and so wanted. She was doing her best to process her emotions. "I…thank you."

"May I kiss you here?" Strong fingers traced along her inner thighs from just above her knees to slightly below her center.

"Yes, please, yes, I—"

"Thank you."

Carrie had glimpsed the confident person she thought Dylan truly was, but nothing could have prepared her for this. The woman kneeling before her was beyond any fantasy Carrie could've imagined. Taking a breath, Carrie coached herself to just relax and enjoy what was happening.

Even though she knew it was coming, Carrie jumped when a warm tongue followed by soft lips began to worship her inner thighs. Dylan was in no hurry, no matter how much Carrie needed her to be. Lick, kiss, lick, kiss. She inched her way up, a few inches on one side and then a few inches on the other. Lick, kiss, lick, kiss, until finally she reached Carrie's center. She knew she had to be soaking through her panties at that point. Carrie could feel the tickle as her wetness dripped onto her panties. Dylan could surely see the evidence right in front of her face. Carrie couldn't possibly hide how excited she was, and in that moment, she wasn't embarrassed. She wanted this woman more than she'd ever wanted anyone and had no shame about showing her the evidence of her attraction.

"Care?"

Carrie released a shaky breath. "Yes?"

"May I remove your panties?"

Jesus Christ. Carrie was pretty sure she'd died and gone to heaven. When she'd asked Dylan to take charge, she had no idea she was going to get this type of behavior. "Please touch me, Dyl. I need you so much."

"I know, sweetie. I promise I'm going to make you feel so good. Your patience will be rewarded." Dylan placed a kiss on her cloth-covered center before sliding the panties down her legs and dropping them onto the growing pile of clothes on the floor. "You doing okay?"

"More than okay. I'm going to burst."

Dylan's lips were back on Carrie's inner thigh, and she chuckled as her teeth lightly grazed Carrie's sensitive skin. "You've been a very good girl. I promise this will be worth the wait."

"Even if we stop right this second, this is already the best sex I've ever had."

"We haven't even begun." Dylan traced her fingers around the edge of Carrie's lower lips, sending a fresh flood of wetness to her increasingly swollen center. "You're so beautiful, Carrie. Absolutely perfect."

Part of Carrie was desperate to beg Dylan to fuck her right then, but the other part wanted nothing more than to allow her the control she'd so expertly taken. This was a master class in anticipation, and Carrie was happy to be the recipient of her attention.

"Dylan…"

"I'm right here, baby. Are you ready for me to make you feel good, to give you what you need?"

Carrie gripped the sheets on either side of her hips, nearing her breaking point. "Yes." She inadvertently held her breath and lifted her hips as Dylan once again placed kisses along the inside of her inner thigh. These were faster, more focused, and unstopping until she reached the juncture of Carrie's legs. She was so overheated the tongue almost felt cool at first touch, but it quickly warmed as Dylan licked the soft but rigid folds of her labia. The touch was gentle, pulling first one side, then the other into her mouth to give each a gentle suck. Carrie was in heaven. This was what the ethereal kingdom, if it truly existed, would be like. She'd never believed in heaven before this moment, but this was too good not to be this sensational.

"You feel so good. It all feels so…"

Dylan gave a low rumble from her chest, and Carrie knew she was quite proud of herself. She deserved it. "Ah." Carrie gasped as Dylan flattened her tongue and started to work on her clit—gently at first, with long, wide laps, before carefully sucking it into her warm mouth and giving it a slight tug. The rhythm Dylan set became the drumbeat guiding her breathing until it quickened enough that Carrie felt light-headed. She focused on slow, measured breaths. In, then out.

Dylan dragged Carrie even closer to the edge of the bed and began a new stroke of sucking her clit into her mouth and swiping her tongue across the tip, then releasing it with a gentle, teasing lap. Carrie's orgasm grew closer, and she wanted to hold it off to make this moment last yet usher it in so she could experience what she could already tell would be fucking amazing.

"Don't stop, Dylan. I'm so close."

Carrie sucked in a breath when a finger traced the edge of her entrance. "May I stick—"

"Yes, fuck, yes. Please, Dylan. I need you inside me."

Dylan groaned a primal noise and slipped her finger inside. "God, Carrie, you're so fucking tight."

"I…I haven't had sex in a while."

"Mmm. I can tell. Do you mind if I stretch you a bit? May I add another finger?"

"It'll make me come." Carrie could hear the regret in her own voice. "If you do that, I'll definitely come."

The fingers inside her never ceased their movement, but Dylan raised her head to study Carrie's face. "Do you want to come, or should I make this last longer?"

That was the million-dollar question. If this continued, Carrie was quite sure she would literally pass out. She'd never been this turned on, and much more of this might be too much of a good thing. Was she—

"Carrie?" Dylan's voice broke through her thoughts.

"Yeah, sorry."

"Baby, this is only the beginning. This is only the first in what I hope will be many orgasms to come. Pun intended. Let me make you feel good, and then you can rest up for the other ways I plan to worship your gorgeous body tonight and for all the nights ahead. If you'll have me."

Carrie laughed. "Oh, I plan to *have* you for a very long time, so please...make me come. I want you inside me when I do."

"Your wish is my command." Dylan resumed her position between Carrie's legs and reestablished the rhythm on her clit. She gradually pulled her finger out and gathered as much of the copious amounts of wetness as she could before gently pushing two fingers back inside. It took Carrie only a few seconds before the slight sting of penetration turned into pleasure and Dylan increased the speed of her thrusts. "I'm going to make you come now, sweetheart."

Carrie gripped the sheets tight and screamed her release as Dylan pushed into her deeply enough to send her careening off an edge she'd had no idea even existed. Saying this was the biggest orgasm she'd ever had was an understatement. Nothing had ever compared to this feeling, which stole her breath. She wanted to scream, say Dylan's name over and over and tell her how thrilled she was that they'd found each other, but no words would come out, only silence.

When she could take no more, she found her voice. "Enough, Dylan. I'll die."

Dylan stopped, then carefully pulled her fingers from Carrie's center. "Are you okay? I didn't hurt you, did I?"

The concern on Dylan's face tugged at Carrie's heart. "Oh, sweetie, that was the single most pleasurable thing that has ever happened to me."

"Really?" Dylan's broad smile made Carrie laugh.

"Get up here, you big galoot." Dylan climbed into bed and pulled Carrie up to lie with her on the pillows.

"We haven't even taken our clothes off yet. I haven't even seen your boobs." Dylan's look of excited wonder warmed Carrie's heart. How could anyone make this woman feel anything less than perfect?

"You're amazing, Dylan Fleming. I'm not only saying that because you just gave me the greatest sex of my life. You're everything I've ever wanted, and I need you to know that you're enough. No matter what anyone has said to you or made you feel in the past, you are more than enough, and I hope you'll allow me the chance to prove that fact to you."

Carrie couldn't interpret Dylan's expression. She was starting to worry she'd said something wrong...until a tear trailed down Dylan's cheek. "Thank you."

"They aren't just words. I intend to show you how much you mean to me for as long as you'll have me."

Dylan grinned. "You've got a big job ahead, because I don't intend to let you go. Let's get naked and do more fun stuff."

"You just might be the death of me, Dylan Fleming, but oh, what a way to go."

EPILOGUE

Thanks for coming out, everyone, and for donating to such an important cause. Every dollar counts and means so much to the families affected by the wildfires last season. I want to dedicate this last song to a special someone sitting on a blanket amongst y'all holding a beer with my name on it. Let's do this." Carrie turned to her band and counted them down.

The cheer from the crowd surrounded her, and the music filled her soul as they played their most popular song. They were only a local band but had a modest following, and every time Carrie stepped onto the stage, she felt such joy. Knowing Dylan was in the crowd, cheering them on, was the icing on the cake.

The song ended, and Carrie and her bandmates took their last bow before leaving the stage. She hadn't played with them in a few months, but the half hour they'd spent onstage today reminded her how much fun they used to have. She silently promised herself that she would invite them over soon to start working on new music.

She safely locked her guitar away and made her way to the section where she knew Dylan would be waiting. As she walked through the crowd, people held up their hands to give her a high-five and complimented her on the set. She loved being a part of this community and was proud of how they all came together to support those who needed extra help in these trying times.

"Hey, sexy," Carrie said as she plopped down next to Dylan on the blanket.

"You were awesome, Care. Thanks so much for inviting me."

"Thanks for coming. Was it okay that I mentioned you?" It had been a spur-of-the-moment decision to dedicate their last song to Dylan. Carrie hoped she hadn't embarrassed her.

"Are you kidding?" The excitement in Dylan's voice made her heart swell. "Who wouldn't be honored to have a stunning, talented woman dedicate a fantastic song to her in front of a crowd? I can't wait to tell Val. She's going to be so jealous."

Carrie kissed Dylan on the cheek. "I'm glad that made you happy. Now, where's my beer?" They both laughed as Dylan pulled a beer from the cooler and handed it to her.

"You're a very demanding woman."

Carrie guided Dylan's head down into her lap and threaded her fingers through her short hair. "I thought you liked it when I'm demanding?"

"Oh, I like it very much. Especially when——" Dylan stopped mid-sentence to stare at two women in the distance who appeared to be walking toward them. The tension on Dylan's face told Carrie all she needed to know. She had no doubt that one of these women was Michelle.

Well, this should be interesting.

Dylan remained silent as the women weaved their way through the crowd of concertgoers sprawled out on blankets. The smaller of the two wore a dress Carrie was sure must have cost the equivalent of one month of her salary, along with Louboutin shoes that had no business at an outdoor event. That had to be Michelle.

Carrie watched Dylan carefully. The next few minutes would speak volumes about where they stood as a couple and where Carrie fit into Dylan's life. She was surprised by how nervous a test like this made her. Dylan had been very clear she was over Michelle, but seeing the beautiful woman in real life left a lump in Carrie's throat, one she was struggling to swallow around.

"Hey, Dyl," the leader of the two said.

"Michelle. Hey, Tammy. How are you?"

"I'm good, Dylan. It's great to see you again," Tammy said.

Michelle rolled her eyes and stuck out her hand to Carrie. "I saw your set, Carrie. It was…cute. I'm Dylan's ex-girlfriend, Michelle, and this is my friend Tammy."

Tammy looked like she wanted to be anywhere other than where she was. Carrie didn't blame her. She felt that way as well.

"Hey." Carrie assumed that the less ammunition she gave this woman, the better, so she kept her response short.

"So Dyl—"

"I don't want to be rude, but we don't have to do this, Michelle. Things between us weren't exactly friendly, and I'm not ready to pretend none of it happened. No matter how happy I am now." Dylan turned to Tammy. "It was good to see you, Tammy."

"You, too," Tammy said, noticeably trying not to smile.

Carrie was pretty sure actual steam escaped from Michelle's ears at the cold brush-off. If they weren't adults, it would be almost funny to see this situation play out. As a grown-up, it was just plain uncomfortable.

Michelle dug into her Coach bag and extracted a blinged-out phone. Dylan muttered an apology to Carrie as they watched her frantically locate a photo that she showed off with a smirk. "This is my new girlfriend, Jael. She's a doctor and, not to get too personal, fucking amazing in bed. Probably the best sex I've ever had." The image was of an admittedly hot butch woman, but Carrie looked at her own girlfriend and knew they didn't even compare. Dylan had a warmth that this Jael chick looked like she lacked.

"Great. Good for you. Tell Jael I said good luck with that."

"You're so fucking rude, Dylan. This is what happens when you don't have someone to teach you some manners." Michelle directed her glare at Carrie while delivering that final dig.

"I don't need—" Dylan stopped mid-sentence and took a deep breath. Carrie could see the effort it took to control her emotions, and she was so proud to see her not play into Michelle's juvenile games. "I'm done with you, Michelle. Like, for real. I'm asking you politely to leave us alone. If you don't, we'll have to get out of here, and I'd much rather make out with my beautiful girlfriend, who makes me feel like the biggest stud in the world every time she looks at me. I'm enough for her, and she's more than I could ever hope to have in a partner, so if you don't mind, take your negativity and hatred somewhere else."

Carrie was speechless. Everything out of Dylan's mouth was precisely what she'd wanted to hear. It was everything Carrie had needed to hear her say. It wasn't about Michelle, but about the confidence Dylan had exuded. This hot, take-control, take-no-prisoners confidence had Carrie wishing they weren't in the middle of a park full of people at that moment.

Tammy took Michelle's phone and shoved it back into her bag. "You take care of yourself, Dyl. I'm happy for you." With that, she pushed a noticeably shocked Michelle back the direction they'd come.

"I'm so sor—"

"Hey," Carrie said. "You have no reason to apologize. That woman deserved everything you said to her, and I couldn't be prouder of you."

"Really?"

Carrie couldn't stop her emotions from bubbling to the surface. She pushed Dylan onto her back and kissed her deeply, right there on the blanket in the middle of a field of people. "Really."

"Wow. If I'd known standing up to some crazy woman would make you hot for me, I'd have done it months ago."

"This wasn't just any woman. This was the woman who stole your dignity for much longer than she should have. She deserved everything you said to her, and I'm just so happy you didn't back down." Carrie watched as a mixture of emotions crossed Dylan's face. Thankfully the one she finally settled on seemed to be satisfaction.

With a slightly puffed-out chest and a huge grin, Dylan brushed her lips against Carrie's and whispered, "Thanks."

Carrie shifted so she was lying next to Dylan on the blanket. "Hey, I know it's only been a few months, but what do you think about moving in with me?"

Dylan's eyes went wide with shock. "Move in with you?"

Carrie's heart sank. "I was worried it might be too soon to ask, but things between us have been so good, and you practically live at my house already. I'm so—"

"Carrie, I would love to move in with you. I've wanted to for a while but wasn't sure how to ask. Especially since it would be me moving into your house."

"I should have asked sooner. I wasn't sure if you'd be ready and didn't want to mess up what we had."

"Oh, baby, you aren't going to mess up what we have. We're in this together. I love you."

The crowd around them cheered for the band that had just taken the stage, but Carrie couldn't help but feel like it was also for them. They'd come a long way since that disastrous first date, and Carrie was ecstatic she'd given Dylan another chance to show her who she truly was. "You should take me home right now, Dylan Fleming. I need you to do things to me I've been fantasizing about all day."

Dylan smiled. "Yes, ma'am." She stood, helped Carrie to her feet, and picked up the blanket and cooler before she led them toward the parking lot. When they reached the car, Dylan opened the door for Carrie and knelt next to her while she buckled her seat belt. "Are you sure you're okay, sweetie? I'd hoped we would never run into that troll, but I guess it was inevitable. The town we live in isn't that large."

Carrie placed her hand on Dylan's warm cheek and ran her thumb along the edge of her lips. "It's okay. You were everything I'd hoped you would be in that moment, and I'm so turned on right now, I just want to get you naked. You're everything I've ever dreamed of in a partner, baby. Everything. Let's go home so I can show my appreciation."

"Let's go home." The pride that shone in Dylan's eyes was a good look on her.

AN EPIPHANY IN FLANNEL

Meghan O'Brien

Meet-Cute at Midnight

Maisie Davis tucked her favorite romance novel under the counter at Moe's Fine Diner, snatched back to reality by the door's chime mere pages before a love scene she knew by heart but couldn't stop rereading. The unexpected interruption had sent her scrambling like a guilty child, so she took a deep breath and pushed aside her frustration, determined to be gracious despite the literary coitus interruptus. She looked up with a smile, ready to welcome her first customer in over an hour, when it suddenly dawned on her how good-looking the man in front of her was. The greeting died in her throat. All she could manage was a quiet, "Hello."

"Evening." Entranced, Maisie watched as the most beautiful man she'd ever seen in real life strolled into the otherwise empty dining room and nodded at a corner booth. "Mind if I sit there?"

"Not in the least." Having lost the chance to play it cool, Maisie almost wasn't fazed when she dropped two menus on the floor while reaching for an entirely different one to offer the handsome stranger. "I'll be your waitress *and* your cook tonight, so I wouldn't recommend the omelet. I'm not very good at those."

The man stopped to give her an amused look. "What about pancakes?"

"Much better. Pancakes are the perfect food, so I want them when I want them." Did she sound as stupid to this absolute dreamboat as she did to her own ears? "Which is why I taught myself to make my own when I was a kid."

He chuckled, blue eyes sparkling like the deepest sea. "Pancakes it is."

With a tip of his hat, the man ambled to his chosen booth and took the seat with the best view of the parking lot. Maisie grabbed a clean glass and went to the ice and water dispensers, glancing out the front window to where the man's attention had drifted. A decent-sized big rig was parked at the edge of the lot, the logo painted on its side as unfamiliar to her as the man it had carried here. Careful to hold the glass steady, she walked to the trucker with a single mission—to convince this nice man that she was more amiable than awkward.

Maisie cringed inside. When had she ever cared what random customers thought about her personality? Embarrassed to be acting like a lovestruck dope, Maisie set the glass on the table and put on a congenial face. "Welcome to Moe's, by the way. Would you like coffee or juice with your pancakes?"

The trucker pulled the ball cap from his head, raked remarkably delicate fingers through his tousled hair, and flashed a little grin. "Coffee, please." Then he shrugged off his leather jacket to reveal the chest-hugging, hint-of-cleavage-revealing blue flannel shirt beneath, shattering Maisie's poise for the second time.

The trucker was a woman—the most magnificent woman Maisie had ever laid eyes on. Her attraction to the stranger increased a thousandfold, as did her fear. This was hardly the first time she'd admired the fairer sex, but it *was* the first time any person of any stripe made her feel like this—desperate to know them, to kiss them, to be held by them. She'd always figured her brain must be wired differently than other peoples', that she would never be unambiguously attracted to a real flesh-and-blood human being despite her quiet fascination with sex and romance. But this situation proved her brain could be just as horny as anyone's.

All it took was meeting the right trucker.

"Care to join me?"

Maisie blinked, cheeks burning anew at her ignorance. Now that she was paying attention, the trucker's voice wasn't even all that deep. Why had she assumed this stunning creation was a man? Was she really that sexist? "Sorry," Maisie said, embarrassed by her own naïveté. At the stranger's bemused expression, she changed her inflection. "I mean, sorry?"

"If you're up for a late-night short stack, that is." The trucker rolled up the cuffs of her blue flannel shirt, drawing Maisie's attention to how perfectly the fabric accentuated her soulful eyes. "If you are, it's on me. Quiet as this place is, you might as well take a load off and share in a perfect midnight feast. Assuming you're hungry."

Maisie scanned the deserted diner, all too aware that she had nothing better to do. She'd agreed to cover this shift for the copious reading time, not the tips. If she was lucky, she'd see maybe five customers before Linda arrived at six for the breakfast shift. And it wasn't like she *didn't* want pancakes. That was rarely the case.

"My feelings won't be hurt if you say no." The lady trucker's swagger seemed to be fading. "Just seems dead in here…and it's been about a week since I've had any kind of meaningful human interaction. But that's the cost of living on the road, obviously, and most definitely not your problem."

Maisie was starting to feel like a real asshole. Forcing her brain and mouth back into proper working order, she said, "Sure, but I'm not charging you for my portion."

"Fair enough." The trucker's broad grin made Maisie tingle in places she hadn't realized existed. "I'm Aiden, by the way." The introduction was accompanied by a friendly smile and a work-worn hand. "It's a pleasure to meet you…Maisie."

Following Aiden's gaze down to the name tag on her chest, Maisie wondered what else those smoky eyes had noticed. "You, too." She shook Aiden's hand. "Though I can't promise I'll be very good company. You may leave here disappointed."

Aiden squeezed her fingers, then let go. "Don't worry about that. I'm not."

Easy for a stud like Aiden to say. Maisie floated to the kitchen, tying an apron around her waist before throwing together a fresh bowl of batter. On autopilot, she poured six largish circles on the hot griddle and watched nervously for tiny bubbles to appear on top. She was almost afraid for the pancakes to finish. Once they were done, the socializing would begin.

Sharing a late-night meal with a customer was unprofessional, at best. Chatting up the type of woman who would have her narrow-minded parents frothing at the mouth in righteous judgment felt downright dangerous. Yet she couldn't seem to hit the brakes on whatever was happening. Like a child with a hurricane at her back, Maisie stumbled ahead, powerless to escape whatever force of nature was driving her into the unknown.

She'd rejected plenty of male customers in the past. What was so different about Aiden? Even when she'd believed "he" was just another long-haul trucker, Maisie had been stirred in ways she still didn't quite understand. Why hadn't she *wanted* to say no? And why was she so desperate for Aiden to enjoy this meal—and her?

Hands shaking, Maisie stacked three pancakes on each plate and called out, "Do you like butter?"

"Even more than I like breathing."

Maisie chuckled and plopped two small scoops of butter atop each of their piles. "One more thing we have in common."

"I knew I liked you for a reason." Aiden slid out of the booth and strode toward the counter, oozing charm. "Will you let me carry those for you?"

Too busy replaying her latest verbal slip-up to register the gallant request, Maisie didn't answer. *One more thing we have in common.* What if Aiden thought she meant they were compatible for reasons beyond a mutual love of flapjacks and butter? She didn't even know if Aiden liked women. What if she was reading too much into the short haircut, the sexy flannel shirt, and the length of time Aiden's attention had lingered in the vicinity of her name tag? She might be guilty of stereotyping again. Maybe Aiden was a badass heterosexual lady trucker in dire need of a friendly late-night chat to help her stay awake—and Maisie just so happened to be the only candidate in the vicinity.

Aiden reached for the plates. "May I?"

Confused, then self-conscious, Maisie drew her arms closer to her chest. "I've got it."

Judging from her stricken look, Aiden hadn't anticipated a refusal. "Oh. My apologies." She stepped away from the counter, gesturing Maisie toward their corner booth. "You are the professional here. I wasn't trying to suggest otherwise."

Maisie's stomach dropped at her knee-jerk reaction to a well-intentioned offer of good, old-fashioned chivalry. "No, I'm sorry." She held both plates over the counter. "How about you carry these? I'll grab the syrup."

"Sure thing." Aiden tipped her head, wearing a mile-wide grin as she took their meals. "This smells amazing."

Somehow even such banal praise had the power to make Maisie's cheeks burn anew. "Thanks. It's, uh...not my recipe or anything."

"But you brought them to fruition." Aiden honored the minor effort with a stately bow. "Respect."

Was that flirting? Maisie had no clue how any of this worked. Romance novels could only get her so far, seeing as she wasn't trying to seduce a multi-millionaire executive or some literal knight in shining armor. Could she safely assume that Aiden was more than likely attracted to her? Or was she reading too much into friendly banter? Maisie swiped a bottle of maple syrup from under the counter and followed Aiden, glad she'd decided to surrender control of the grub. Her hands were shaking.

Aiden set their plates on the table and slid back into her seat, taking yet another peek out the window in the direction of her dark, silent rig. Maisie deposited the syrup in the center of the table, then sat down across from Aiden. Following her gaze, Maisie said, "There's no need to worry about your truck. Hardly anyone's out at this time of night, and nothing ever happens in this town anyway."

Nodding, Aiden faced her head-on and unwrapped the napkin from around the set of utensils in front of her. "I'm not concerned about my ride so much as I am my dog." Maisie watched the strong hands across the table slice into and then spear a forkful of pancake. "He didn't want to wake up when I tried to take him out to potty, so I decided not to push it since he tends to get lonely when I'm gone. I'm hoping he'll sleep through this pit stop so I can stay inside and chat with you a while longer."

Maisie didn't know what to say. What was actually happening here? Aiden could be a dashing butch with an inexplicable crush or else a serial killer intent on luring innocent, skirt-and-sandals-clad waitresses into her mobile torture chamber with tales of the adorable puppy waiting inside. It would be stupid to ignore the potential danger and focus on Aiden's chiseled features and delicious body instead. Right?

Maisie studied Aiden's contented chewing, her kind eyes, and the open, unguarded expression on her face. "What kind of dog?"

Aiden lit up. "Pit bull." She balanced her fork on the plate and extracted a smart phone from her jacket pocket. "I hope you want to see a picture, because I'm showing you one. Or twenty."

Well, she wasn't faking this affection for her canine friend. That was plain as day. Swallowing the small bite she'd taken, Maisie leaned forward to look at the image on Aiden's phone. "Aww!" Serial killer or not, Maisie's heart melted at the goofy, open-mouthed grin on the precious face of the white pit bull on her home screen. "He's darling." She cooed again when Aiden flipped to the next photo, a selfie she'd taken with her arm around the dog's shoulder. "What do you call him?"

"Major. After the street I found him on." Aiden swiped left to reveal a ridiculous image of the pit bull wrapped in a blanket like a giant burrito, tongue lolling from the silly face that stuck out of one end. "I keep telling him I'll promote him to lieutenant general once he stops farting in the cab—and not a moment sooner."

Maisie laughed, tickled by the begrudging affection in Aiden's complaint about her almost-certainly-real companion. "Poor boy. What are you feeding him?"

"Raw, meaty bones are his favorite. Other than that, kibble." Aiden lowered her face and wolfed down another mouthful of pancakes. "And perhaps a few too many cubes of cheddar cheese. They're one of my favorite daytime snacks. Major's, too."

Rolling her eyes, Maisie realized that she'd started to mirror Aiden's steady rate of consumption, no doubt because this conversation was easier than she'd expected and far less awkward than she'd feared. "You feed your dog cheese, then chastise him for passing gas. Kind of cold, don't you think, after you've set him up to fail like that?"

Aiden snorted. "He loves it, though. And makes the cutest faces when he begs. You have no idea how hard it is to say no," Aiden's smoky eyes locked onto hers, triggering a flash flood of desire between Maisie's already trembling thighs, "to something that irresistible."

Realistically, what *were* the odds Aiden was a truck-driving murderer engaged in an after-hours hunt? Not zero, she supposed, but probably less than five percent, tops. Ten at the most. It seemed far more likely that Aiden was exactly what she seemed—a basically good-natured, masculine-presenting, working woman who had a cute dog waiting in her truck. A dog who might currently be hungry. Without questioning herself, Maisie said, "I'm almost positive we have some raw, meaty bones in the back. If you wanted, you could take a couple to

Major as a peace offering. You know, to make amends for your lengthy absence."

Aiden's laughter grew. "Oh, man. See? You're wrapped around his paw, and you haven't even met him yet."

Want to see my puppy? Well, follow me, little girl. He's right over here. Here in the back of my murder van. Maisie shivered, unsettled by her lingering paranoia about Aiden's intentions. At the moment, she didn't know what she was more afraid of—being killed or being kissed. Or rather, she did know...but it was a damn close call. Flustered, Maisie shoveled more food into her mouth to avoid answering the subtle invitation.

"I'd love to purchase a couple bones for him, as long as you have enough to spare."

"Definitely." Maisie paused to swallow before going on. "But as the cutest dog I've seen all month, Major qualifies for the good-boy discount. So the bones are on the house. A gift from me to him."

"Would you like to present them to the good boy yourself?"

Maisie's attention flicked out the window, first searching the darkened cab of the truck for any trace of white fur, then scanning the parking lot and adjoining streets for any sign of life. Nothing. They were alone. Unwatched.

"Once we've eaten, I can go grab him and meet you right out front." As though sensing her hesitation, Aiden said, "Unless you'd rather have us go around back. Whatever works for you." She paused to swallow. When Maisie made no attempt to respond, Aiden stared down at her nearly empty plate, rosy-cheeked and full of a brand-new awkwardness that was painful to see. "Or maybe I should deliver his windfall on your behalf. Given that you're at work and probably have other things to do."

Much to her own surprise, Maisie shook her head. "Not really." They were both done eating, and as nervous as Maisie was, she still didn't want to say good-bye. "I mean, I love dogs."

Not yet.

MAISIE'S MAJOR MILESTONE

Maisie waited at the entrance until she saw a white pit bull jump out of the driver's side door of the big truck, tail wagging happily as he wound his leash around Aiden's calves. Maisie winced at the all-too-predictable stumble that followed, then laughed at the dirty look Aiden shot Major while clumsily disentangling herself from her enthusiastic companion. Pushing open the front door, Maisie stepped out of Moe's Fine Diner with a shit-eating grin on her face.

"*This* is the dog who refused to get out of bed?" She tilted her head, frowning. "You sure about that?"

Aiden tightened her grip on Major's leash to keep him from bounding over to greet her. "I just told him that a very pretty lady wanted to give him some gourmet bones. Can you blame the guy for being a bit overexcited?"

Maisie's grin eased as she flushed with a mixture of desire and disbelief. *That* was flirting. It had to be. Taking a step away from the safety of the diner, she waved Aiden closer so as not to give away her complete and utter confusion about what might come next. "You can bring him closer. I'm used to overexcited dogs, so I don't mind."

"I apologize in advance if he comes in a little hot. He's totally friendly, just…a bit of an overgrown puppy who still hasn't quite mastered his manners." Aiden bent and patted Major on the head, and the dog nuzzled into her arm so contentedly that Maisie couldn't help but coo out loud. Seeming to recognize Maisie's ability to see past the young dog's exuberance, she relaxed her shoulders and said, "He loves women. Especially feminine ones, with kind voices." She stroked the dog's ear as he strained at the leash. "I'm not sure what happened to the poor guy before I found him, but he's not the biggest fan of men. Which kind of sucks considering how much time we spend at truck stops."

Maisie took another step forward. "I can only imagine, living on the streets." She set the plastic bag in her hands on top of the newspaper dispenser beside her, then went to the curb and crouched down to address the good boy face-to-face. "Hi, Major. Your mommy told me what a cute, stinky boy you are. I happen to be a sucker for overgrown puppies, so this is a good night for both of us."

Aiden walked him a few feet closer, then stopped short and said, "Sit."

Major slammed his butt onto the pavement without hesitation, tail wagging furiously. His entire body quivered as though on the verge of exploding, yet it was clear that he was desperate to do whatever Aiden told him was right.

"Good boy." Aiden delivered the praise in a higher-pitched voice than Maisie had yet heard from her, a voice that made Maisie hotter than any love scene she'd ever read. "Stay calm and be polite, okay? No jumping, no knocking her over, no nothing that will make Maisie regret meeting us. Got it?"

Major stared up into Aiden's eyes, panting hard, then turned his longing gaze toward Maisie with an insistent whine. Heart melting, Maisie said, "You're torturing both of us at this point. Just bring him over, will you? I've spent my whole life around dogs. Jumping, nipping, even plain, old-fashioned bad manners don't faze me." She noted the relief on Aiden's face. "It's obvious his heart is in the right place."

Aiden nodded, then allowed Major to move a few feet closer on his fairly short leash. "Cool. Not everyone sees that right away, if ever. Major is the sort of dog who makes even the occasional dog lover take a step back. Until they get to know him, that is. Everyone who knows Major absolutely adores him."

Maisie held out her arms to encourage them onward. "I believe it. Look at how handsome this guy is." Greeting Major's boisterous nudge of her hand with friendly pets across his silky chest, Maisie forgot her inhibitions and said, "You two make quite a pair."

"Because I'm handsome, too?" Aiden's voice was playful but tentative. "Or because we're both awkward around the women we're attracted to?"

Any shred of doubt about Aiden's orientation and intentions faded away. The only question that remained was how Maisie felt about them.

Major chose that moment to nearly bowl Maisie over with a wild burst of energy, spinning in place before forcing his head between Maisie's thighs to bulldoze his way through her legs en route to the newspaper box. "Whoa, whoa, whoa." Her hands flew to her uniform, keeping the knee-length skirt from riding up any higher. "Maybe buy a girl dinner first?" Once she'd regained her balance, she scooted out of Major's single-minded path. "Next time?"

"Oh, for the love of—I'm so sorry." To say Aiden sounded mortified would be a massive understatement. Lunging forward to give Major's leash a firm tug, Aiden appeared to be wishing the earth would crack open and swallow both her and her dog whole. "That was *very* rude, Major! Bad boy!"

"Never without consent!" Maisie added. Unable to suppress a giggle, she turned and patted a salivating Major on the head. "But I forgive you, buddy. Can hardly blame a hungry pup for figuring out *the bones are right there!*"

Aiden didn't seem all that reassured by Maisie's easy acceptance of the stunt. "Sure, but he knows better than that." She aimed a glare in his direction, then returned her focus to Maisie, scanning her from head to toe. "You all right? He didn't hurt you?"

"I'm fine." Maisie walked to the newspaper box and grabbed the fragrant package from on top. She extracted the biggest bone, then handed the other to Aiden. "For later."

Aiden accepted the bag and gave a jaunty salute. "Yes, ma'am."

At her feet, Major was positively vibrating—and had been since the moment he laid eyes on what was in her hand. Holding the bone above his head, Maisie said, "Sit."

Responsive as ever, Major parked his butt onto the pavement and waited. Wiggling madly, puppy dog eyes engaged and dialed to maximum cuteness, he made it impossible for Maisie to deny him.

Aiden chuckled. "He knows how to work you."

"Yes, he does. A major cutie-pants is what you are." Maisie bent and held out her hand. "Can you shake?"

Doggy-grinning from ear to ear, Major lifted a big, clumsy paw and plopped it onto her hand. "Good boy!" Maisie offered him the bone as a reward. "Enjoy the late-night snack."

Major lowered himself onto his belly, both paws wrapped around the bone to hold it still enough to gnaw in earnest. A contented growl emanated from somewhere deep inside his throat, low and long and downright hysterical, given the context. Maisie chuckled when several more vocalizations followed the first one.

"Sounds like he approves." Aiden beamed at her dog, then at Maisie. "Who says you're not an accomplished chef?"

Maisie snorted. "Your average dog's culinary bar is disgustingly low. One of my daddy's old hounds used to feast on cow shit like it was filet mignon."

Aiden's nose wrinkled in the most adorable way. "Then I suppose Major has at least one thing going for him. As far as I know, not a fan of poop."

"Impressive credentials." Maisie looked down at the thoroughly distracted pup, wishing she knew what to say after their banter about Major ran its course. Wishing she knew where this was going, what Aiden wanted.

"Trust me, we're both more than satisfied with the food *and* service at Moe's Fine Diner."

Maisie wondered if, by service, Aiden meant flirting. Because they *were* flirting. Or was Aiden hoping for more? Maisie had no idea how she would react if Aiden tried to kiss her, let alone if she didn't.

"Seriously, though." Aiden caught her gaze, trapping Maisie in those bottomless blue eyes. "Thanks for joining me in there. I've been hauling for weeks on back-to-back-to-back interstate jobs. Major's decent enough company, but he can't hold a conversation worth a damn. Not to mention he takes a *lot* of naps." She cracked a smirk and scolded the feasting dog. "Rather smelly naps, I might add. So my social life is…a bit pathetic at the moment."

Maisie shrugged, embarrassed for Aiden to think her life was any more glamorous. "I don't get out much, either. Mostly work, helping out around the house, school. Doesn't leave a whole lot of time for a social life."

Aiden took half a step back, as though stricken by her candor. "School?"

Maisie understood immediately. "*College* classes. I'm twenty-four."

"Oh, thank God."

Now she had no doubt about Aiden's intentions. Only her own. "Worried I was too young?" Maisie couldn't help poking fun, despite where it might lead.

"Too young for what?" Aiden's eyes sparkled in the moonlight, full of mischief and playful affection. "Pancake-making? It's never too early to start, as you yourself can apparently attest."

Maisie bit the inside of her lip, lacking the nerve to nudge their interaction back into semi-romantic territory. "I'm so glad they hit the spot."

Aiden's lips quirked. "They sure did."

"Well..." Maisie bent and patted Major's head. He paused his chewing long enough to lick her wrist, then returned to his bounty. "I don't want to keep you—"

"You're not." Aiden was quick to interject. "Unless you need to go inside and clean up, or whatever."

After a scan of the empty parking lot, Maisie debated for only a moment, then sat down on the curb. Adjusting her skirt around her knees, she waited to find out if she was making an ass of herself. For his part, Major wagged his tail even harder, damn near hard enough to throw him off balance. A few seconds passed before Aiden took a seat next to her, settling in with a tired groan.

"You okay?" Maisie couldn't bring herself to glance sideways, afraid to initiate any kind of physical escalation. "Would you be more comfortable somewhere else?"

"No. I'm good right here." She heard Aiden angle her body closer, then lean in. "Next to you."

Maisie trembled at the soft-spoken come-on, a line that rivaled her favorite romance novels. She really hadn't misinterpreted. The attraction was mutual, and Aiden hadn't been the slightest bit hesitant to say so. With a belly full of butterflies and nervous anticipation, Maisie whispered, "You should probably know that I've never kissed a woman before."

She swore she heard Aiden's vertebrate stiffen. "Oh. I'm sorry if I misread—"

"You didn't." Maisie finally mustered the courage to face her, but she kept her head down so she wouldn't have to witness Aiden's reaction to her pathetic sexual history—or lack thereof. "The truth is, I think you're the hottest woman I've ever met…but I've never actually been with anyone yet. Male, female, or otherwise. My folks didn't let me date in high school, and I'm taking all my college courses online, so it's not like I've had a wild and crazy undergraduate experience with all the normal milestones."

"But you're so…" Aiden gestured at her face. "Wonderful, inside and out. It's hard to believe nobody ever tried to sweep you off your feet before I rode into town." She lifted the hand closer to Maisie's, then just as quickly lowered it. "I can't be the only one who's noticed how extraordinary you are."

Flushing, Maisie said, "Sure, I've been hit on. Only by guys, though. Usually drunk ones."

"Does that mean your inexperience comes down to a lack of desirable options?"

"That, and never knowing what I wanted." Maisie gathered her nerve, then reached over to put her hand on Aiden's. "Until you walked through the door and showed me."

Aiden let out a low, shaky breath, turning her hand over to thread their fingers together. She tightened her grip ever so slightly, then murmured, "Is this okay?"

Maisie felt like she might die of happiness right on the spot, a big smile on her face to complement the freshly soaked pair of panties under her skirt. Her heart was racing out of control, her palm sweating. Would Aiden think she was clammy and gross, and let go? She was awkwardness incarnate, knocked senseless and incoherent by the utterly innocent act of holding another woman's hand. Terrified Aiden would retreat if she didn't verbally consent, Maisie managed a strained "Yes." Then she shut up and tried to take everything in.

Maisie's senses were aroused. Aiden's spicy but subtle cologne, a traditionally masculine scent not unlike her former volleyball coach's aftershave. The tempting warmth of the body next to hers, then the scorching heat of their newly physical entanglement. Aiden's skin against her own, the tender but work-roughened hand to which she clung, the hitch in Aiden's breathing when Maisie rubbed her thumb along the inside of her wrist.

The deafening blast of a dog's asshole not two feet to her right. Then, an odor she instantly wished she could forget.

"*Fuck,* Major." Aiden dropped her hand and stood up, grabbing Major's leash to lead him away to a patch of grass farther along the sidewalk. "I am *so* sorry."

Maisie couldn't help it. She had to laugh. So hard, in fact, that tears soon filled her eyes. *Or maybe that's the gas.* Aware that she'd left Aiden hanging, she simmered down long enough to say, "It's not your fault. And I can't say you didn't warn me."

Aiden grunted. "Timing is everything." She looked down at Major, who had squatted over the spot on offer. "Rotten dog."

Relieved by the lack of real anger in Aiden's tone, Maisie got to her feet and went to join them. "It's all right. When nature calls…"

"My fault for not making him go before I brought him over to meet you." Aiden shrugged, then gave her a self-conscious nod. "Maybe it's good. That he stopped us."

"Good?" Maisie didn't understand. They were only holding hands. She never even got her first kiss.

"Before anything went too far."

"We were holding hands." For the first time since they'd sat down, Maisie made direct eye contact. "That's a long way from 'too far,' isn't it?" When Aiden didn't answer right away, bending to bag up Major's waste instead, another, more awful thought occurred. "Oh."

Brow furrowed, Aiden took a step closer to drop the tied-off bag into a nearby trash can. "Oh, what?"

"It's fine if you're not into me. I get it." Ashamed to have pushed, Maisie retreated a step so as to maintain the safety buffer between them. "I shouldn't have been so forward."

Judging by her expression, Aiden was downright mystified. "Forward?" She chuckled. "No. You weren't—Why would you think I don't want you?"

Now Maisie was the one with no idea what was going on. "Because you said you were glad Major stopped us?"

"I'm almost positive I said, 'Maybe it's good,' not 'Good, I'm glad *that's* over.'" Aiden withdrew a bottle of hand sanitizer from her jacket pocket and squeezed a dollop into her hands. Rubbing her palms together, she closed the rest of the distance between them in three long strides. "I was giving you an out. If you needed one."

"How about if I need an out, I'll tell you?" It felt surreal to be throwing herself at a complete stranger after a lifetime of celibacy.

What would her mother think? Or, God forbid, her father? *Who cares what they think?* whispered a familiar voice in the back of her head, and for once, Maisie listened. "I liked holding your hand. And...I wouldn't have minded a kiss."

Aiden's chest rose then fell, her breathing shaky and audible. "Wouldn't have minded, huh?" She licked her lips—and Maisie couldn't stop staring at the sheen her tongue left behind. "Was that it? Or was it more like you *wanted* a kiss?"

Maisie's face burned with deeply ingrained shame. Maybe her mother was right about the romance novels turning her into a wanton whore. She'd known Aiden for all of an hour, yet here she was, practically surrendering her body to a woman she might never see again. Outside her workplace. In the company of a flatulent pit bull.

What in the devil was wrong with her?

"Hey." Aiden ran a knuckle along Maisie's jawline, a feather-soft caress that ended up going straight to her nipples and clit. "I wasn't trying to make you feel bad. The opposite, actually. I have this rather unfortunate habit of teasing women I like before they know me well enough to enjoy it. Or at least tolerate it." Sounding contrite, Aiden dropped her hand and laced Maisie's slim fingers through her own. "It goes without saying that I'm more desperate for that kiss than you are. I was just stoked to hear that the attraction is mutual."

It took all of Maisie's courage to meet Aiden's steady gaze. "Maybe we should go around back for a few minutes. You know, if we...if you still wanted..."

Aiden let her off the hook by taking over. "How about I escort Major to his bed and then meet you there? It'll be quick."

Surprised by how concerned Aiden sounded about whether she'd wait, Maisie said, "That would be nice." She was all too aware of the ache between her thighs. "Kissing only, though. Is that okay?"

Aiden squeezed her hand, then let go. "It's perfect."

After what felt like an hour later but was no doubt closer to five minutes, Aiden rounded the corner of the diner and squinted into the dark. "Maisie?"

She stepped out of the shadows and waved Aiden forward. "Over here."

Aiden looked almost nervous upon reaching the far side of the dumpster. "Is it safe for us to be out here? If someone caught us, I mean…" She exhaled, ducking into the darkness to join Maisie near the rear entrance. "I don't want to cause you any trouble."

While she wasn't one hundred percent confident this wasn't a stupidly dangerous decision, Maisie was short on ideas. They couldn't retreat to Aiden's truck because, well…she wasn't about to get into a vehicle with someone she barely knew. Make out with her, sure. But more or less volunteer to be kidnapped? No way, even if her would-be captor *was* drop-dead gorgeous. Inside the diner also wouldn't work. Her boss had installed cameras outside the restrooms six months ago, in addition to the security cameras already pointed at the cash register, kitchen, and front entryway. Henry already had footage of Maisie exiting the diner with Aiden; leading the trucker back inside would only invite more questions.

"Maisie?" Aiden's hand found her shoulder in the darkness. "Maybe we—"

Maisie didn't want to hear whatever Aiden was about to say. "Don't worry. We'll be able to hear any cars coming our way long before anyone sees us."

When Aiden didn't object, Maisie moved close enough to feel the heat pouring off her. That warmth, along with Aiden's scent, only deepened her hunger for the forbidden fruit of another woman's lips on her own. Though she couldn't see Aiden's face, Maisie could both feel and hear the effect their proximity had on her. Aiden slid the hand on Maisie's shoulder down to grip her forearm, then took hold of her other forearm with equally shaky fingers. Walking her backward a couple of steps, Aiden leaned in once Maisie was trapped against the wall. "And you're sure?" Gentle lips ghosted across her forehead, nearly crumbling Maisie's legs beneath her. "This is what you want?"

"Yes." She didn't even have to think about that one. Even if she'd never fully understood the inner workings of her heart before today, Maisie knew for a fact that this was all she'd ever wanted. "Please." She inhaled at the exquisite press of supple breasts against her own heaving chest. "Before I kiss you first."

Maisie froze when those tender lips first brushed against her cheek, then trailed a string of kisses along the curve of her jaw. She knew it was coming, her first romantic kiss, and the anticipation was killing her. What if she didn't feel anything? Or, worse yet, hated how it felt? The fear of being abnormal, of feeling desperate for physical intimacy without any hope of finding the partner she desired, sped up Maisie's heart and hastened her increasingly shallow breathing.

"Hey." Aiden retreated a couple of inches, giving her time to inhale, then exhale at length. The gentlest hands Maisie had ever felt cradled her face—precisely the reassurance she needed but wouldn't have been brave enough to ask for. "It's me. Aiden, truck-driving guardian of a socially awkward pit bull. There's no reason to be nervous with me. Not when you're by far the prettiest girl I've ever had up against a wall."

Maisie closed her eyes, clit pulsing in response to the quiet, delicious words. She couldn't stop her hips from bucking against Aiden's, no more than she could stop her moan at the rough scrape of denim over her skin as Aiden slipped a firm thigh between Maisie's bare knees. No longer concerned about not feeling anything, Maisie latched onto a brand-new worry. What if it turned out she was one of those women who could be brought to orgasm by a mere kiss? How would Aiden react if she wound up with some random waitress's cum all over her sexy, skin-tight jeans?

Aiden shut down her fretting with the briefest, barest meeting of their lips, a fleeting caress that left Maisie wanting so much more. "Did you like that?" Aiden murmured.

Beyond caring about her mother's perspective on blasphemy, Maisie whispered, "God, yes." She looped her arms around Aiden's neck, tempted to drag her in for another. "You feel incredible."

"So do you." Another semi-chaste graze of their mouths, followed by the thrilling flick of Aiden's tongue against her lower lip. "And you taste like maple syrup." When Maisie giggled, Aiden gave the same spot a second lick. "The ultimate turn-on."

Maisie was still grinning when Aiden finally delivered the kind of kiss she'd only read about in novels—searing, impassioned, hungry. Transformative. It went straight to her core, a flood of ecstasy and relief and fiery lust unlike anything she'd ever experienced or expected. Maisie gasped when her legs wobbled, terrified she might pass out and miss the greatest moment of her life. Aiden leapt into action, wrapping her in a bear hug and holding her in place against the wall.

"Hang on to me, baby." Aiden slid her tongue across Maisie's in an unhurried demonstration of the delicate interplay necessary to ensure their mutual pleasure. Clutching Aiden's flannel shirt in both fists, Maisie wished she hadn't set such a strict boundary. Aiden broke their kiss, panting, then brought her lower body flush against Maisie's. Pinning her to the wall, she said, "I won't let you fall."

Maisie couldn't get over how sincere Aiden sounded. How respectful she was. She also couldn't believe she'd landed such a prodigious kisser as her first. Gazing up into Aiden's shaded, glittering eyes, it occurred to Maisie what a mistake she'd made.

How could *any* woman live up to the standard set by this flannel-clad goddess? Her high school friends had always told her that first kisses were supposed to be awful—clumsy and awkward and out of sync, or so they claimed. Despite the grandiose expectations created by her collection of steamy romances, Maisie had been mentally prepared to have a mediocre time. But this? Kissing Aiden was the opposite of mediocre. It was transcendent, the best of the best, and so far beyond what she'd expected from an illicit hookup next to a semi-pungent dumpster that she had no idea what to do or say. As the ideal against which all future partners would be judged, Aiden had sealed her fate as the "what if" scenario Maisie feared would haunt her until the day she died.

So yeah—a *huge* mistake.

Unable or perhaps unwilling to stop a train wreck in motion, Maisie initiated yet another kiss, this one a heated clash of lips and teeth and tongues she couldn't believe she was part of. Aiden tasted like liquid fire—searing and intoxicating and oh so dangerous to consume. Maisie imagined moving her hand to Aiden's breast, the warmth and weight and curve of it cradled in her palm, and nearly fell down a second time.

Aiden left Maisie with a peck on the forehead, pulling back to search her face. "Still okay?"

"Better than that." Maisie tugged on Aiden's shirt, urging her closer until she could feel Aiden's heartbeat in her own chest. Too overcome by hormones and adrenaline to care if Aiden thought she was silly or immature for saying so, Maisie told the truth. "I'm…transformed." Letting go of her flannel shirt, Maisie reached up to stroke the silky hairs on the nape of Aiden's neck. "You've just shown me who I am."

"A smokin' pancake chef in a short skirt that shows off her killer legs?"

Eyes rolling, Maisie tugged lightly on the delicate strands between her fingers. "It's not *that* short." Drawn to the breathtaking expanse of skin exposed by Aiden's partially unbuttoned shirt, Maisie bent and kissed one of the spots she'd been trying not to stare at until now.

Aiden's groan made Maisie feel like the most powerful human on the planet. "Short enough to get me so hot and bothered and stupid that I agreed to steal a first kiss you probably should've saved for someone special."

"You are special." Apparently, Maisie's mouth had decided to work independent of her brain. Flushing, she said, "Remember?"

Tugging gently on her ponytail, Aiden ran the tip of her tongue along Maisie's exposed clavicle, a delectable tease that only served to highlight exactly how much bare skin she had on display. "Because I showed you who you are?"

Maisie nodded, unable to speak with Aiden's face so close to her breasts. Aiden tilted her head to glance up at her, eyes sparkling with mirth and genuine curiosity. "And?"

Maisie had to take a deep breath for courage before finally speaking her truth out loud. "I'm a girl who likes girls who look like boys."

Aiden's whole countenance lit up, elevating her beauty to a level Maisie wasn't sure she could handle. "So you're saying I'm your type?"

Maisie nodded, not trusting that her mouth wouldn't betray the depth of her feelings about their too-right-to-be-wrong chemistry. She already felt more vulnerable than was comfortable, trapped in place by a near stranger and wetter than she'd ever been.

Slowly, Aiden brought her lips to Maisie's for their sweetest kiss yet. She drew away some time later, murmuring, "If you haven't already noticed, you're also my type. And then some."

A shiver ran through Maisie from head to toe, making her feel ecstatic and alive. Ravenous for more, she stared up at Aiden with as much confidence as she could muster. "May I..." The question died in her throat, too salacious to make it past the critical voice in her head.

"Anything," Aiden said, without waiting or seemingly caring about what Maisie intended to ask. "Tell me what you want, and I'll do anything."

Floored by the invitation, Maisie let go of her upbringing and asked for what she wanted. "May I...touch you?" She wet her lips, ruing the migration of all available moisture to her southern hemisphere. "Like, maybe your..." Another pass of her tongue over parched lips. "Chest?"

Without missing a beat, Aiden thumbed open the next three buttons on her shirt. Parting the blue flannel with one hand, she used the other to take hold of Maisie's wrist. "Yes, please." Aiden guided Maisie inside her shirt, then her bra, until her fingers instinctively curled around the softest, smoothest mound of flesh they'd ever felt. "Touch me as much you want. Any way you want."

Maisie gasped as Aiden's nipple hardened against her palm. She'd never felt anything so miraculous. With the tempting offer still in the air between them, Maisie froze at the familiar rumble of an approaching car. She jerked her hand out of Aiden's shirt like a kid caught feeling up the cookie jar, then twisted sideways and squirmed out of her grasp. Aiden raised her hands over her head and retreated a few steps. Even in the dark, Aiden's naked fear was plain to see.

"Car," Maisie said, and Aiden's shoulders actually relaxed.

"Go." Redoing her buttons like it wasn't the single biggest disappointment of Maisie's life, Aiden nodded in the direction of the rear door. "Get back to work. You have other hungry mouths in need of your talents."

Maisie adjusted her now-messy ponytail, as though the sweat-soaked armpits of her uniform and most likely smudged lip balm wouldn't be enough to arouse suspicion on their own. It wasn't until she registered Aiden's advice that real panic set in. "Oh my God."

Maisie brushed off the front of the skirt, then knocked the dirt from her shoulders, back, and rear end. This late on a Tuesday night, she'd assumed she wouldn't get another customer until the lone bar in town closed at two. Although she hadn't the foggiest idea what time it was, Maisie knew for certain that this was far too soon to say good-bye to Aiden, let alone interact with friends and neighbors in her current state. The car slowed down, then pulled into the front parking lot, and Maisie still didn't have a plan for how to act nonchalant once inside.

Stomach in her knees, Maisie jogged around Aiden and the dumpster to key open the back door. "What the hell am I doing? I can't go in there like this."

"Sure you can." Aiden shot her a cautious smile. "You're a professional, remember?"

"But my makeup—"

"Is beautiful. As are you." Aiden walked to the corner of the building, slowing at the sound of two car doors opening and three or more male voices carrying over the night air. Glancing over her shoulder, she whispered, "You'll be fine. Nobody will know."

Maisie already had the door unlocked and open, poised to sprint to the front register before those seminal moment-spoiling interlopers could wonder where everyone was. The easiest way to avoid raising anyone's suspicions was to be where she was supposed to be, and do what she was supposed to do. If she played it super cool in there, maybe no one would notice how Aiden had changed her life forever. "Sorry to run out on you, but…" She glanced over her shoulder at the kitchen, beyond which lay the comfort of her banal existence. "Sorry."

Too impatient to wait for a reply, Maisie turned to sprint madly across the tiled floor—barely picking up Aiden's hushed send-off. "Thanks for the best kiss of my life."

Maisie wished she had time to echo Aiden's gratitude, but her trio of drunk locals took precedence over a drawn-out farewell. Rip the bandage off. Isn't that what her father always said? Take the pain, and then get on with your life.

If only that made her feel less shitty about running like hell from the trucker of her dreams.

A Semi-Sweet Parting

Once the drunken pie-and-coffee crowd finally dissipated a few hours later, Maisie could no longer avoid looking at the parking lot she knew would be empty. Her miraculous interlude with Aiden was over, and she needed to accept that, for now at least, the life she wanted remained maddeningly beyond her reach. It was time to wake up and readjust her expectations, to put on her happy face and get through another day in her quest for independence. Prepared for a reality check, she peered through the window with a longing sigh.

Except the lot wasn't empty. Positioned along the far edge, Aiden's truck hadn't budged from the spot where she'd parked it. Baffled and almost a little annoyed, Maisie slung a jacket over her short-sleeved blouse before venturing outside for the second time that night.

Why in the world hadn't Aiden left? Earlier, she'd mentioned needing to deliver her cargo before noon the following day or else risk losing a hefty bonus. Already behind schedule due to three-plus hours spent in bumper-to-bumper traffic earlier that day, Aiden hadn't sounded altogether confident about whether she could make such a tight deadline. Now, after having wasted a few more hours hanging out at a rinky-dink small-town diner, did she have even the slightest chance of pulling off an on-time arrival? Maisie didn't know for sure, but it seemed unlikely. Queasy at the thought of Aiden forgoing money on her account, she prepared for a potentially awkward conversation. She'd never asked her to stay. Would Aiden expect something from her in return?

Assuming Aiden was asleep, Maisie approached the driver's side door and stood on her tiptoes, hoping to catch a glimpse inside. She squeaked in surprise when the window rolled down and a blocky white head emerged to unleash an exuberant whine. By the time Aiden pulled Major away and hastily took his place, Maisie no longer knew how she felt about this turn of events.

On the one hand, Aiden was still here. Still sexy. Still interested. Still a possibility. But on the other, the longer Aiden hung around, the more likely it was that someone in town would see them together. She shuddered to imagine gossip of that flavor eventually making its way to her parents. God forbid.

Unnerved, Maisie arched an eyebrow at the guilt in Aiden's bright eyes. To give her the benefit of the doubt, Maisie stayed calm and kept it simple. "Hey. You all right?"

"Of course, yeah, sorry." Aiden frowned as she shoved Major off her lap for the second time, before turning to flash Maisie a self-conscious grin. "Everything's cool. As you can see."

Maisie snorted at the dog's frantic efforts to reach her idle hands. "Clearly." She gestured at the driveway to their left and, fighting to keep the frustration out of her voice, asked, "Shouldn't you be at least one hundred eighty miles from here by now?"

"I decided to close my eyes for a few. Must've napped longer than I meant to."

Maisie narrowed her gaze and studied Aiden's bright eyes and flawless hair. "You were asleep just now? I woke you up?"

Aiden hesitated, then released a heavy sigh. "No, I'm sorry, I—" Another sigh. "Couldn't fall asleep."

"You told me you'd have to drive straight through to Tacoma in order to meet your deadline." Maisie folded her arms over her chest, remembering all too well how it felt to be pinned between a brick wall and the most appealing woman she'd ever met. Her panties weren't even dry yet, and here she was, craving more. "What happened to that plan?"

She watched Aiden consider her options, then settle for honesty. "Earlier, I heard those guys mouthing off before they went inside. Stupid drunk, all of them."

Maisie straightened, instantly on the defensive. "You don't think I can handle a few drunk customers? Do you *know* what I do for a living?"

Aiden's jaw tightened. "They were speculating about your ass—whether it tasted as good as it looks."

Rolling her eyes, Maisie said, "I've known those guys forever. One of them mows my grandmother's lawn every weekend, and has for years. They're harmless, each and every one."

"You were alone in there. Middle of nowhere, dead of night..." Deflated, Aiden gave up on blocking Major from joining her at the window. "I don't think it's right to have anyone work a graveyard shift by themselves. I'm sure you're very capable—"

Losing a bit of her bravado, Maisie downplayed her imaginary self-defense prowess in favor of an explanation about her family's position in their very small town. "My father's the preacher. My mother taught Sunday school to half the population. And my grandfather retired as sheriff last year. Nobody's about to mess with me. Promise."

"Well...I didn't know those boys were locals." Aiden shifted uncomfortably beneath Major's bulk. "Or that your daddy's relationship with God has afforded you special protections."

Maisie couldn't stay mad. Not with Major doggy-grinning up a storm and Aiden looking like a puppy who'd just been kicked. Stepping up onto the footboard, Maisie ended Major's misery with a scratch behind his ears. She stared into his wide green eyes but directed her apology to the chivalrous butch trucker whose only crime was sticking around in case she needed help.

"Look, I'm sorry. I'm not upset you stayed, only that you've lost out on a bonus because of me." Maisie checked Aiden's expression, relieved to see her lips curve into the hint of a smile. "You really didn't need to do that."

Aiden bit her lip, then exhaled and said, "I know, but..." She let go of Major's collar and raked her fingers through her hair. "I didn't stay only because of those guys. Truth is, I couldn't bring myself to leave. Not like that, without a proper good-bye."

Maisie gave Major one final scratch, then stepped down from the window. She wasn't sure what Aiden considered a "proper goodbye" but knew it wasn't smart to linger if it meant finding out under the glow of a blinking Moe's Fine Diner sign. "It's all right. I had a wonderful time with you earlier...despite the abrupt ending."

"Me too." Sweeping Major off her lap once again, Aiden opened the door and hopped out. Major let out a pitiful whine when she shut the door before he could follow. Startled by the unexpected movement, Maisie backed away a few steps to give Aiden plenty of room to disembark. Aiden jumped off the footboard, landing maybe twelve inches in front of her—close enough to smell her shampoo. "Listen, Maisie…"

Maisie swallowed and took another step back. "Not here. We're right out in the open."

Aiden cocked her head, brows furrowed in the most adorable way. "No. I wasn't—" She placed her hands behind her and retreated until her shoulders rested against the wheel well to her right. "I promise I won't touch you, *ever*, unless you ask me to."

In spite of the danger and her own internal conflict, some part of Maisie wanted nothing more than to finish what they'd started. Or to go a little farther, if nothing else. She hadn't even gotten to see the breast she'd felt up. There was still so much to taste and feel and explore. So much to learn about the only person to ever make her body come alive in the real world. So much to *do*.

But her shift was over in less than ninety minutes. The breakfast crowd would start to drift in even earlier than that. As much as Maisie wanted to pursue her sexual education, she had no choice but to get her libido under control and usher Aiden into her truck and out of this small-minded town. "Sorry for the overreaction. It's not like I thought you were gonna throw me down and take me right here—"

A tiny, luminous smile on her irresistible lips, Aiden hushed Maisie with a shake of her head. "I get it. Small town, gossip travels fast. Daddy's a preacher, Mama teaches Sunday school…you can't let anyone see us together. Whether or not they identify me as a woman."

Ashamed to be living under her parents' authoritarian rule at the not-so-tender age of twenty-four, Maisie gazed up at the sky while justifying her lack of independence. "After I graduated high school, my parents told me they'd only help me pay for college if I continued to live at home and keep up my weekly chores. Between the housework, my job at the diner, a minor addiction to books, and my own half-assed attempts to write, I've had no choice but to take classes part-time— even if it means being treated like a child well into my twenties."

"Understandable. College isn't cheap." Aiden looked her up and down, the smile growing. "May I say one more thing before I go?"

Maisie's heart ached at the thought of Aiden actually *going*. Like

Schrödinger's butch, she wished for Aiden to be both here and *not* here. Like a dirty little secret no one could possibly discover. Resolve weakened, she said, "Yes, of course."

Aiden took a deep breath, then let it out slowly. "I need you to know that what we did meant something to me, too. It would kill me if every time you think back on your first kiss, you can't help but wonder if you were just another notch in some horny trucker's dashboard." She swallowed. "Because you're not."

It dawned on Maisie that regardless of how dead sexy Aiden happened to be, she wasn't any less human and vulnerable than everyone else. Just because Maisie saw the patently obvious, Aiden didn't have the clarity to do the same. She understood how it felt not to see what others claimed to see, perhaps better than most. Heart tugged by the earnest declaration, Maisie dropped her guard and met Aiden's honesty with her truth. "I appreciate you telling me. You're right. I probably would've wondered, starting tomorrow at church, if the past twenty-plus years are anything to go on."

Aiden chuckled, then tilted her head and studied Maisie's face. Self-conscious for reasons she didn't entirely understand, Maisie steeled her spine before pulling Aiden's focus to her narrowed eyes.

"What?" Maisie checked her blouse, then her skirt. "Are you laughing at me?"

Aiden relented with a bashful shrug. Blinking, she met Maisie's fierce stare head-on, with affection. "No. I'm enjoying you." She lowered her voice. "Admiring you."

If only she had time to drag Aiden behind the dumpster for a second round, Maisie would drop her inhibitions and do exactly that. But she had no time. Soon the sun would come up and awaken her friends, family, and neighbors to a brand-new day—and, if she wasn't careful, to a brand-new version of the preacher's daughter they all thought they knew. Her only option was to send Aiden away as quickly and politely as possible, yet she no longer wanted to. The thought of never seeing Aiden again, of never finding out how their unconventional story would end, made Maisie's chest ache. It was downright *painful*.

"Anyway…" Aiden sounded ready to change the subject—anything to get Maisie talking again. "It was well worth the five hundred dollars for this chance to let you know where I stand. You know, as far as tonight being the best kiss I've ever had, and the most excited I've ever been." She waited a beat. "So…thank you. I really did have a wonderful time."

"Me too." Maisie shifted her weight from foot to foot, jittery about the possibility of being seen from the road. "It's a shame it ended the way it did, but…" Joy overwhelmed her anxiety and brought an unthinking grin to her recently kissed lips. "Tonight will always be one of my favorite memories." She flushed as the next confession slipped out. "And I'll never forget you—or the way you blew off your deadline to reassure me that I wasn't just another piece of ass for your travelogue."

Aiden chuckled. "It's a pretty slim volume, if I'm being honest. I've never been much of a love-'em-and-leave-'em type. Not really my nature, I guess."

"Does that mean I'm the first waitress you've ever kissed?"

Grimacing, Aiden removed her hands from behind her back, then shrugged. "Uh…"

"Mm-hmm." That was hardly a surprise, but jealousy slithered through Maisie anyway. "Don't worry. I'd figured I wasn't your first anything. I assume women throw themselves at you wherever you go."

Aiden stuffed her hands into her pockets and rocked back on her heels, clearly uncomfortable with the subject of her past exploits. "I've been with my share of women, but never someone like you. That sounds like a line, but it isn't. At the risk of freaking you out, I want you to know…" She pushed off the wheel well and squared her shoulders. "I'm interested. So if you're ever in a position…" She cleared her throat. "To go on a date, that is."

Maisie's mind whirled, reeling from the bombshell Aiden had lobbed at her feet. Date? Like girlfriends? Or long-distance acquaintances who occasionally met for casual sex? What would it even mean to "date" someone she didn't want anyone to know about? Although she found the fantasy of a secret lover titillating, Maisie suspected the reality wouldn't be nearly as much fun. Even so, it might be worth considering. Otherwise she might never see Aiden again.

If only she could jump into Aiden's truck and run away with her. Maisie's heart raced at the errant thought and how alluring it was in that moment. What if she did? What if she begged Aiden to take her away from this place, and her parents, once and for all? Would Aiden say yes? Did Maisie even *want* her to?

Too confused to speak, Maisie nodded and looked down at her shoes.

"I mean if you're also interested." Aiden sounded almost as nervous as Maisie felt. "Obviously."

Maisie summoned the courage to give Aiden the eye contact she deserved. "I am interested, just..." Just what? She faltered, at a loss about how to make Aiden understand exactly how stuck she was—in this town, in her family, and in her life.

"Not in a position," Aiden said. Her smile was as kind as her eyes. "I get it. I'd offer to give you my number for the future, but I'm not sure you want that kind of evidence in your possession."

Feeling smaller than ever, Maisie tipped her head in gratitude. "Yeah. As much as I'd love to keep in touch—"

Aiden gave a dismissive wave. "No worries. The last thing I want is to fuck things up for you. With your folks, or school...or anything, really."

Until that moment, Maisie's resentment toward her parents and their stipulations had been manageable. Ever present and moderately infuriating, but not so terrible that she'd ever seriously considered striking out on her own with less than a thousand dollars. Sure, she daydreamed now and then about leaving everyone and everything she knew behind. Of reinventing herself somewhere nobody knew her as the preacher's kid or the sheriff's granddaughter. Of finding a place where she fit in.

Later. Someday. When she was ready.

Tonight, with a potential escape route laid out before her, maybe she *was* ready. After a kiss like that, and feelings like these, how was she supposed to go home and pretend nothing was different? How could she brush off her father's judgments and her mother's insults now that a woman like Aiden had accepted her exactly as she was? She couldn't predict how Aiden would respond if she begged to be taken anywhere but here, yet Maisie had never been more tempted to upend her entire world with one simple choice.

Throw caution to the wind? Or keep playing it safe.

It wasn't much of a decision. Twenty-four years of programming wasn't easy to overcome, no matter how tempting the incentive might be. Resigned, Maisie checked the parking lot and the road, then walked to Aiden for a tentative hug. Strong arms encircled her waist without pulling her in, a loose embrace that exuded affection rather than expectation. Not at all like the last time they touched.

A lifetime of celibacy and now—three hours post-making out—Maisie already missed the euphoric rush of mutual desire. How long until she experienced the pure bliss of another lover's caress?

Fully aware of the danger she was courting, Maisie let her heart have its say. "Even if we can't text…" Aiden hugged her tighter. "You know where to find me if you're in the mood for another midnight short stack, or whatever."

Aiden didn't answer for so long Maisie feared she'd made a mistake. Why hadn't she left well enough alone? Aiden didn't seem like someone who would be interested in occasional no-strings-attached reunions—but only when circumstances permitted. Why would she sign up for *that*? When you can get any similarly inclined woman you want, why bother with a lame virgin who's only good for a few secret kisses when nobody else is around? Besides, Aiden clearly didn't have or want to have a girl in every diner along the highway. From what Maisie could glean, Aiden was looking for a girlfriend, not a horny, inexperienced waitress to coach to second base.

"You sure?"

Swallowing at the unexpected response, Maisie let go of Aiden's shoulders and moved a safe distance away. "About cooking you more pancakes?" She tried to smile, not wanting to show how shaken she was. "Yes, ma'am."

Aiden licked her lips, cheeks flushing with what Maisie assumed was arousal. "It won't be awkward for you? Serving an extremely butch dyke who shows up every so often in her very conspicuous truck alongside her even more conspicuous dog?"

Maisie assumed it would be awkward. At least a little. Awkward enough to let Aiden disappear from her life forever? Maisie shook her head. She would survive a bit of awkwardness. What she wouldn't survive was living in a world without Aiden's talented mouth and comforting embrace, without the ability to learn more about this woman who'd stolen a piece of her heart forever.

Ignoring her mother's many warnings about inviting divine punishment for her wickedness, Maisie borrowed a page from one of her romance books and left their story open for further development. "I don't want this to be the last time I see you. It'll be somewhat awkward, I'm sure, but better that than never getting to pet Major again."

Aiden chuckled. Climbing onto the truck's footboard, she turned to blow Maisie a quick kiss. "Deal. It may be a while before I come back this way, but when I do…"

"I'll keep the griddle hot." Maisie's chest ached when Aiden opened the door, pushing the dog out of her seat to reclaim her place behind the wheel. *Take me with you!* Her jaw contracted from the strain of keeping the desperate cry out of her throat. Sad about tonight but exhilarated for the future, Maisie waved to Aiden and her copilot, then blew a couple of her own kisses their way.

Once the truck left the parking lot and her line of sight, Maisie returned to the diner for the rest of her shift. She'd never refuse a graveyard shift again, despite the tower of dirty dishes waiting for her in the sink.

HOME LIFE IS NO LIFE

"Well, it's about time."

Maisie cringed at the snide greeting from her mother, deployed well before she'd made it past the foyer. Familiar with their routine, Maisie stopped at the entrance of the sitting room and forced a smile for the sake of the woman scowling at her from the lounge chair nearest the fireplace. "Morning, Mom. Sorry I'm a little late. The breakfast crowd was a lot bigger than usual for some reason, so I ended up staying another fifteen minutes to help the kitchen catch up."

"Moe pay you extra for that?" Bernice Davis clucked her tongue before taking a long sip of her morning mimosa—a concoction consisting of no less than eighty percent champagne and twenty percent orange juice. The tipsier her mother got, the more scathing her inherently sharp tongue became. On topics like Maisie's boss, her job at the diner, college tuition, boys, her love life, and anything else she disapproved of, drunk Bernice always had plenty to spout off about. "Didn't I tell you to stop giving that man your unpaid labor? If you never act like you're worth anything, how do you expect people to treat you?"

Having adored and respected sweet, grandfatherly Moe Jackson since he'd hired her as a waitress one day after her sixteen birthday, Maisie struggled not to rise to the bait. "I'm being paid fairly, Mom. Don't worry."

"'*Don't worry.*'" Bernice mimicked her with a roll of her eyes. She snorted and took another drink. "Meanwhile I'm the one who pays for your tuition, room and board, internet connection, and health insurance. You don't think I'm entitled to an opinion about your piss-poor money-management skills? Is that it?"

Based on the fullness of her mother's glass and the intensity of her combative mood, Maisie could only assume she'd been unlucky enough to interrupt one of her infrequent two-mimosa breakfasts. Double the champagne, double the venom. Dread crawled up Maisie's spine as she considered probable causes for Bernice's foul mood.

Treading lightly, Maisie forced a gracious smile. "I appreciate everything you and Dad do for me. You know that." How could she not? For years Bernice had browbeaten her into daily demonstrations of gratitude, dangling Maisie's education over her head to ensure lengthy groveling sessions anytime she needed the extra validation. Eager to flee upstairs as soon as possible, Maisie cut straight to the display of remorse her mother would need to let this go. "I apologize. I'm tired, that's all."

Bernice's eyes narrowed. She summoned Maisie closer with her free hand. Only after she crossed the room to stand in front of her mother's chair did the interrogation continue. "Late-night crowd also bigger than expected?"

On guard, Maisie decided to stick as close to the truth as possible. "Smaller, actually. The place was more or less dead before two, maybe three o'clock, but the kitchen didn't get behind until closer to five."

"So you barely worked half your shift, yet somehow strolled in here too exhausted not to disrespect your own mother in the house where she *allows* you to reside." When Maisie hesitated, at a loss for the least risky answer to give, Bernice took another long swig of her mimosa, then slammed her tall glass down on the nearest end table. "What else were you doing last night? Tell me the truth."

Maisie swallowed. She'd checked her appearance in the mirror before she left work, but her mother's scrutiny always put her on edge. Her scrutiny, and her tendency to assume the worst about Maisie in every situation. Even if she hadn't somehow found out about Aiden, Bernice was clearly convinced Maisie had done *something* to deserve her ire. "Just working—and studying."

"Who were you with?" Bernice steamed full speed ahead with a new line of questioning. An old standby and favorite, the twisted fantasy of her daughter the town slut had been her mother's preferred way to inflict shame since the day of Maisie's first period. Usually the accusations barely made her flinch, but after the time she'd spent with Aiden, it was hard to maintain her composure.

"Nobody." Maisie tried to play it cool, praying her mother was too drunk to see the nerves she couldn't hide. "Customers."

"Then why does it look like you've been out whorin' it up?" Disgust etched onto her impeccably made-up face, Bernice visually inspected Maisie from head to toe. "I don't remember your skirt being this wrinkled when you left last night."

Resisting the urge to fix her hair and hemline, Maisie trusted in the once-over she'd given herself before driving home. "You can ask Brian. He came in around one in the morning with the rest of the boys. They all saw me."

"Probably reading that trash again." The woman was never happy, always critical. "Filthy books full of shirtless men. It's no wonder everyone thinks you're easy."

Maisie suppressed her chuckle at the notion that *anybody* in town thought she was easy. Or that all she read were novels about shirtless men. Some of them were—those her mother knew about. The more taboo titles in her collection stayed under lock and key in a secure locker at the diner. "Lots of women read romance novels, Mom. It's better than going out and doing those things for real, right?" Unable to resist, she added, "Don't you think?"

Her mother narrowed her eyes, lips pursed in disapproval. "Go get some sleep. I want you up and dressed for church by nine."

Less than three hours to recharge. Wonderful. Taking a chance, Maisie shot her a pleading look. "Would you mind—"

"No. Your father spent all night at the office, slaving away on a new sermon he's eager for us to hear. If you want more sleep, tell Moe to stop giving you night shifts."

That explained the mood. Bernice hated it when her husband spent the night elsewhere. Maisie didn't exactly blame her. She'd noticed her father's roving eye, and the way some of the single women in their congregation would flirt with him after services. "Night shifts give me more time to study during the day."

"Too bad. The world doesn't revolve around you, missy, so buck the hell up and do what I tell you." Swiping her half-empty mimosa off the table, Bernice drained the rest of the glass in three long swallows. Maisie waited for the parting shot she knew was coming, painfully aware that she hadn't been dismissed yet. "I don't know what I did to deserve such a wicked daughter. Spent my whole life being a good Christian, and *this* is what I get. An insolent brat who can't keep her legs closed long enough to grow up and move out."

There it was. Reliable as ever. If she hadn't already heard this same vile shit a thousand times, it might have actually unsettled her. But this was her mother's usual script, uninformed by last night's secretly groundbreaking encounter. Maisie relaxed her shoulders, too tired to argue or defend herself against the verbal onslaught. At this point the easiest way out was to stay strong and wait for the tirade to end.

Another minute of choice insults and Bernice was done. Slumped in her chair, she closed her eyes and waved Maisie away with a pained expression. "Go to bed. I've got a killer headache, thanks to you, and will require a couple hours of solitude to recover."

"Feel better," Maisie murmured, then tiptoed up the carpeted stairs and into her bedroom. Once inside, she fell onto her mattress and released a slow, shaky breath. Deflated about being treated like a child only hours after engaging in some very adult making out, Maisie focused instead on how thankful she was that her mother hadn't somehow found out the truth about Aiden.

Aiden.

Crawling beneath the covers without removing her blouse and skirt, Maisie closed her eyes and hoped to dream about the extraordinary woman who'd not only ignited her passion but awakened a fierce thirst for independence she didn't yet know how to resolve.

More Pancakes, Less Privacy

When a month passed without any sign of Aiden or her big rig, Maisie began to wonder if the whole experience had been a fever dream conjured by her sex-starved, romance-bingeing brain. She had no physical evidence from her encounter with Aiden, no real way to prove that the striking butch trucker existed at all. Though she couldn't fathom creating such a visceral, specific fantasy out of thin air, the imaginary-butch theory sure beat the alternative.

What if Aiden had simply moved on? She could be on the other side of the country by now, on the prowl for a nice girl who was ready to settle down and raise a couple of kids together. It was entirely possible she'd blown her chance by refusing to take Aiden's number. Why would an out-and-proud butch goddess want anything to do with a closeted, small-town virgin who still lived in her childhood bedroom, two doors down from the deeply religious—and constantly judgmental—parents whose financial support she relied on? Aiden had a choice about whether to get involved in her sad little life, and Maisie hardly blamed her for opting out. She'd run away and never come back, too, given the chance.

One day. Her mantra since the first grade and a promise she intended to keep. *One day, I'll be gone, and they'll be sorry.*

Less than an hour before the end of a relatively slow Friday lunch and dinner shift, Maisie exited the kitchen carrying three trays of burgers and french fries for a table of high-tipping regulars—only to practically drop them at the sight of a familiar figure seated in the corner booth. Forcing her eyes away from the flannel-clad trucker who probably wasn't even Aiden, Maisie did what she could to deliver the

Carter grandparents and grandson their meals without letting on that anything was out of the ordinary.

Grabbing a menu on her way past the register, Maisie took a deep, calming breath before she walked to the corner booth and placed the laminated list of offerings on the table in front of the man-or-woman who might not be Aiden at all. "Welcome to Moe's. May I get you a drink while you look over the menu?"

"Oh, I already know what I want." Her voice was every bit as sexy as Maisie remembered, if not more. "I've had this massive hankering for pancakes…for maybe a month now?"

Afraid to look, but even more nervous not to, Maisie raised her eyes to take in the not-so-make-believe lady trucker. Somehow, Aiden was even more handsome than she remembered. Piercing blue eyes, dark, close-cropped hair made for running fingernails through, those full, eminently kissable lips—

"And water to drink."

Grateful to have been snapped out of what had almost turned into an extremely not-safe-for-work flight of fancy, Maisie put the tip of her pen against the order pad in her white-knuckled hand and agonized about how to proceed. No way could she say any of what she wanted to, or ask what she wanted to, out loud and in front of everyone. If she was going to pass along a message, it needed to be committed to paper.

But her mind had gone blank. She wasn't positive she knew how to spell anymore, let alone compose a coherent sentence. Maisie lowered the pen and pad, flashing an awkward grin instead. "Yes, sir. I'll have those right out for you."

Sir? Maisie cringed at the unintentional slip. While it *would* be easier if those who saw them together assumed Aiden was male, she hadn't intended to lie. Nor had she planned to misgender Aiden a second time.

It was official. Maisie really, truly sucked at this romance thing.

Afraid of Aiden's reaction—and keenly aware of how long she was spending on the simplest order imaginable—Maisie spun on her heels and all but ran behind the counter and into the kitchen. Once the door swung closed behind her, she stopped to breathe in, breathe out, trying to calm down. She was able to regain her composure in under a minute, one of many neat tricks she'd honed through years of hiding her true self from everyone she knew. As soon as she trusted herself to speak without emotion, she peered into the pass-through counter at their junior chef, Ralph, who hovered over the prime rib he was tending with all the anxiety and tenderness of a new mother.

"How's it coming along, Ralph?"

The stocky teenager's eyes never strayed from the partially cooked cut of meat. "Couple more minutes and it should be perfect."

Taking advantage of his hyper-focused state, Maisie pitched an idea that would keep her in the kitchen a little while longer. "Got an order here for one short stack of pancakes. Want me to make them so you can finish off your meat?"

"Pancakes?" If Ralph had caught on to her double entendre, he didn't show it. "Sure. Why not? Knock yourself out."

Maisie walked around the counter to collect the ingredients for another kick-ass plate of made-from-scratch pancakes. As long as she kept her mind occupied, she wouldn't have to speculate about whether Aiden was still out there waiting for them in the wake of her disastrous exit. Or consider how awful it would feel if the cowardice of choosing to run away rather than apologize had led Aiden to decide she wasn't worth the heartache. Her eyes welled as she considered what she'd done to the one person she wanted to impress, and how she'd likely blown the chance she'd been praying for all month.

By the time the pancakes were plated, topped with butter, and joined by an individual syrup dispenser, Maisie doubted she had the stomach to return to the scene of her crimes—let alone deal with the mess she'd left behind. Not that she had other options. She could try to bribe Ralph into delivering Aiden's order, but why bother? If the woman of her dreams had left, she'd left. If by some miracle she hadn't, Maisie needed to persuade her to leave as quickly as possible, then drive forty miles south to an address Maisie knew would afford them enough privacy for a real conversation.

Prepared to have her hopes shattered, she walked into the dining room with a warm plate in one hand and an ice-cold glass of water in the other. When Aiden's head popped up to track her progress across the room, Maisie stumbled and almost fell from the sheer relief of having that brilliant smile directed her way once more. She flushed, realizing too late that she'd neglected to write any kind of note or instruction and still couldn't think of anything to say.

"Here you are!" Maisie cringed at the false cheer in her voice, a facsimile of bubbly enthusiasm usually reserved for her more challenging customers. "One short stack and a glass of water. Will you need anything else this evening?"

Aiden's brows knitted together in obvious confusion, but she uttered a simple "No, thank you" and didn't press Maisie to explain the standoffish service.

Sensing Aiden's unease about the signals she was receiving, Maisie managed her first genuine smile since the biggest secret she'd ever kept came strolling into her semi-populated workplace. "Let me get you extra napkins." She met Aiden's cautious gaze, willing her to understand. "Okay?"

"Thanks."

Unsure whether her message had been received, Maisie retreated behind the counter and grabbed a couple napkins, then tore a blank sheet out of her order pad. She scribbled the first thing that came to mind, all too aware of how little time she had to stop Aiden from giving up on her altogether. After a quick scan to confirm the address she'd jotted down was reasonably legible, Maisie slipped the sheet between the napkins before returning to the corner booth for the third time.

"Compliments to the chef." Aiden greeted her with a tentative smile. "These really hit the spot."

Maisie's face burned at the praise and how ecstatic Aiden's approval made her feel. "Well, we aim to please here at Moe's Fine Diner." Tamping down her irrational giddiness at the fact that they remained on speaking terms, she added, "So I very much appreciate each and every piece of feedback I'm given. Even the negative stuff." She set the napkins in her hand right next to Aiden's plate, taking care to expose one corner of the order slip concealed inside. "I'll be back to check on you in a few. Until then, bon appétit!"

Without waiting for Aiden to respond, Maisie marched with purpose to the Carter family's table to check for empty dishes and full bellies. It was a welcome break from the stress of juggling her crush on Aiden with the desire to protect the squeaky-clean image she'd been cultivating since childhood—albeit a fleeting one that ended far too soon when the entire crew packed up and left to catch a late movie. Maisie took the handful of cash they'd tossed onto the table and entered the total into the register, then pocketed the leftover bills and coins as her tip.

Money for Bernice to spend however she saw fit.

"Miss?"

Jolted by the unexpected presence a few feet to her left, Maisie grabbed at her chest and tried to keep her panic on the inside so as not to embarrass them both. The noise that managed to escape was more a whimper than a scream, but every inch as humiliating as any banshee howl she could've produced. Aiden was the only woman to ever make Maisie feel desperate to look cool, and that right there was the *opposite* of cool. She sounded unhinged.

"Forgive me." Aiden stared at her, wide-eyed and seemingly full of regret. "I didn't mean to startle you."

"You didn't," Maisie said, then cracked a grin at how full of shit they both knew she was. "And even if you did, it was my fault for not paying attention."

Aiden lifted one shoulder in a dismissive shrug, eyes sparkling like ocean waves on a steamy summer afternoon. "I'm sure you have a lot on your mind." She passed a fifty-dollar bill over the counter and offered a cordial nod. "Keep the change."

Stunned by the suggestion of a more than forty-dollar tip, Maisie shook her head on instinct. "That's way too generous. Let me give you at least ten dollars in exchange."

"Too generous?" Aiden tilted her head. "According to who?"

Maisie glanced down at the bill in Aiden's strong, undoubtedly skillful hand and noticed a gum wrapper folded around the middle. Intrigued, she accepted the fifty and smoothly pocketed the slip of paper in one fluid motion. Bernice's disapproving tone echoed in Maisie's head, broadcasting an incessant stream of dire predictions about what Aiden might ask for in exchange for this kind of cash. Her mother would be aghast at just how ineffective her usual scare tactics were in a scenario like this.

If Aiden wanted to go all the way, she didn't have to pay for it. Maisie had yearned for an opportunity like this since the day she first realized that sex actually sounded pretty fun. Even if Aiden *did* expect more than she'd planned to give...did she care?

"For tuition," Aiden whispered.

Nodding, Maisie opened the register and made change that went directly into her pocket. "Thank you. That's very kind."

Aiden winked, then withdrew a tattered ball cap from her back pocket that she tipped at Maisie before putting on. "You have a good evening."

"You too." Maisie's palms began to sweat at the sudden, unshakeable suspicion that Aiden hadn't seen her message after all. That she was seconds away from climbing into her truck and driving somewhere other than the proposed meeting spot. What if the tip had been a parting gift? What if her inability to admit what she wanted out loud was about to drive Aiden off for good? Fear and desperation emboldened Maisie to speak. "Until next time."

She hadn't meant it to be a question but heard a hopeful lift in her tone that seemed to compel a response. Luckily, Aiden didn't disappoint. Flashing a split-second grin, she lowered a hand to give her back pocket a subtle tap. "Until then."

It took what Maisie considered to be legendary self-control to not immediately search for the gum wrapper in her pocket and examine it for a secret note. Given that her actions at the register were constantly captured on video, she didn't feel safe taking even a cursory peek at whatever missive Aiden might've penned. A task like that called for total privacy—especially if the gum wrapper was blank or carrying a rejection. Snapped into reality by the urgent need to flee to the restroom, Maisie glanced at the clock over her head to check how long it would be until her shift ended.

Thirteen minutes—and no customers in sight. Maisie sighed, buckling down on her willpower. She could do this. The alleged note could wait.

Two minutes later, Maisie poked her head into the kitchen to find Ralph staring at his smartphone. "Mind if I run to the bathroom? The place is dead, and Deirdre should be here in the next few minutes, anyway."

"Uh-huh," Ralph said, most likely without having any idea what he'd agreed to.

"You may want to keep an eye on the dining room." Maisie tried not to sound as annoyed as she was. Sometimes she felt like the only one who cared about customer service around here. Most of her coworkers didn't hesitate to regularly slack off during their shifts—if they showed up at all—secure in the knowledge that Maisie would do whatever it took to keep their customers happy and coming back for more. "Or at least listen for the door."

"Sure." After a moment, Ralph tore his eyes from his phone's screen and squinted up at her with a confused frown. "I said go on, I got it." He returned his attention to whatever video he'd been watching before her interruption. "Don't go pissing yourself on my account."

Disgusted, Maisie wrinkled her nose and walked past him to the employee-only unisex bathroom at the far end of the hallway. She locked the door behind her, then leaned on the sink to dig through her apron pocket for the slim strip of white paper among the green bills and coins. When her fingers brushed against it, all the blood in Maisie's body rushed from her head to her already pounding heart.

With shaky hands that felt like they belonged to someone else, Maisie unfolded the gum wrapper and flipped it over to reveal a single word.

Yes.

A Magical Date

Maisie turned down the long driveway of the empty farmhouse where she'd sent Aiden, hands tense on the steering wheel as she searched the darkened shadows that obscured the house and accompanying barn from the public road. She assumed Aiden had beaten her here by forty minutes or more, thanks to the nightmare traffic she'd encountered due to their local high school football team's semi-final playoff game ending at the same time as her shift. Her late start had triggered a vague malaise that continued to fester and build over the course of the forty-mile journey, until she no longer knew why she'd bothered to haul her butt all the way to Lowell this late at night. To confirm the inevitable? Even if Aiden had puzzled out the scribbled instructions and found the place, it didn't make sense for her to linger around a stranger's poorly lit property for more than thirty minutes, tops, before thinking better of the idea.

Once she made it halfway up the drive without spotting Aiden's telltale rig, Maisie was ready to make a U-turn and leave so she wouldn't have to endure the brutal slap of being stood up. Or given up on. Either way, she didn't want to feel it, didn't want to accept that she'd screwed up with the only person whose opinion mattered to her right now.

Then a white figure emerged from behind the house and ran in frenetic circles beneath the oak tree where the tire swing her grandfather made for her fifth birthday used to hang. Maisie forgot to breathe as she drove closer to the house, desperate for hard evidence that she wasn't hallucinating the hyper pit bull as a defense mechanism against emotional trauma. At the sight of a dark truck parked behind the barn, she let out a relieved whimper. "Oh, thank goodness."

Aiden met her at the driver's side door after she parked. "You sure this place is safe? We're allowed to be here?"

Empowered by her certainty on at least this one matter, Maisie climbed out of her truck and greeted an exuberant Major with a calm pat on the chest once he sat. "It belongs to my grandparents, Mom's folks, who always treated me a whole lot nicer than their daughter ever has."

Aiden's jaw tensed for a moment before she spoke. "I'm sorry about your mother. Are your grandparents still around, or...?"

"Grandma died a couple years ago. They just moved Grandpa into my uncle's house last weekend. Dementia." Maisie surveyed their gloomy surroundings, aglow with the nostalgia of countless childhood memories. "I'm pretty sure they plan to list this property for sale, but for tonight at least..." She paused, breathless at what she was about to utter. "It's all ours."

"Awesome." Aiden eased into a shy grin, then looked down to watch Major soak up her affection. "We've missed you." As if on cue, Major spun in an excited circle before quickly settling down for more pets. "I'm a little more deft at playing it cool, but rest assured that's exactly how I feel on the inside. Just...out-of-my-mind excited to see you again."

Maisie licked her lips. Were they going to kiss like the last time? Would Aiden want even more than that? She wasn't sure how she'd react, in the moment, if Aiden asked for something she wasn't ready to give. Conscious of how long her silence was stretching, Maisie said the first thing that came to mind. "Me too."

"Hey." Aiden advanced a step, then ducked to study her face without making physical contact. "Maisie, I need you to believe what I'm about to tell you. All right?"

She nodded.

"Whatever happened between us last time, I don't expect or feel entitled to any part of you. Not tonight or any other night." Aiden paused either for effect or to await a response, then went on. "That's not why I left you a big tip. I have no interest in pressuring you into anything you don't want to do. Even if that means we never have sex. I'd be fine with that." She swallowed, voice wavering on her last few words. "All I want is to know you. Be your friend or...whatever."

"And if I wanted to be more than friends?" Maisie's throat went dry, like it did every time she thought about doing what she wanted instead of what her parents expected. "Would that also be fine?"

"That would be amazing." Aiden waited a beat, then said, "May I give you a hug now?"

Maisie moved forward, melting into her open arms with a drawn-out sigh. Her body reacted to Aiden like a live wire, hands trembling, knees wobbling, thighs shaking, feet sweating, clit jumping. Poise entirely nonexistent. She suspected most women didn't get this worked up over an innocent hug, but every touch from Aiden was pure ecstasy. If they did ever have sex, it might send her to an early grave.

"I've been waiting for this all month." Aiden tightened her arms around Maisie's waist, drawing them together until Maisie gasped at the friction of Aiden's knee easing between her thighs. "To hold you again, without all the paranoia...it's heaven."

Maisie couldn't claim to be paranoia-*free*, exactly, but she'd always felt safe at her grandparents' farm, and tonight was no exception. No one had any reason to visit the property this late on a Friday, making it the ideal spot to finally cede control to her hormones and enjoy Aiden every which way she could. Unsure how to express the depth of her hunger, Maisie tucked her face into Aiden's neck and shyly kissed her throat. "Same."

Aiden took Maisie by the shoulders before stepping out of their embrace. "You're nervous. Why?"

Maisie bleated out a full-throated laugh, too tickled by Aiden's sincerity to stifle herself. "Surely I'm not the first girl to be intimidated by your good looks and endless charm. Or those lips..." She stopped, regretting the decision to expand beyond one-word answers. "You know why."

"Can't say I understand it, though. On the off chance I haven't been clear, I happen to be carrying a massive torch for you, Miss Davis. So there's no need to worry about impressing me, 'cause I already think you're wonderful."

"Except you barely know me." Maisie's insecurities crept in to plant doubt and sow despair. In what world was a stud like Aiden this enamored with a nobody like her? She didn't know how to make sense of the attraction Aiden professed to feel, which meant it couldn't possibly be true. "Maybe your opinion will change once you do."

"Maybe it will. I may end up liking you even more." Aiden quirked her mouth into a wry smile. "Only one way to find out."

She was right. What happened tonight would likely determine how both of them felt about their tentative friendship and the hassle of keeping it secret. After the awkwardness of their earlier interaction at the diner, the least she could do was show Aiden enough of the real Maisie for her to make an informed decision about whether she was worth all the bullshit.

Emboldened by Aiden's encouraging words, Maisie closed the distance between them in a single stride and rose onto her tiptoes to crush their mouths together. It was a terrible attempt to initiate a passionate kiss, a move fit for an inexperienced teenager but downright pathetic from a woman three years past the legal drinking age. Aiden brought her hands up to cradle Maisie's face in a valiant attempt to fix the disaster-in-progress, only to pull away a moment later for a prolonged chuckle.

"I wasn't ready." Aiden licked her lips, already shiny from Maisie's clumsy efforts, and inched closer. "Mind if we try again?"

Blaming her own lack of preparedness for that awful clash of lips, teeth, and tongues was so thoroughly *Aiden* that Maisie had to smile. "You're very kind."

"For wanting a do-over?"

Soothed by Aiden's inherent decency, Maisie followed her lead and set aside the shame of her ineptness for later. She met Aiden's eyes, desperate to get it right this time. Who sneaks around a shitty backwoods town to hook up with a virgin who can't even *kiss?* Her novelty would wear off fast if she failed to keep up with Aiden's patient guidance. Even if Aiden didn't expect anything, to be disappointed by what Maisie freely gave would surely make her reconsider whatever bright future she might've envisioned for them.

Figuring it was wisest to let Aiden make the first move, Maisie took a deep breath and prepared for redemption. Aiden used both hands to cup Maisie's red-hot cheeks, the same as before, but kept her approach slow and deliberate so they had time to align their mouths for a truly stellar kiss. Maisie moaned at the easy slide of Aiden's tongue against hers, matching its rhythm without even trying. How Aiden managed to pull off kisses like this with someone as clumsy as her was one of life's great mysteries, she supposed, but Maisie had never needed to understand magic to appreciate it. She was content to simply enjoy the ride.

Aiden ended their kiss much sooner than Maisie would've preferred, but she hid her disappointment behind a satisfied grin and fanned her face with a trembling hand. "So *that's* how it's done."

"You're such a good kisser." Aiden's groan was the most sensual sound to ever grace Maisie's ears. "I could do that all day. Every day."

"Then why don't you?" Maisie inched forward to loop her arms around Aiden's neck. Not wanting to ruin the moment with her impatience, she waited for Aiden to take the hint and go in for a third kiss. "I won't say no."

Aiden chuckled, then backed out of her embrace. "Actually—"

"Oh." Mortified by her misreading of Aiden's intent, Maisie reached down to tug on the hem of her skirt. "Sorry, I thought—"

"Wait." Aiden's hand shot into the air, cutting her off mid-sentence. "I *do* want to keep kissing you, all night if possible, but…"

Maisie swallowed. *But?*

"Would you…is there somewhere we can sit and talk for a while?" Aiden sounded sheepish but sincere, and maybe even nervous, about asking. "I don't want to get distracted by…" She gestured at Maisie. "This, and miss my chance to get to know you more. Especially when it'll only make the kissing part better."

That was hard to imagine. "Better?" Maisie doubted her heart could endure anything hotter than what they'd already done. "I can't promise I'll survive that."

"You will." Aiden extended a hand in silent invitation. "I'll protect you."

Shivering at the heartfelt words, Maisie accepted Aiden's hand and pointed toward the house. "On the porch. There's a swing big enough for two people."

"Perfect." Despite not knowing exactly where they were going, Aiden led Maisie up the front steps and paused at the top. She waited until Major caught up, then said, "Left or right?"

Intimately familiar with every inch of the wraparound porch, Maisie took the lead and tugged Aiden's hand to guide them to the right. "Over here."

They had to walk around to the side of the house to find the handmade wooden swing her grandfather had built for his wife on their twenty-fifth wedding anniversary. As a child she used to love sitting out here squeezed between the two of them, begging Grandpa to use his legs and make them swing, then laughing with Grandma as they rocked back and forth at his whim. She claimed the right side of the swing—her grandma's side—and invited Aiden to sit in her grandfather's spot.

To break the ice, Maisie shared the memory of her grandparents and the swing—its significance as a handcrafted gift, the way they'd almost always be camped out in their respective spots when Maisie and her parents arrived for a visit, and the thrill of being able to join them for an occasional ride. By the time she exhausted her anecdotes on the subject, Aiden was beaming at her like a maniac.

"What?" Self-conscious about how much info she'd dumped, Maisie lowered her gaze to her lap and awaited Aiden's reaction. "Sorry for the long and boring tangent."

"Boring?" Aiden snorted, then laced their fingers together and squeezed. "Are you kidding? That's the most I've ever heard you talk—and your grandparents sound *amazing*." Mirth fading, she said, "I'm sorry you don't have them to swing with anymore."

Maisie shrugged and, without thinking, said, "I have you."

"Yes, you do." Aiden eased an arm around her shoulders, pulling Maisie tight against her side. She planted both feet on the porch and rocked the swing lazily to and fro, a soothing pace that threatened to lull Maisie to sleep. "For however long you want me."

Maisie blinked, unsure whether Aiden had meant the murmured declaration the way it sounded. Pulse racing, she fumbled for an acceptable response. If it were up to her, she'd take Aiden forever, no questions asked. But there was so much about her life she didn't control, so many decisions she didn't have the money, education, or freedom to make. Unable to commit to next month, let alone forever, Maisie changed the subject to the only thing she *really* wanted to talk about.

"Anyway, tell me about you. Family, friends, hobbies, childhood, trucking…" Maisie chuckled. "Anything you're comfortable sharing, really. I want to know it all."

"Well, I grew up near Flint, Michigan, where my father was a machinist at General Motors. Mom worked for Ford Motor Company, so we were always an automotive family." Aiden spoke without emotion, a simple recitation of facts. "I'm the oldest of three—one girl, two boys—and was always the biggest tomboy in the family. My brothers would get pissed at me for running faster, climbing higher, belching louder—whatever—because they hated losing to a girl. School was... school. Never had a lot of friends in middle school, or high school, since most of the girls thought I was a pervert, and the boys treated me like a freak."

Maisie angled her body toward Aiden's and pulled her into a tight hug. Aiden tensed, then relaxed against Maisie's chest and brought their foreheads together. "I'm over it," Aiden said, running her fingers along Maisie's spine. "It honestly doesn't bother me anymore."

"It bothers me." Maisie slid her hand up Aiden's back to play with the short, fine hairs on the nape of her neck. "Kids can be so cruel. Especially when you're different."

"Were they cruel to you?"

Maisie shrugged, abashed to have somehow compared her relatively uneventful adolescence to Aiden's personal hell on earth. "Not really, but then I never gave them much to work with. Is it sad to admit that after only three hours in each other's company, you know more about me than any of my high school classmates did?"

"A bit." Aiden kissed the corners of her mouth, both sides, then put her lips on Maisie's for a sweet kiss. "It's also smart. The less people know, the harder it is to hurt you."

"But at what cost?" Maisie drew away, surprised by how badly she wanted to see Aiden's face. "I'm a twenty-four-year-old virgin with no friends and no life of her own. I still live in the same bedroom where I got and then hid my first period at age thirteen, under the thumb of one and a half parents who don't even realize yet how much they hate me. I've never had a boyfriend, or a girlfriend, and until I saw you, I wasn't sure if I'd ever feel sexually attracted to anyone." She held Aiden's stare, dumbfounded by her own honesty. "I've done such a bang-up job of hiding who I am that even I didn't know."

"Until me?" Aiden radiated quiet exhilaration at her admission. "That's...I'm flattered."

"Yeah, yeah," Maisie said, deflecting with humor. "You managed to rev the little engine nobody thought could."

"It's the flannel, right?" Adopting the same tone, Aiden smirked and popped open her leather jacket to reveal a new green flannel shirt beneath. "I decided to go with the same theme, in case it was my butch uniform that hooked you."

Maisie was stunned by the girlish giggle that bubbled out of her in response. Good gravy, she sounded like a flirt—not unlike the cheerleaders and pretty girls she couldn't stand in high school. She should've felt dumb, channeling a breathless, starry-eyed fangirl, but she knew Aiden didn't see her that way. Judging by the flared nostrils and flushed skin, Aiden found this side of her to be the opposite of dumb.

Eager to prove her right, Maisie said, "The leather jacket, the flannel, the face, the cleavage…"

"Cleavage?" Aiden snorted. "And here I thought it was my ass that caught your eye."

Fresh humiliation washed over Maisie at the memory of Aiden's entrance into the diner. "Everything about you caught my eye. Even before I knew you were a woman."

Aiden's arm snaked around Maisie's waist to draw her into a loose embrace. "Don't be embarrassed. You aren't the first, and you sure as hell won't be the last." She kissed the crown of Maisie's head, inhaling at length. "Happens all the time."

Maisie arched into Aiden's solid heat, unable to stop her body from seeking out the relief it badly needed. "Sorry."

"About being attracted to me as a man?" Aiden's smile permeated her voice. "Don't be. Means you want me regardless of what's in my pants."

"You're stunning. Inside and out." She shot Aiden a sidelong glance, thrilled by the light the compliment brought to her eyes. "That said, the cleavage was a game-changer. Finding out you were a woman kicked my crush into the stratosphere."

"Nice to hear they're good for something." Aiden chuckled. "Other than ruining my golf swing."

Maisie shivered at a vivid memory of Aiden's hard nipple poking into her palm. What she wouldn't give to touch her like that a second time. "They're incredible."

"Not as incredible as your legs in that skirt." Aiden tilted her head to gaze at the skirt in question. "Or any part of you, as far as I'm concerned." As though realizing that she'd set them on a crash course to ending their conversation for some nonverbal communication, Aiden changed the subject in the most unexpected fashion. "My mom says hello, by the way."

Maisie blinked, taken aback that *anyone's* mom knew about her, let alone Aiden's. "You told your *mom* about the slutty waitress you made out with behind a dumpster?"

"No." Aiden tugged on a lock of her hair, a gentle correction. "I told my mom the story of meeting a woman I can't stop thinking about." Her voice softened. "Used to be she didn't want to hear about my love life, but we've made a lot of progress over the years. She says you sound darling."

Ashamed by her relative lack of transparency, Maisie said, "I'm not sure when I'll feel safe enough to talk to my parents about you."

"That's okay." Aiden stopped the swing's motion. "I didn't share that with you so you'd run home and tell your folks about your new trucker girlfriend. I only...I want you to understand how serious I am." She trailed her fingers down Maisie's forearm in an adoring caress. "About you."

Maisie licked her lips. *Girlfriend?* So Aiden truly did want more from her than sex and small talk. Enough to inspire a heart-to-heart with her mother. Shouldn't she be ecstatic about that? If not for the impossible situation in which she was trapped, maybe she would be. But to divulge their brief encounter to her formerly homophobic mother, Aiden had to want far more than Maisie could reasonably give. Why confide in any parent about the random, top-secret make-out session you had with a closeted waitress whose father happened to be the town preacher? Unless, of course, Aiden saw her as more than a random, closeted waitress in search of a horny time.

"What are you thinking?"

Aiden's murmur interrupted her silent rumination, forcing her to share her anxiety without the benefit of a prepared answer. "I'm thinking I'm not sure I can give you what you want. Or what you deserve."

"Maisie, what I want is you." Aiden shifted to face her more directly, revealing the mild panic in her eyes. "Forget about what I deserve, 'cause it can't possibly be anyone as sweet and pretty as the girl in my arms. That's why I'm content to take whatever I can get, even if it isn't everything I'd like."

Maisie smiled despite her insecurity. "Dang, you're good."

"Good enough for another kiss?" Aiden puckered her lips and leaned in, eyes shut tight.

God, she was cute. Amused, Maisie pressed a brief, loving peck atop the bridge of Aiden's nose. She eased away, tickled by the grumpy pout she'd put on Aiden's previously hopeful face. "You never said what kind, or where."

Aiden lowered her hands to Maisie's sides, unleashing a tickle attack that left Maisie quaking with tearful guffaws. "Listen, young lady. I can think of *five* places I'd love to kiss you—none of which is your nose."

Maisie's laughter faded as her brain jumped to assemble a list of potential locations. Lips, of course—though maybe those didn't count. Did she mean five places *besides* the usual suspects, or her mouth plus four more? Didn't matter. Mouth, neck, cheek, chin— She rolled her eyes at the innocent acts she'd reverted to on instinct. None of those spots were where Maisie most wanted Aiden's mouth.

Soft lips grazed her earlobe. "Yes, baby. Your nipples are tied for first."

Maisie cried out at a violent pulse from her clit and the weak pleasure that followed. Did she dare inquire about the runner-up? She exhaled through her nose, calming herself before she said or did anything to derail their trajectory. "Whenever you're in the mood to tick a few items off that list, let me know. Sounds like we may have some overlap."

"Mutually beneficial kissing?" Aiden's breath danced over the sensitive flesh at the juncture of Maisie's neck and shoulder, raising goose bumps down both arms and across her chest. "Yes, please."

As grateful as she was for Aiden's manners and sense of propriety, Maisie thought she might explode if they didn't act on at least some of this teasing. She wanted to learn absolutely every detail about Aiden's life, truly, but the sun would rise soon enough, and their stolen moment would be over. Until who knew when? What if they never had another opportunity like this one? Total privacy, multiple cozy spots to fool around, and Maisie wasn't on her period. It was impossible to say if the stars would ever align this perfectly again.

Aiden retreated a few inches, creating a sliver of distance between them. Then she exhaled, ran a hand through her hair, and released a shaky laugh. "Wow. I, uh…need a second."

Maisie didn't want her to rein in whatever had made her back off. She yearned to know this Aiden, too, every bit as much as where she grew up or what her parents were like. The memory of being caged against the brick wall, Aiden's heavy body holding her in place, nearly pushed her to ask for another kiss. Not wanting to disrespect Aiden's request to take their time, she settled for a subtle shift of her weight to squeeze her thighs together. The mild friction wasn't nearly enough to dull the edge of her intense arousal.

"Maisie..."

To hell with propriety. After a lifetime of repressing her desires, Maisie lacked the will to be a good girl and stay quiet. "Aiden, it means everything that you like me enough to attempt a mini-courtship, and I'm happy to keep talking about our hobbies or whatever if that's what you truly want, but you can't work me up like this if all you're looking for is conversation."

With her eyes adjusted to the darkness, Maisie saw the shift in Aiden's body language and knew she'd made the right choice. She wasn't used to getting what she asked for, but Aiden didn't hesitate to comply. Scooting back over, Aiden wrapped her arms around Maisie's waist to tug her up and onto her lap. "Yes, ma'am."

WITH A HAPPY ENDING

Gasping at the unexpected move, Maisie put her arms around Aiden's shoulders for balance. A million thoughts flitted through her head, one after the other in a rapid-fire assault on her psyche. Had Aiden meant to echo her heinous verbal slip at the diner? Why did her tummy flutter when Aiden called her "ma'am"? She hated hearing the word from anyone else. What if she was heavier than Aiden expected? Would she let Maisie crush her, too polite to shove her off? Then, once the reality of her situation registered, she worried some more. Had her skirt ridden up during the transfer? Were her panties in direct contact with Aiden's lap? How soaked were they? Enough to leave a stain behind for Aiden to clean up?

Aiden stopped her anxiety train before it got too far down the tracks, rubbing a hand over Maisie's hip, then giving her a firm squeeze. "Whatever you're spinning out about, don't. Talk to me, let me know how you're feeling, and I'll do everything possible to ease any worries or doubts you can't seem to shake."

Being a twenty-four-year-old virgin, Maisie had never imagined her first sexual partner would end up being the sweetest person she'd ever met. She'd assumed her options were inherently limited, that she had no chance of attracting anyone worthwhile, and that holding out for the perfect suitor was a fairy tale she'd never get to experience. But here Aiden was, setting an impossibly high standard for absolutely everyone who came after.

Maisie blew out a shaky breath, then half smiled at Aiden's obvious concern. "No. I'm fine, it's just..." She weighed which confession was least embarrassing, then said, "I felt terrible about calling you 'sir' earlier, at Moe's. It wasn't on purpose. I was just…nervous."

Aiden's brows furrowed in apparent confusion. "Please tell me you haven't been beating yourself up over that."

"Only a little." Dumbstruck by Aiden's nonchalance, Maisie wondered if it had been a mistake to bring up an incident Aiden seemingly hadn't read anything into. "I didn't want you to think I was trying to pretend you're something you're not. You know, around other people."

Aiden's expression softened. "Sweetheart, I don't blame you for being nervous. I dropped by your workplace without any kind of warning or advance notice, knowing full well you wouldn't be able to acknowledge me until everyone else was gone. I wasn't sure when you'd be working, so I planned to wait for your shift to end, then catch you in the parking lot before you drove away. But when I pulled up and saw you through the window…" She winced, shooting Maisie a guilty frown. "It was my fault for going in. I knew you had other customers, but after a month of waiting and dreaming…"

"Literal dreaming?" Awed by the thought of Aiden lying in bed thinking about *her*, Maisie traced a fingernail over Aiden's collarbone and savored the answering shudder of the body under and around her. "Sex dreams, or…?"

"Sex, cuddling, grocery shopping, a trip to outer space…" Aiden cracked a roguish grin, reaching around to give Maisie's bottom a playful pinch. "My unconscious mind likes to keep us busy." Her grin widened. "And naked."

Aiden had pictured her naked. More than once. Maisie breathed out, fighting off her fear of being a disappointment. She reminded herself of Aiden's unimpeachable character, her deep empathy, and the sincerity of her consistent encouragement and praise. She basked in the absolute elation of being wanted. Newfound confidence flowed through her, bolstered by the knowledge that Aiden would never hurt her on purpose. Even if her body didn't live up to the fantasy, Aiden would worship it all the same. Because it was hers.

"Have you thought about me?" Aiden prompted Maisie with a light nip of her earlobe. "Naked or otherwise?"

"Yes," Maisie answered, then giggled. If Aiden wanted more details, she'd have to ask for them. Maisie was way too bashful to reveal exactly how often her thoughts had turned to Aiden over the past four weeks—or the frequency with which she'd used her hand and pillows as a poor substitute.

"Naked?" Aiden repeated. She tickled Maisie's bare knee, making her squirm. "On the moon?"

Disarmed by the goofy line of questioning, Maisie admitted, "Naked. Sadly, we never made it to the moon." She bit her lip, tempted to offer Aiden another crumb. Her internal battle ended without any shots fired. "Never really made it anywhere except my bedroom."

She swore she could feel Aiden's heart pound harder. "Like you dreamed I was in your bedroom, or…?"

Giving Aiden what she wanted to hear, Maisie closed her eyes and told the truth. "Fantasized, more like. Asleep, awake…you've dominated my thoughts more than I should probably admit."

Aiden curled her fingers around the nape of Maisie's neck and brought their lips together for a long, sensual kiss. Maisie moaned into Aiden's hungry mouth, hips rolling in an uncontrolled hunt for relief. If her skirt had ridden up, Aiden was about to find out. Firm hands gripped her hips and guided them back and forth, back and forth, across Aiden's receptive lap. Maisie felt her juices trickling out before being smeared across her panties and realized it didn't matter if there was one layer or ten between her and Aiden's jeans. Nothing would hinder her out-of-control arousal. Aiden was going to get wet, and she couldn't do anything to stop it.

Maisie broke the kiss with a muted cry, hips bucking as she chased the elusive peak just beyond her reach. Shaking, Aiden unbuttoned her flannel shirt and pulled the two sides apart. Then she took Maisie's hand and placed it on her left breast, teaching her where and how hard to squeeze. "This where we left off?"

Breathless with wonder, Maisie nodded and rubbed her palm over the pebbled tip. What she wouldn't give for a lamp right about now. Or the afternoon sun. She could feel the tantalizing curve and weight of the breast in her hand, but her eyes were also keen to join the feast. Overwhelmed by the tremendous honor of being in this position a second time, Maisie licked her lips and asked a favor she'd rehearsed hundreds of times in her head. "May I kiss them?" She flexed her fingers on Aiden's breast, just in case she had any doubt about where she wanted to put her mouth. "Please?"

"Yes," Aiden said, then added, "But first I want you to tell me something, and be honest." She paused, lips quirking into a wicked smile. "Did you ever touch yourself while you were thinking about me?"

Maisie froze. She'd never talked to anyone about that. Ever. As a kid, her mother would go ballistic anytime she found Maisie with one or both hands under the comforter, convinced her daughter was a compulsive pervert without a shred of self-control. No exceptions, even in the dead of winter, when Bernice insisted on keeping the house like an icebox to combat the hot flashes that had plagued her for years. Better to wake up with icicles for fingers than risk abusing your own body in defiance of the Lord. The shame had been drilled into Maisie so thoroughly that her stomach turned over at the prospect of admitting her most sinful secret.

Aiden dialed down the heat with a disclosure of her own. "I have. Last time was right after I woke up this morning. Stroked my clit until I came—twice. Both times while thinking of you." She waited a beat. "In this skirt."

Made brave by Aiden's candor, Maisie whispered, "I pretended it was your hand. Touching me."

Aiden's hips rose beneath her, increasing the friction she so desperately craved. Maisie ground herself on the firm thigh she sat upon, far too horny to care how she looked or what Aiden thought. Or even how wet she was. Watching Aiden react to her words filled Maisie with self-confidence, along with a sense of power and control she'd never thought possible. The only thing that mattered was Aiden, their bodies, and the pursuit of pleasure. She ran her thumb over Aiden's engorged nipple, then trapped it between her fingers for a tentative tug.

"Oh." Aiden moaned, chest thrust out to give Maisie easier access. "Fuck, baby, that feels good." When Maisie responded with a careful twist of the hardened peak, Aiden grabbed her ass and convulsed in ecstatic abandon. "You're making me so wet." She brought her lips to Maisie's ear, licking the edge. "And hard for you."

Pleasantly stunned by Aiden's suggestive dialogue, Maisie did what she could to participate. "*You* feel good." She gave Aiden's nipple another twist, then flattened her hand against the distended nub. "I can't believe I'm touching you. Again."

"Meanwhile, I'm trying to figure out why I'm *not* touching you."

Aiden smoothed a hand up and down Maisie's flank before pausing at the spot where her blouse met her skirt. "May I feel your skin?"

Maisie nodded, too excited to speak. When Aiden didn't move, she managed a strained, "Yes."

"Thank you," Aiden murmured, sliding beneath Maisie's blouse to caress her bare stomach. "You're so soft." Maisie tensed, adjusting to the foreign sensation of another person's hands on her. Nobody had ever touched her stomach before, let alone any of the other places Aiden now had access to. "One day I'd love to kiss you all over. Every inch of your gorgeous body, head to toe."

Maisie jolted at the slow journey of Aiden's hand from her belly to just below the cup of her plain white bra. Aiden traced the shape of her top rib with lazy fingertips, ratcheting Maisie's anticipation to perilous heights. If Aiden didn't touch her soon, it seemed feasible that she might literally die from wanting. "Please," Maisie breathed. "I'll do anything if you'll just—"

Already one step ahead of her, Aiden unhooked the front clasp of her bra and pushed the material out of the way to make room for the hand she placed on Maisie's uncovered breast. Maisie hissed in relief at the warmth against her nipple, which had stiffened into an excruciating peak only made worse by the evening breeze. Pressing herself into Aiden's large, capable hand, Maisie forgot to wait and captured Aiden's lips in another passionate kiss. This time Aiden met her halfway, and they established the perfect rhythm together.

Time fell away as they kissed and stroked and discovered each other, until Maisie lost track of how long they'd been entangled on the porch swing. Every touch from Aiden brought her closer and closer to the edge—without pushing her over. Maisie wasn't confident she could climax from this alone, and by now she *needed* release. She'd never sleep without it. Shedding the last of her inhibitions, Maisie moved Aiden's hand from her breast to her bare knee. Then, pointedly *not* second-guessing her boldness, she slid it under her skirt and up the inside of her thigh, inches from her ruined panties.

Aiden turned her head and sucked in a shaky breath. She kept her hand exactly where Maisie had left it, so close and yet still so far from where Maisie most needed it to be. Sounding like she'd just finished running a marathon, Aiden asked, "Are you sure?"

The lack of certainty in her voice led Maisie to a moment of pause, wherein it occurred to her exactly how promiscuous her behavior was. Practically begging a woman she barely knew to touch her vagina... Maisie snorted at the irony. Virgin preacher's daughter throws her untouched lady garden at the first butch lesbian she sees—to be fair, it wouldn't make for a bad romance novel. She'd read it, at least.

Aiden leaned back to study her face. "Maisie." She ghosted her thumb over the delicate flesh of Maisie's unexplored inner thigh. "Whatever you want, I'll do. But I need you to tell me. I refuse to cross any lines you aren't ready to cross."

Appreciative as always of Aiden's focus on enthusiastic consent, Maisie nonetheless found it easier to speak with actions rather than words. She locked eyes with Aiden, then reached under her skirt to urge the hand on her thigh farther up to rest atop her vulva. They both moaned at the contact, and Maisie threw her arms around Aiden and buried her face in her neck. "Yes," she said, in case she hadn't been clear. "Please, *yes.*"

Aiden's fingers curled around Maisie's covered mound for a tender but possessive squeeze. "I can't believe how wet you are." She rubbed the flat of her hand up and down the sodden crotch of Maisie's panties, nostrils flaring at the slickness her fingers glided across. "I'll bet you taste even better than pancakes."

Maisie half laughed, half sobbed as the steady motion of Aiden's hand threatened to prematurely finish her off. An image of Aiden kneeling beside the bed, head between her widespread thighs, triggered a clenching ripple inside Maisie that further coated Aiden's talented fingers in hot, slippery satisfaction. Aiden growled under her breath, palming her one last time before letting go. Maisie's disappointment didn't have time to register before Aiden trailed a finger along the elastic leg of her panties.

"Mind if I get these out of the way?"

"Yes," Maisie said, falling back on her standard one-syllable reply. Then she mentally reviewed Aiden's wording and amended her response. "No. I don't mind." Frustrated by her own incoherence, Maisie said, "Get them out of the way."

Maisie expected Aiden to yank the panties down her legs and toss them onto the porch, but what she actually did was so much more thrilling. She snuck two fingers beneath the elastic band, took hold of the soaked strip of cotton, and dragged the material aside to expose

Maisie's heated flesh to the cool air and Aiden's attentive hand. Out of breath already, Maisie released a strained whimper in advance of the contact she knew was imminent.

Finally.

At the first graze of Aiden's fingertip across her hypersensitive labia, Maisie jerked in shock and awe. How did Aiden's touch feel *so* different than her own? To not be in control of the direction, pressure, and speed of the sensual massage transformed the familiar ritual into an entirely new experience. The unpredictability of the hand between Maisie's thighs sharpened her arousal to a fine point, obliterating whatever self-control she might've still possessed. Spreading her legs as far as she could without tumbling off Aiden's lap, Maisie surrendered her body and soul to the only person to ever see through the facade and appreciate *her.*

Aiden kissed her cheek, teasing the edge of Maisie's labia in an unhurried exploration of the slick, swollen folds. "Does that feel good?"

Maisie nodded quickly, afraid Aiden might stop if she didn't get an answer. To demonstrate exactly *how* good, Maisie rocked her hips against Aiden's hand in a silent plea for more. Aiden chuckled but didn't give in. Painting a tight circle over her clit, Aiden positioned her lips just below Maisie's ear and spoke in a calm, authoritative murmur.

"I'm proud of you for being able to make yourself come." Aiden paused to kiss her neck, slowing the fingers on Maisie's labia to an infuriating crawl. "Know why?"

Maisie shook her head, inexplicably bashful despite the hands reaching up her skirt. "Growing up I was told it's a sin. Made me feel guilty every time."

"Fuck that." Stroking the hood of her clit, Aiden rested her head against Maisie's and spoke into her ear. "There's nothing sinful about learning your own body and what it likes. Makes it easier when the time comes to share yourself with someone else."

Maisie sank her teeth into her lower lip, using the painful sting to stave off the orgasm she could already feel. When Aiden stopped her ministrations a moment later, Maisie wasn't sure whether to thank her or burst into tears. "Aiden." Her voice cracked on the name. "Please, don't stop."

"I'm thrilled you already know what you like because it means you can tell me." Aiden withdrew her hand from Maisie's skirt, then returned a moment later with Maisie's free hand in tow. Aiden guided the hand between Maisie's thighs and positioned it near her clit. "Or show me."

None of Maisie's fantasies had come anywhere near this. She hadn't even known to imagine something so delicious. Too self-conscious to masturbate on Aiden's lap—not this time, at least—Maisie covered Aiden's hand with hers and brought it back to her wetness. Manipulating the fingers beneath her own, Maisie demonstrated her favorite way to stimulate her clit. Two fingers. Large, light circles around, then over, the swollen tip. Slow at first, fast at the end. Once Aiden adopted her tried-and-true technique, Maisie released her to finish the job.

"Yes?" Aiden groaned along with her, fully aware of the answer.

"Just like that." Maisie tried to hold back a moan, but she couldn't. It felt too amazing. Aiden was amazing. "Don't stop. Keep going *just like that*."

She tensed, thighs quaking on either side of Aiden's busy hand. As much as she didn't want this to end, Maisie wasn't sure how much longer she'd be able to hold off the inevitable. It was a miracle she'd hadn't come apart already.

Aiden, perhaps sensing her impending climax, abandoned Maisie's clit to run a finger around the entrance of her vagina. Maisie froze, transfixed by the novel sensation. She'd never penetrated herself before and wondered how it would feel. Toying lightly with the narrow opening, Aiden kept her suspended on the knife edge of ecstasy.

"Aiden." Maisie's eyelashes fluttered, every bit as out of control as the rest of her. "Don't stop."

Aiden drew another circle around the tight channel, chest heaving. "Have you ever touched yourself here?"

"No," Maisie said. That was one act she wasn't interested in doing alone.

"Maybe next time I'll put my finger inside you and show you how to fuck, but not tonight." She combed through the juices gathered at Maisie's entrance, then resumed drawing circles around the painfully distended clit she'd worked to full rigidity. "Tonight I'm going to play with your pussy until you can't stand it anymore. Until you beg me to stop."

Blown away by Aiden's rough language, Maisie rocketed to climax in record time. She crushed her mouth to Aiden's so she wouldn't scream into the night, shattered by an orgasm far more intense than any delivered by her own hand. Aiden slipped her tongue into Maisie's open mouth, kissing her hard and deep while continuing to manipulate the throbbing clit between her fingers. Maisie convulsed again and again on Aiden's lap, for what felt like forever, until finally she slammed her thighs shut on Aiden's arm and breathed, "No more."

Aiden stilled her fingers, then flattened her hand atop Maisie's twitching mound. "You're breathtaking." She kissed Maisie's cheek, her chin, her mouth. "Thank you."

Maisie shook her head in disbelief. "Thank *me*?"

"For trusting me." Aiden removed the hand from under her skirt, adjusting the hemline before she shifted Maisie to sit sideways across her lap. Encouraging Maisie to rest against her chest, she tightened her arms to engulf her in a warm bear hug. "For sharing yourself with me."

Sobering as the afterglow began to fade, Maisie blinked to try to stop the tears that were already falling. "Thanks for being so nice to me."

"I can't wait to be even nicer." Aiden nuzzled into her, cupping Maisie's breast through her blouse. "Soon, I hope."

Reminded of their difficult circumstances, Maisie let her tears flow even harder. "Me too."

"Maisie, hey." Gentle fingers grazed her cheek, urging her to turn and meet Aiden's worried eyes. At the sight of her tearstained face, Aiden went from looking troubled to deeply distressed in half a heartbeat. "Are you all right? Did I...do you regret letting me—?"

"No! Not at all. I've never been happier."

"I can see that."

"I've never been happier," Maisie said again. "And it's almost over. I have to go back to my crappy life in this crappy town living with my crappy *parents*, and you'll drive away...and who knows when I'll see you again?"

"Soon." Aiden pulled her close, swaying them back and forth as though to calm Maisie's tears. "I've already made some adjustments to my work schedule that should allow me to swing by again in a week, ten days at the most."

After what they'd shared, a week might as well be forever. Still, it wasn't like Maisie hadn't known what she was getting into. "I'm sorry. I don't know why I'm so emotional."

"Because you were just made love to by a woman who wishes she could spend every day with you?"

Aiden's heartfelt words didn't make their impending separation any easier. Embarrassed by the sadness she'd invited with her own behavior, Maisie wiped the tears from her eyes with a tremulous laugh. "Nailed it."

"Next time we'll find a bed and really take our time." Aiden's hand wandered over the curve of Maisie's hip, molding around her bottom to give one cheek a lusty squeeze. "There are so many things I want to show you. So much I can't wait to do." She inched lower, pressing her fingers into the gap between her closed thighs. "Maybe you'll let me clean up whatever messes you make. It may take a while, but I like to be thorough and let my tongue work at its own pace."

Maisie nearly came a second time at the thought of being taken into Aiden's mouth for a lengthy tongue bath. The prospect of having someone's face inches from her vagina was daunting, to be sure, but also exhilarating. Having *Aiden*'s face inches from her vagina…Maisie assumed it would send her to another world. "I'd like that."

"Yes, you will." Aiden graced her bottom with a lively slap. "For now, though, I have but one favor to ask."

Maisie's mind raced through dozens of possibilities. Did Aiden want her to do the same thing? Or more? Would she ask to be fingered? Licked? Some other sex act she'd never heard of? Determined to be game for whatever it was, Maisie put on an eager smile. "Anything."

"Will you come to the truck and lie with me for a while? I have a mattress in there, nothing fancy, but…" Aiden sounded almost scared to ask. "I'd love to have a proper cuddle before you go. So I can remember how your body feels curled around mine."

"Until next week?" Maisie hoped she didn't sound as pathetic as she felt.

"Ten days at the most." Aiden sat up, helping Maisie off her lap so she could get to her feet. Holding out the hand she'd just used to change Maisie's life, Aiden broke into a goofy smile. "Now, have you ever been spooned?"

Not entirely sure what that meant, Maisie took the proffered hand

and allowed herself to be pulled off the swing and into Aiden's waiting arms. "I don't think so."

Hopping down the porch steps, Aiden gawped at her in wonderment. "Wait...I also get to be your first big spoon?"

"I guess?" Maisie still had no clue what Aiden was talking about—but she was dying to find out.

THE UNWELCOME HOME

Spooning, Maisie realized as soon as she woke up in Aiden's arms to dim sunlight and chirping birds, was simply another word for a sleep-trap. She'd never meant to close her eyes after lying down on Aiden's surprisingly comfortable mattress, but between the warm safety of the body wrapped around hers and Major's heavy breathing from his bed in the corner, she fell to post-orgasmic exhaustion within minutes of assuming the role of little spoon. Her last memory before dozing off was Aiden petting her belly like she was the most precious treasure on earth. Then, after what felt like a blink of an eye, Maisie woke up and dove off the mattress in a madcap scramble to fix her hair, face, and clothing before she started her forty-mile drive straight to hell.

Now on the porch of her "home sweet home," Maisie paused to take inventory of her appearance. She'd washed off the lip gloss smeared by her illicit homosexual kissing, used the spare brush in her glove compartment to tame her messy hair, re-fastened her bra, and triple-checked the buttons on her blouse for proper alignment. Surely she'd thought of everything Bernice might scrutinize. Heck, she'd even left her dirty panties with Aiden to make sure they couldn't be held up as proof of her wicked nature.

All the prayers in the world wouldn't save her from the verbal lashing she knew awaited her inside. She'd long since gotten used to being yelled at and called names, so assuming her mother didn't stray from the usual playbook of unfounded accusations and wild insinuations, Maisie could make it through the next five to thirty minutes relatively unscathed. But if Bernice did happen to notice something amiss, or smell the sex on her, or somehow manage to divine that her panties had gone missing during the night, Maisie didn't have the foggiest idea what would happen. She'd never come home with such an explosive secret before.

Taking a deep, sobering breath, Maisie put on a neutral expression, opened the front door, and walked inside. She didn't bother to rush past the foyer, aware that her mother had likely known about her absence since dawn broke, if not earlier. Instead, she made a beeline for the sitting room and poked her head inside. "Morning, Mom." Before Bernice had a chance to articulate the anger behind her flashing brown eyes, Maisie deployed the best excuse she'd invented during the longest car ride known to humankind. "I'm sorry I'm late. I drove down to the campus library after work last night to cram for Monday's midterm and ended up falling asleep in my study pod. Woke up this morning with no clue where I was. Once I realized…" She slowed down, afraid to tip off her mother with an overly manic performance. "I drove home as fast as I could. I apologize if I made you worry."

Her mother didn't say anything, just stared at Maisie while sipping her extra-tall mimosa from an oversized pint glass. Though it killed her to do so, Maisie mirrored Bernice's calm silence and returned the steely look without any flicker of emotion. Bernice sucked down another five or six swallows of her spiked orange juice, then set the glass down on the end table and stood up.

Maisie's heart sank. Whatever was happening, it scared her to death. Her mother rarely got this quiet. Maisie could only remember a handful of times when Bernice had come at her with something other than immediate and explosive anger or frustration. Those run-ins were the worst—slow burns that continued to build until her mother's unpredictable fury finally overtook her self-control and she lost it completely. After last night, Maisie didn't have the energy for a knock-down, drag-out with her drunk mother—who still hadn't said a word. Maybe Bernice was considering giving her a rare pass from their welcome-home inspection and interrogation routine?

Or maybe not. When Bernice ran skeptical eyes over her face and body, then snorted, Maisie knew she was in all kinds of trouble. The low volume of Bernice's first question hinted at exactly how much. "So why didn't you call? If you knew you were making me worry."

Maisie blinked, stunned that after forty-five minutes of careful planning, she had still managed to overlook the most obvious hole in her story. "Uh…" *I didn't want to wake you?* Sure, at nine in the morning. When had her mother ever slept in past six? Desperate for a fast answer, Maisie grabbed onto the first lie that flew into her mind. "My phone died. At the library when I was asleep. I didn't notice until I was already in the car on my way home. At that point it seemed silly to turn around and charge it—"

"What happened to the charger in your car?"

Damn it. Another hole, possibly larger than the last. She was off her game this morning. *It broke?* How stupid would that sound? What a perfect storm of simultaneous mishaps— "It broke," Maisie said, doubtful she'd ever come up with a stronger explanation than that. "Like a week ago, I think. I kept meaning to tell you, but—"

Her mother folded her arms over her chest, nodding in pseudo-sympathy. "Sounds like you had quite the night."

"Work, library, studying, sleep…" Maisie forced herself not to break eye contact. Once she did, she'd lose whatever crumb of power she might have. "Definitely made for a long night, that's for sure."

"And a lonely one?"

So it began. Used to this line of questioning, Maisie tried to channel the girl who never had anything to hide. "A little, but I didn't mind. Bev and Miles Carter brought their grandson in for dinner, so I got to catch up with them a bit. I also ran into my girlfriend Naomi later at the library, and we chatted about our accounting homework for a while. That's part of the reason I stayed late enough to doze off."

"Where does Naomi go to church?"

She was prepared for this one. "In Lowell. That mega-church in the center of town."

"Who else did you see last night?"

Apparently Naomi's church-going habits hadn't bought her any slack. "Nobody, Mom. I swear."

"On our Bible?" Bernice took a couple steps to the left and removed the large, leather-bound heirloom from its place on the tall bookshelf next to her chair. She held it out to Maisie, a fake smile plastered across her painted lips. "Go ahead, Maisie. I think it's a wonderful idea. I'd like to see you do that."

Maisie took the weighty book without hesitation, unwilling to waver in the selling of her story. The Bible no longer held any power over her, at least not in the way Bernice wanted. There was nothing wrong with liking sex. Nothing wrong with loving another woman. Aiden had embraced her own identity with such courage and pride, and look what it had gotten her. The freedom to be who she was, and the inner peace to relish what that meant. Exactly what Maisie wanted for herself.

Looking her mom dead in the eye, Maisie said, "I swear I wasn't sneaking around meeting up with boys or anything like that."

Bernice's eyebrows popped. "*Boys?*"

"Boy." Maisie corrected herself. "I meant one boy."

She realized her mistake as soon as Bernice's face lit up at the opportunity in front of her. "*Boy,*" she enunciated. "Which boy weren't you sneaking around with last night?"

"Mom, I *swear.*" She lifted the Bible so Bernice would remember it was still in her hand. "I swear I didn't do anything wrong."

She saw Bernice wind up just in time to brace herself for a vicious smack across her face. Before she could recover, her mother ripped the Bible out of her grip and slapped her twice more. "Lying to your mother with a *Bible* in your hands?" She shot Maisie a withering look before stalking over to reshelve the book in its place of honor. "If you'll do that, God knows what other sins you're willing to commit."

"I didn't do anything wrong," Maisie repeated, holding back tears she refused to shed. "I'm sorry you don't believe me, but that's the truth."

"Alma called me this morning about seven, wondering if you'd made it home safely last night. I checked your bedroom and told her no, actually you didn't. What made Alma think to ask, I wondered?" Bernice went to the end table for another long drink of her mimosa. "She tells me she noticed you flirting with a young man at Moe's not long before your shift ended, and the way he looked at you got her worried enough that she thought about following you home in her car to make sure he didn't try anything once you were alone."

"What?" Maisie's head spun, and not just from the vicious blows. She hadn't noticed Alma at the diner last night. Had Bernice actually recruited friends to spy on her behalf?

"Do me a favor, *sweetie*, and shut your lying mouth while I'm talking." Bernice slammed her glass down on the end table, causing it to wobble and spill onto the white carpet she'd long admonished Maisie to protect at all costs. Her mother's head snapped up from the scene of the self-inflicted catastrophe, cheeks red with alcohol and anger. "Look what you've done now, you little bitch!"

Genuinely afraid for the first time she could remember, Maisie retreated into the foyer to put some space between her panty-less ass and the woman who gave birth to her. Shrinking from the relentless advance across the white-carpeted floor, Maisie nearly bolted once her mother reached striking distance—but what was the point in running away? This was her home. She had nowhere else to go. She didn't even have Aiden's contact information. To deescalate the situation, Maisie relied on Bernice's constant desire for sympathy. "I'm so sorry, Mom. You've had such a hard morning already, not knowing where I was, and now this…I feel awful."

"You should."

"Please forgive me. I'll clean up the mess, it'll be like it never happened." Head lowered in deference, Maisie willed her mother to accept the apology and move on. It was entirely possible the story about Alma was a lie. They'd been so careful. "After I pour you another drink."

Bernice's expression softened ever so slightly. "No." She exhaled, rubbing her temples as though to douse the furious inferno within. "You'll only make it worse. I'll take care of the stain, like I do everything else around here."

"Yes, ma'am." Maisie fought to keep the resentment out of her tone. In reality, she handled well over half the household chores as part of the tuition agreement she'd struck with her parents. But Bernice was nothing if not a martyr, so Maisie let her bask in the fantasy of being locked into indentured servitude. "Thank you, for everything."

Her mother met her gratitude with a derisive snort. Turning to survey the splotchy orange mess on the carpet, she performed a long-suffering sigh. "I will take that drink, though. Use whatever's left of the champagne in the fridge, easy on the orange juice."

One more round of fury fuel—why not? "Yes, Mom." Conflicted about pushing another drink on a bona fide alcoholic, even as an act of self-preservation, Maisie welcomed the opportunity to flee to the kitchen for a moment to regroup. If Alma *had* called and Bernice believed her tale of illicit flirting and dangerous men, her entire world was teetering on the precipice of life-altering, relationship-ending disaster. Her mother *would* find out, eventually. How had she ever fooled herself into thinking she could hide a secret butch girlfriend from the nosiest woman in heaven or on earth?

By the time Maisie returned from the kitchen, her mother was down on all fours treating the carpet with her favorite spray bottle of spot remover. Like a soldieer traversing a minefield, Maisie took small, gingerly steps across the room to deposit the champagne-with-a-splash-of-orange-juice on the table beside her mother's chair. "Is there anything else I can do?" She hovered over Bernice awkwardly, wishing for a speedy dismissal and no more accusations or lectures. "Besides pray over the bad judgment I showed by making you worry?"

Her mother stopped scrubbing the carpet and stared up at her. Skepticism etched onto her tired face, she said, "Watch yourself."

"Yes, ma'am." Maisie waited for more. There was always more.

"Stop flirting with your customers. It's unprofessional, and whorish, and embarrassing for both me and your father." Bernice ran her critical gaze up and down Maisie's work uniform, reminding her of what wasn't under her skirt. "You're the one who should feel humiliated, not us. We raised you better than to giggle and blush and shake your tits for every man who looks your way."

"Mother, I'm not interested in any of them. I promise." She hoped, in this case, the truth really would set her free. "Please believe me. I'm not looking for a boyfriend *or* a casual fling. There's no room in my life for anything like that, not until I've finished school."

Red-rimmed eyes narrowed. "You don't think someone will take you up on *this* eventually?" She jutted her chin at Maisie's bare legs. "Trust me, they will. Whether you like it or not."

Time to retreat. Angling for a clean exit, Maisie aimed to appease just enough to prevent their confrontation from regaining its previous intensity. "You're right, Mom. Even if I don't intend to entice, the result will be the same." It was hard to swallow her pride past the lump in her throat. She was twenty-four years old. This was ridiculous. "I'll be more careful in the future."

"Start by wearing a cardigan over your blouse, especially at work." Bernice set the spray bottle aside and rose to examine her face and body, standing uncomfortably close to the blouse Aiden had unbuttoned, the skirt she'd reached under, the breast she'd cradled— close enough to literally expose the truth. She wrinkled her nose, then added, "I'll buy new tights for you to wear under that skirt. I mean, I can see your *knees*." Before she had time to react, her mother grabbed hold of her hemline and lifted the knee-length skirt to expose her upper thighs. "Filthy old man, putting young girls on display like this. And for what? *Money*. Moe Jackson ought to be ashamed of himself."

Moe, as far as Maisie knew, was still having the time of his life on an extended vacation to Florida. Best not to mention that to her mother, however. Maisie tried to change the subject, afraid she'd be baited into defending her boss—which would do nothing except incite another outburst. "Would you like me to set my alarm for this afternoon's church service? I'm happy to drive you."

Bernice met the offer with loud, condescending laughter. "Drive *me*?" She shook her head, then dropped Maisie's hemline and held out her hand. Giving her a smug, expectant look, Bernice said, "Oh no, honey. After last night? You won't be driving anywhere for a while. Not until you've regained my trust."

Trust she never had in the first place? Not even at seven years old? Maisie's chest tightened at the threat of having her only access to the outside world, and Aiden, taken away. Throat dry, she argued her case in the calmest voice she could muster. "Mom, I accept full responsibility for being gone all night and making you worry. It was a huge mistake, one I'll *never* make again. But my truck...I need it for work, and school, and—"

"Your truck?"

Maisie bit her lip, debating, then said what she was thinking. "I paid for it."

"Is your name on the title? No?" Bernice grinned, seemingly heartened by Maisie's obvious despair about her choice of punishment. "The truck belongs to your father, and therefore to me, as we explained when he agreed to cosign on your loan."

Her mother's snide, self-satisfied smirk made Maisie want to claw her own eyes out. Fuming, she said, "I paid off that loan over a year ago."

"Yet never asked your father if he would transfer the title into your name." Bernice clucked her tongue, head shaking in faux sympathy. Then she snapped her fingers and gestured at the purse that still dangled from Maisie's wrist. "Your keys. They're mine now."

"But—"

"Keys. Before I paddle your ass like the brat you are." The dark eyes locked onto hers flashed dangerously, cold and contemptuous and capable of unbelievable cruelty. Even at twenty-four years old and roughly the same size as her bitter, alcoholic rival, Maisie didn't dare test her mother's sincerity when it came to corporal punishment. "I've done it before, and you damn well know I'm willing to do it again. So try me, if you'd like. Give me an excuse to teach you some respect."

This was a no-win situation. With Bernice atop her self-righteous hill to die upon, Maisie's only choices were to surrender her keys and freedom or engage in a literal brawl with a woman who wasn't above violating her privacy in the name of righteous discipline. Even if she managed to get away before her mother noticed the missing panties, where would she go? Sure, if she had her keys she could always get in her truck and drive—but where? The only place Aiden knew to find her was Moe's. So no matter how badly she yearned to flee her overbearing parents and this dead-end life in Nowhere, USA, she had no other option but to stay. She couldn't afford to strike out on her own without a plan or anyone to lean on—and Aiden wouldn't know where to find her if she did.

Maisie opened her purse and removed the key ring she'd carried with her since the day after her eighteenth birthday. Averting her gaze from the triumphant smile less than a foot from her face, she surrendered the only access to autonomy her parents had ever permitted her to possess. Bernice swiped the keys from her hand with an amused chuckle. "Clever girl." The mirth vanished from her face, replaced by disdain. "Now go upstairs and take a shower so no one at church mistakes you for a homeless streetwalker who accidentally wandered into the afternoon service in between johns."

Cut by her constant, demeaning jabs, Maisie hardened her heart against the harsh judgment. *I didn't do anything wrong* she told herself over and over again in her head—a mantra meant to keep her firmly anchored in her own worldview and committed to the independence she would do anything to achieve. "Yes, ma'am."

HER BUTCH IN FLANNEL ARMOR

A week and a half went by without any sign of Aiden, eleven long days during which Maisie struggled to adjust to a new routine of chaperoned rides to and from work in her mother's car. Some part of her was relieved Aiden hadn't returned, given the wretched state of her personal life. Bernice had her under what felt like constant surveillance, both at home and around town via a network of embedded spies. Every parishioner Maisie served or neighbor she greeted was a potential informant, if only by virtue of their susceptibly to Bernice's manipulative, coercive dirt-digging tactics. She'd never been under more pressure to cloak herself from everyone's radar and play the role of the meek, boring virgin her mother wanted her to be. A visit from Aiden would be disastrous in that regard, as Maisie couldn't predict how she'd react if her secret lesbian suitor rolled into town before the fallout from their overnight rendezvous had a chance to settle.

Torn between fear and longing, Maisie spent all day, every day, thinking about bold, beautiful Aiden and her silly dog. Daydreaming about when they'd next be together. Dreading an ill-timed visit that would set her up for even more misery at home. Wishing Aiden would force her into the truck and take her somewhere Bernice would never find them. Worrying about whether Aiden planned to come back this way at all. Maybe she'd gotten what she wanted and wasn't interested in anything else. Maybe she'd met someone, someone out and self-assured and proud to hold her hand in public.

Maybe Maisie was too mediocre a kisser to waste another minute on.

On the Thursday evening Aiden walked into Moe's Fine Diner for the third time, an instant, gut-churning foreboding overtook whatever vindication of her kissing skills Maisie might've otherwise taken from the repeat business. Aiden couldn't have timed her entrance any worse. Along the front windows, at a table only a few feet from Aiden's usual booth, sat two of her mother's closest friends, Alma the snitch and Candy the drama queen, town gossip, and resident shit-stirrer. Like two hawks on the prowl, they locked their narrow, suspicious gazes onto the flannel-clad trucker the instant she came through the door.

Having apparently read the muted terror on her face, Aiden barely glanced Maisie's way before she gestured at a booth on the opposite side of the room.

"Seat yourself." Maisie acknowledged the silent request with a cordial nod, beyond thankful for Aiden's intuition—and discretion.

Pointedly not paying her mother's busybodies any attention, she grabbed a menu and silverware and half-floated to Aiden's booth in a semi-dissociative haze. Her heartbeat boomed in her ears, her hands were numb, and she wasn't sure she remembered how to form complete sentences. What if Alma recognized Aiden as the person she'd flirted with the night she hadn't come home? Or one or both of those vultures realized Aiden wasn't a man at all?

"Welcome to Moe's," Maisie said, voice cracking on the name. She licked her lips and swallowed against the nausea rising in her throat. "May I get you a drink?"

"Water's fine." Aiden handed over the menu without meeting her eyes. "And one short stack, if you don't mind."

Maisie's knees buckled when Aiden's finger grazed the inside of her wrist under cover of the menu they both held. She regained her balance seconds before landing on the floor but had to assume Alma had taken note of the bodily reaction. Needing to breathe, Maisie scribbled the word pancakes and nodded. "Coming right up."

She spun to execute a hasty retreat, only to stumble on a nonexistent obstacle that sent her falling onto her face in front of everyone. *Nearly* falling onto her face. If not for two strong hands catching her around the waist, Maisie would've had to process this tragedy on the floor. Instead, she stayed on her feet, facing Alma and Candy's blatant stares at the strapping young trucker whose hands were still on her. Squirming away from Aiden like the deadliest of poisons, Maisie misjudged her footing and tumbled forward to crash into the empty booth in front of them. The loud impact knocked the wind from her lungs and left her bent in half and gasping.

"I'm so sorry." Aiden's nervous apology drew even more attention to their plight, not as though every eye in the place weren't on them already. "I saw you trip and…didn't mean to startle you."

Maisie straightened, longing for a merciful God to smite her right then and there. So much for acting casual and not drawing attention. Before she could reassure the rattled patron she'd supposedly never met in her life that she was unharmed, Alma piped up from their table by the window. "You all right, Maisie?"

"Yes, ma'am." Maisie turned to Aiden, pleading with her eyes for Aiden to go, now, before this nightmare got any worse. She couldn't imagine her mother wouldn't hear about this later, and there was no telling what might set her off.

"It was my fault," Maisie told Aiden, faking a bright smile. "Not the first time I've made an ass of myself in public, and undoubtedly not the last."

Aiden tipped her head, then sat and pulled her phone from her pocket to stare at the screen in awkward silence. Eager to put some distance between them, Maisie decided to visit Alma and Candy's table for some damage control. Mustering a sheepish smile, she deployed the cover story she'd concocted on the way over. "I tripped and—" She stumbled again, this time over her words, upon realizing what a perplexing dilemma she'd trapped herself in. Either pretend Aiden was a man and risk offending the woman she loved, or tell the truth, even if it meant having her secret life unravel at the speed of the local rumor mill. Maisie opted for option number three—redirection. "Turns out I'm so clumsy I can't even accept help without almost breaking my neck in the process. Not that I didn't appreciate the chivalry. I would've landed on my face if not for those quick reflexes."

"Mm-hmm." Alma leveled a disapproving look in Aiden's direction. "I'd watch yourself around that one. I don't like how he looks at you."

A droplet of sweat rolled from Maisie's hairline to the base of her spine. Was that Alma's way of implying that she recognized Aiden from last time? Or was that her own paranoia talking? Another rivulet of sweat wended its way down Maisie's chest and into the crevice between her breasts. Damn cardigan.

Maisie agreed with a nod, hoping to convince Alma that the mysterious trucker meant nothing to her. "Thank you, ma'am. I appreciate you looking out for me."

Candy studied her with bright, curious eyes. "You've always been such a sweet girl, Maisie." Her lips curled into a condescending smile. "Maybe a bit *too* sweet at times, but I do believe you mean well."

Thanks? Unsure how to respond to the backhanded compliment, Maisie shoved aside her pride and tried to look pleased. "I try my best."

With that, she retreated to the kitchen to relay Aiden's order to Ralph and fill two glasses with ice and water. She drained the first glass in four large swallows, then picked up the second for Aiden in case she hadn't left. When Maisie reentered the dining room, the first thing she noticed was Alma and Candy whispering and stealing glances at the booth Aiden continued to occupy. Thankfully, Aiden appeared to be too fixated on her phone to notice the unwelcome attention. Maisie tensed when Alma's narrow gaze shifted to the doorway where she stood paralyzed by performance anxiety.

Sooner or later Alma would learn the truth—if she didn't know already—and Maisie could do absolutely nothing to stop that. She couldn't avoid the inevitable outcome of her duplicity. Even if she somehow evaded Candy and Alma's suspicions this time, it wouldn't be long before they or someone else worked out that she and Aiden knew each other. That they passed messages to each other at the diner. That Maisie wasn't the girl this town thought she was.

That she didn't belong.

Aware that the smallest misstep had the potential to expose her secret, Maisie steadied her nerves and stepped into the dining room as though she had nothing to hide. She averted her gaze from the older women and went to Aiden as though she were any other customer.

"Here you are." Maisie set the water glass in front of Aiden at the same time Aiden placed her unlocked phone faceup on the table. In a large, bold font, she'd typed a simple, three-word question.

Should I go?

Maisie was stumped. Should she? A few minutes ago that was all she wanted. Now she wasn't so sure. Wouldn't it be even more suspicious if Aiden left before her pancakes came off the griddle? And where exactly did she plan to go? How would they ever find each other without a phone number or social-media-account information?

Seeing no easy answers, Maisie erred on the side of keeping Aiden in her life for as long as possible. The idea of screwing up what they had scared Maisie far worse than the threat of disownment by her parents or the loss of the tuition money they provided. Reminded of where her true priorities lay, Maisie said, "Your pancakes will be out shortly."

Aiden glanced up and into Maisie's eyes, then busied herself with the phone once again, erasing the note and locking the screen in one fluid motion. "Thanks."

Maisie strolled away from the booth—not too fast, not too slow—and paused next to Alma when she gestured with her hand. "Yes, ma'am?" She noticed their empty plates and bowls for the first time. Rushing to collect them from the table, Maisie said, "Ready for dessert?"

"We sure are." Candy clapped her hands, then rubbed them together. "I'll have a slice of strawberry-rhubarb pie, please, with a scoop of vanilla ice cream. Alma?"

Maisie looked at the other woman. "And for you?"

After a brief pause, Alma said, "One scoop of vanilla ice cream. Plain."

"All right." Maisie suppressed a smirk at the predictable order. "Coming right up. More coffee?"

"Decaf." Alma sniffed.

"None for me." Candy flashed her bleach-white grin. "Or else I'll be up all night."

Maisie waited to jot down their order until she was safely behind the kitchen door. She passed the ticket to Ralph, who handed over a plate of golden-brown pancakes in return. "Try not to eat them on your way to the table."

"Funny." Maisie rolled her eyes, pretending to be calm enough to joke around. She *had* been eating a lot of pancakes lately. They reminded her of the night when everything changed and her true life began. "I make no promises." She nodded at the ticket in Ralph's hand. "Do me a favor and speed that one along, will you? My mother's church friends are working on my last nerve out there."

Ralph chuckled, all too aware of Alma's withering, judgmental ways. "You got it."

"You're the best, you know that?"

"Yup." He glanced at the ticket and scoffed. "I'll have this ready by the time you return."

Maisie exhaled and used her shoulder to push open the kitchen door. Alma and Candy had resumed their intense, whispered discussion— about what or whom, Maisie didn't want to know. Blocking them out, she made her way past the front register and presented the pancakes to Aiden wearing a not-too-friendly smile. "Here you are. Hot off the griddle."

"That was fast."

"I assumed you would be eager to get back on the road." Maisie wanted to slap herself across the head the moment the words left her mouth. Why had she said that? The last thing she wanted was for Aiden to take off before they had a chance to exchange more than a handful of pleasantries. Flustered, Maisie met Aiden's neutral stare and shook her head once. She could only hope Aiden understood the mixed messaging. "May I get you anything else?"

Aiden glanced at her plate, then the table, before flashing Maisie an apologetic frown.

She saw the problem immediately. "Syrup." Ralph had topped Aiden's pancakes with a dollop of butter, but Maisie was supposed to have filled a syrup dispenser before delivering the dish to the table. "I'm so sorry. I'll have that out for you right away."

"No worries." Aiden's warmth and compassion wrapped Maisie in a blanket of safety she was loath to ever discard. "Thanks."

Feeling like an idiot, Maisie hurried behind the counter and grabbed the first syrup dispenser she saw. She wiped it clean of the sticky residue she'd dripped onto the side courtesy of her unsteady hands, then turned to rush it over to Aiden so she could start eating.

"Maisie, honey." Candy waved her over to their table. "A word?"

Teeth gritted, Maisie lamented Candy's reliably lousy timing. "I'll be right with you, ladies. Just a moment."

Any hope of further nonverbal communication with Aiden thwarted, Maisie swung by her booth just long enough to drop off the syrup before circling back to check on her least-favorite customers.

"Your order should be up any second now," Maisie said, barely slowing on her way past their booth. "If it isn't already. I'll check."

"Maisie!" Candy's tone took on a finely honed edge. "Slow down. It won't kill us to wait another minute for ice cream."

Alma frowned. "I'd rather not eat a melted puddle, thank you."

"Oh, Alma. Stop being dramatic."

Maisie had to stifle her laughter at that one. These two were the proverbial pot and kettle, far more alike than either would ever admit out loud. "Yes, ma'am. What can I do for you?"

Candy's eyes twinkled. "I thought maybe you could help us settle a bet. About your trucker friend over there."

"Friend?" Maisie resisted the urge to steal a look in Aiden's direction, afraid of what Alma and Candy would see on her face before she returned her attention to their mysterious bet. Playing it safe, Maisie said, "I don't know about that."

Alma shook her head, nose wrinkled in what looked like disgust. "Oh, Candy, stop it."

"What?" Candy taunted her dearest friend. "Afraid to be wrong?"

Maisie's heart sank in her chest, deeper and deeper until it sat cold and unmoving in her belly. She knew what they were going to ask. What the bet was. The only thing she didn't know was how to respond. "I'll let you two hash this out while I che—"

"No need." Ignoring Alma's death stare, Candy beamed up at Maisie like a middle-aged, bleached-blond Cheshire cat. "Simple question. Man or woman?"

"Excuse me?"

Candy huffed, seemingly annoyed by her unwillingness to play again. "Boy or girl. What *is* it?"

Maisie blinked, offended on Aiden's behalf. "A paying customer."

Rolling her eyes heavenward, Candy shook her head, then pinned Maisie with an admonishing stare. "So you don't know? Or you don't want to tell us?"

Grasping for something to say that wouldn't explode her life or make her feel like shit later, Maisie projected every ounce of confidence she possessed—which, admittedly, was not a whole lot—and met Alma's eyes. Fingers crossed that the older woman found the speculation as distasteful as she did, Maisie said, "Ma'am, I'm not permitted to gossip about other customers, especially in the dining room. Sorry."

Candy grunted and folded her arms over her chest. "Well, I'm telling you both that the individual who put 'his' hands on Maisie is most definitely *not* a man. She may be the butchest of butches, but that there is a stone-cold dyke if I ever saw one."

Alma's lips pursed and she shook her head. "God forbid."

"Why?" The simple question popped out of Maisie's mouth before she had a chance to censor herself. "Because you'd rather see a strange man touch me than another woman?"

"Stop." Maisie had never seen Alma's expression so severe. Eyes blazing, she scorched Candy with a venomous glare of pure disdain. "Enough. This is *highly* inappropriate, both of you."

Annoyed to be scolded about a conversation she'd hadn't asked to be invited into, Maisie said, "I'll have your coffee and ice cream out to you shortly."

"And pie!" Candy called out as she walked away. "Don't forget my slice of strawberry-rhubarb."

Maisie didn't bother to reply before entering the kitchen for a brief respite. Ralph met her appearance with a toothy, self-satisfied grin. "Perfect timing." He slid a bowl of ice cream and Candy's strawberry-rhubarb pie—plus ice cream—across the counter. "Order's up."

"Fantastic," Maisie muttered, making no move to grab the dishes or leave her temporary refuge.

"Everything okay?" Ralph slung a dish towel over his shoulder, head cocked in what appeared to be genuine concern. "You don't look too great."

"Gee, thanks." Maisie leaned against the pass-through window and sighed. "My mother's church friends keep staring at me and whispering like I'm under some kind of microscope, and I know damn well they're judging every move I make. There's only so long I can pretend not to care."

Ralph snorted, ducking his head to shoot her a knowing grimace. "Alma and Candy, huh? Judging others is the only joy they have left, I reckon. Don't let them rattle you."

"I'm trying not to. But Alma has a direct line to my mother's ear, so there's no telling what I'll get talked to about tomorrow morning."

Embarrassed to be twenty-four and still at the mercy of her mother's deeply held beliefs, Maisie said, "I know that's beyond pathetic. I shouldn't care what my mother thinks."

"You shouldn't care what anyone in this backwards town thinks." Ralph pulled the dish towel off his shoulder and fiddled nervously with one end. "Neither of us should."

Maisie searched Ralph's face, trying to decide if he was coming out or merely identifying with the plight of feeling like an outsider. "I know, but...easier said than done, right?"

"I don't know." Ralph pushed the bowl and plate closer. "I'm thinking I may get the hell out of here the day after I graduate. I've always known I was destined for more than this shithole town, so why wait? Why not start my actual life as soon as possible?"

"How much money do you have saved up?" Maisie got a sick thrill from the idea of poking a big hole in Ralph's juvenile fantasy. "Enough to pay first and last month's rent as the security deposit on a semi-livable apartment? What about college? How will you pay for the tuition?"

"Tuition?" Ralph snorted. "Maybe I'll worry about more school in a year or two, after I've found a job and somewhere to live. As for my savings...well, I may not have much, but it should be plenty to get me where I'm going."

"Where's that?"

Ralph shrugged his shoulders, a shy smile on his pink cheeks. "Away."

Maisie was transfixed. She'd never heard someone express the same eagerness to escape their boring, painfully homogenous hometown that she'd always felt, let alone announce the exact day they intended to leave. Her stomach twisted on his behalf. "You aren't scared?"

"Nah." He pulled a face. "No more than I would be if I stayed."

Whether or not Ralph's aplomb was an act, Maisie found the lack of doubt in his voice downright inspirational. "Good for you. I hope it works out."

"It will, eventually." Ralph winked. "For both of us." He glanced at the ice cream, giving her a sympathetic wince. "Anyway, you'd better take these to your friends before Alma gets it in her mind to lecture you about the evils of 'idle hands' or some such bullshit."

Disarmed by the unexpected camaraderie she felt for a boy she'd always dismissed as just another small-minded local, Maisie managed an actual grin. "Thanks. Wish me luck."

"You've got this." Ralph chuckled. "Nobody knows how to handle those old biddies better than you."

Maybe, Maisie mused as she gathered the dishes and grabbed a fresh cup of coffee on her way out the door. But her patience for playing pretend and avoiding conflict had reached an all-time low. She was tired of being surrounded by minds too narrow to conceive of the life she wanted to lead—or accept the woman she loved. Why should she care what Alma and Candy thought? Or her mother, an abusive, alcoholic hypocrite she didn't even respect?

Shoulders squared, Maisie pushed open the kitchen door to discover an even more public stage for Candy's nonsense than the one she'd left. Plastering on a practiced smile, she waved the sheriff and his wife to the table farthest away from where Aiden sat. "I'll be with you two shortly." Glad for an excuse not to linger at Alma and Candy's table, Maisie placed each dessert in front of its owner and set the coffee—decaf—in front of Alma. "Here you are, ladies. Do you need anything else?"

"How about a guess?" Candy asked in a sickly sweet voice. "As a tie-breaker."

Alma made a disapproving noise. "Mine is already half-melted."

"Would you like a new scoop?" Maisie's fingers curled into fists at her sides. "I'm happy to bring you one."

Without breaking eye contact, Alma lifted a spoonful of ice cream to her lips and slurped it off the spoon. "No. It's fine. I'll make do with what I was given, like I always do."

Maisie's skin crawled at yet another performative act of martyrdom from her mother's closest friend. How much longer *did* she want to tolerate this shit? Another year? Two years? Until she graduated and had saved enough money to safely strike out on her own?

Could she even make it that long? *Would* she?

"Excuse me," Maisie said in a brusque tone. "I have other customers to tend to."

As badly as she wanted to check on Aiden first, Maisie knew from experience how unwise it would be to leave the often "hangry" sheriff waiting too long. To avoid any further drama, she made him and his unsmiling wife her next stop on the longest waitressing shift she'd ever worked. Per usual, the sheriff and his wife kept their orders brief and simple—the man clearly valued efficiency over personal taste—so it didn't take long before Maisie was en route to the kitchen once more.

This time she didn't stick around to commiserate. Handing Ralph the ticket with a knowing smile, Maisie was halfway into the dining room before she heard his instant assessment. "Looks like the law's in town."

Maisie cleared her throat to both cover his snarky quip and keep the amusement from reaching her eyes. Lucky for her, Aiden was the next stop on her agenda. With Aiden, she never had to pretend. She could be exactly who she was—and even feel good about it. True happiness welled up inside her at the thought of living every day surrounded by that kind of acceptance and unconditional love.

So why wait?

Broken out of the fantasy by a flash of movement in her peripheral vision, Maisie watched as Aiden tossed a couple bills onto the table and strode purposefully toward the door. *We never even got to talk.* Maisie glanced at the now-empty booth. She scanned the table for any sign of a note or other attempt at communication. She didn't see one, but that didn't mean it wasn't there. Maybe tucked under the salt and pepper shakers, or folded up between packets of jelly, or inside a napkin—

"Dyke."

Maisie stiffened at the audible slur from the table nearest the door Aiden had already pushed open with her shoulder. Pausing, Aiden hesitated for an endless, painful few beats before she turned to look Candy dead in the eyes. "Excuse me?"

Candy's self-righteous smirk tripled in size at the sound of Aiden's unmistakably feminine voice. "You heard me, and that's exactly what you are. Isn't it?" Her defiance grew before Aiden could get a word in edgewise. "If you don't like being called dyke, or *lesbian*, or whatever, maybe you ought to reconsider shoving your 'identity' in everyone's faces."

"Candy." Alma admonished her, motioning for her to hush. "Let's not make a scene."

"Oh, you're just mad that I was right and you were clueless." Candy ignored her companion's angry glare in favor of resuming her venomous attack on the silent, steadfast Aiden. "I *knew* you were getting off on groping poor Maisie over there, but that's probably the only way you can convince anyone to let you touch them. By making believe it was an 'accident' and swooping in like you're their knight in shining armor."

Aiden still hadn't broken the unflinching eye contact Maisie assumed she'd established as an unspoken warning to fuck off, but Candy's accusation caused her stoic countenance to waver for the first time. She opened her mouth to defend herself, but Maisie knew she couldn't stay quiet anymore. Not when the woman she loved was being bullied right in front of her.

"That's not what happened, Candy, and you know it." Maisie stole a sideways glance at the table where the sheriff and his wife sat in silence as they waited for their dinners to arrive. Based on the sheriff's apparent dedication to staring out the window instead of at the noisy altercation less than twenty-five feet away, he appeared to consider himself officially off duty and unwilling to mediate in their dispute. Which, she had to admit, was probably for the best. Pinning Candy with her own stern glare, Maisie said, "I tripped, like I told you, so all you're doing is making a giant ass of yourself. Slinging accusations fit for a schoolyard bully."

The look she received from Candy was sharp enough to cut glass, no hands or tools required. "*I'm* the child? What does that make you? An experienced woman of the world? Still living under mommy and daddy's roof, being disciplined like a bratty teenager when you break curfew?" Candy scoffed, her words dripping with condescension. "Sorry, honey, but you don't have the first inkling how the world works, let alone what deviants like *her* want from naive young girls like you."

"Maybe I'm not as naive as you think," Maisie countered, on the verge of admitting everything. At least then it would be over. The constant fear would abate. Maybe she'd finally be able to breathe. All she had to do was step into the unknown and trust she would be okay—with or without Aiden.

"All I want *for* Maisie is the same thing I want for everyone—happiness, love, and peace." Aiden kept her attention on Candy, as though worried that a stray backward glance at Maisie might incite a new level of violence. "Everyone, including you."

"Don't you worry about me," Candy snapped, nostrils flaring. "I'm very happy, thank you, because I live my life doing right by Jesus. Can you say the same?"

"I don't remember the part of the Bible where Jesus heckles friendly strangers who've done nothing but mind their own business. How about you, Alma?" Incensed, Maisie tore into the blatant hypocrisy she'd lived with her entire life. "What do you think Jesus would say about trading gossip? Or judging others?"

"All right, Maisie. You've made your point." Alma spoke to her in a clear, ominous undertone, then issued her next admonishment to the holy crusader whose strawberry-rhubarb pie remained untouched. "Candy, we get it. You were right, I was wrong. The woman's a freak, so how about we send 'her' on its way before anyone else loses their appetite?"

Rage bubbled up inside Maisie's chest, but before she could expel any of it, Aiden's eyes hardened, and she shouldered open the door. "With pleasure. Have a nice evening, ladies."

Maisie watched her march out the door and across the parking lot, headed for the big rig she'd somehow maneuvered into the three spots farthest from the driveway. Time seemed to slow down with each step Aiden took, yet Maisie could do nothing except stand there— helpless—and start to process the loss.

"Well, that was awkward." Alma shook her head, licking the final traces of ice cream off her spoon. "You and your big mouth, Candy. I swear. God only knows why I take you anywhere."

Giggling, Candy reached over the table to pat a scowling Alma on the arm. "Lighten up. It's not like I picked on someone who wasn't asking for it."

"*Asking for it?*" Maisie repeated, the first words she'd spoken since Aiden's departure. "What the hell is that supposed to mean?"

"*Maisie,*" Alma said. "Watch your language."

"Your middle-aged, churchgoing friend just called a complete stranger—my *customer*—a 'dyke' for doing nothing more than walking nearby, and *I* need to watch my language?"

"Right now, yes, you do." Alma regarded her through derisive eyes. "Now don't push me, or I'll tell your mother *everything* about what just happened. How you *had* to jump into the fray in defense of the indefensible."

Before tonight, a threat like that would've stopped Maisie cold. But after the behavior she'd just witnessed—from women her mother honestly believed were worthy of her respect—the prospect of maternal disapproval barely registered. Who covets the acceptance of bigots and bullies? What kind of fool chooses to live a life of misery when they no longer have to?

A spark ignited in Maisie's soul, filling her with pride and confidence and passion unlike anything she had ever felt—or allowed herself to feel—in the past. What was she *doing* here? Why stay? Any reasons she could discern—school, her parents, this job—seemed pathetically thin, almost inconsequential. School could be postponed. Her parents were only using her as a buffer for their marriage and an outlet for their frustrations. They didn't deserve her presence in their lives. This job? As much as she liked Moe, the thought of continuing to serve bigoted, hypocritical, ugly customers like Alma and Candy made her want to vomit.

She was done. *Beyond* done—with this town, these people, and the empty life she'd tried to make work for far too long. Finally allowing her disdain to show, Maisie answered Alma's menacing words with a disgusted sniff. "What's wrong with you?" She regarded Candy like the trash she plainly was. "Spoiler alert: Jesus would *not* be impressed."

"Maisie, that's *enough*." Alma raised her voice loud enough to draw the attention of Sheriff Del Ray—for a second or two, anyway. "Go on and fetch us our bill. We're leaving."

Maisie shook her head, madder than Bernice on the unholiest of Halloween nights. Madder than she knew a human could be without erupting into flames. "You're right. This *is* enough." She ripped off her apron and tossed it over the closest chair, then dismissed both women with her middle finger. "Tell my mother good-bye, and don't bother to come after me. I'm already gone."

Alma's stern frown barely faltered. "You are, aren't you?"

Alarmed by the bright sweep of truck headlights across the wall, Maisie unfroze her brain and ran out the door. She'd made it only a couple of steps past the curb when Ralph shouted after her. "Maisie, stop! Hold up."

She half turned, ready to brush him off with a clipped good-bye, then realized he'd just tossed her purse into the air. Stopping long enough to catch the precious bundle, Maisie blew him a kiss and took off in a dead run toward the front of the lot. She saw the truck's headlights sweep across the pavement a few feet away as Aiden made the turn to enter the driveway that would spit her out onto the main road to the highway. Driven by the nightmarish possibility of losing Aiden forever, Maisie waved her arms over her head and yelled as she high-tailed it across the parking lot in a desperate bid to get Aiden's attention.

"Wait!" Never had she flown so fast, and so effortlessly, in a pair of kitten heels. Her feet seemed to be barely touching the ground, like some benevolent force was helping propel her into the future she wanted more than the breath in her lungs. "Aiden, wait! Stop!" Aiden's brake lights flicked off as she eased the truck a few inches closer to the road. Screaming like a woman possessed, Maisie swung her purse over her head, anything to be noticed. "Don't leave me! Aiden!"

The truck jerked to a halt, its brake lights back on. With less than ten feet to go before she reached the driver's-side door, Maisie didn't slow down to celebrate. Aiden shifted the truck into park, then rolled down the window. "Maisie," she called out. "I'm so sorry. Are you all right?"

"Take me with you." Maisie skidded to a stop below the driver's side door. "Please, I know it's crazy, but—"

"Get in," Aiden said, disappearing from sight to lean across the cab and open the passenger-side door. She reappeared at the window, voice choked and heartfelt. "I promise to keep you safe and make you happy."

"Maisie Davis!"

She'd recognize Alma's shrill hysteria anywhere. Without looking back at her mother's lackey, Maisie ran around the front of the truck and hauled herself up into the passenger seat. Major whined happily from the mattress behind them, then barked at the crazy woman yelling and screaming after them as Aiden drove out of the parking lot and into the unknown.

MAISIE'S MAIN SQUEEZE

They drove for over two hours before Maisie felt comfortable enough to let Aiden pull off the highway to find them a room for the night. She'd been cuddling Major since they left Moe's, but he was no substitute for his copilot—and Maisie needed to be held. She and Aiden had chatted a bit during their near-surreal journey farther north, then east, mostly about what had happened since their first night together. Bernice's furious accusations and vengeful confiscation of her only mode of transportation. The threats to make her quit waitressing so she could spend more time at church and home. Being under constant surveillance thanks to her mother's network of blabbermouths and unwitting informants.

Aiden had listened to all of it, only occasionally interjecting a word of support or sympathy or frustration. For the most part she simply let Maisie vent, so by the time they reached the hotel her muscles were looser and she no longer felt like she might pass out. Amped but emotionally exhausted, Maisie let her mind move beyond what she'd just done to what would happen next. And how Aiden felt about being used as her ticket out.

After Aiden paid for the room, she walked around the truck to open the passenger-side door. Holding out her hand, she melted Maisie with a cheek-splitting grin. "My lady."

Maisie blushed and accepted the help descending the steep stairs. "Chivalrous to the end."

"For you? Always." Aiden wrapped her arms around Maisie's waist, lifting her before carefully setting her on the pavement. "But especially tonight. I'd say you deserve a whole lot of tender, loving care after what you just did."

Maisie shook her head, still caught between exhilaration and disbelief at her uncharacteristically decisive action. "My mother must know by now. Alma would've called her immediately. My father probably also knows, if he's answering his phone tonight." She exhaled, shaky from the adrenaline of her great escape. "Sorry if I keep repeating myself. I guess I can't stop running through the whole thing in my head."

"Baby, it's okay." Aiden tugged on Major's leash, encouraging the dog to jump down after her. Then she wrapped her arm around Maisie's waist and led the three of them to a nearby patch of grass, where Major could take care of business before they turned in for the night. "Don't worry about repeating yourself. What happened tonight was huge. You chose to run away from everyone and everything you've ever known. With me, a woman whose company you've shared for no more than thirteen hours, tops. All you have is the purse on your back and my promise to protect you until you figure out what you want to do next."

Maisie's eyes watered at the uncertainty in both Aiden's voice and her own heart. What she *wanted* was to stay with Aiden for as long as they made each other happy. She suspected they harbored the same desire, but try as she might, Maisie couldn't fathom what she could offer an independent, self-sufficient, gorgeous stud like Aiden. As of tonight, she had no job, no clothing, no family, and only twenty dollars. She looked down at her work uniform as they approached the room Aiden had reserved, sickened by the realization that she had nothing to change into tomorrow morning.

Aiden unlocked the door, allowing Major to run through first before she tugged Maisie inside after her. "I know it's not exactly the honeymoon suite, but…" She ran her fingers through her hair, then turned to Maisie with an embarrassed smile. "This should do in a pinch."

Maisie walked into the middle of the room, turning to admire the four walls and ceiling her parents didn't own. "It's wonderful."

"I'm not sure I'd go *that* far." Aiden joined her at the foot of the bed, seemingly more relaxed now that Maisie had voiced her approval. "But at least we'll have some privacy here, and a comfortable place to sleep." She raised her hand along with an eyebrow. "Would you like me to hang up your purse?"

"Thank you," Maisie said, shrugging the bag off her shoulder for Aiden. "I'm relieved Ralph had the presence of mind to bring me my driver's license, wallet, and favorite lip gloss before I shot out of there." She watched Aiden hang the purse in the closet, followed by her leather jacket. Maisie's pulse jumped at the sight of her broad shoulders and form-fitting flannel shirt, which Aiden casually unbuttoned to just above her breasts. Leaving the closet, she went to Maisie and wrapped her in a strong, soothing embrace. Maisie swallowed hard as the magnitude of her decision finally sank in. "Aiden?"

"Yes, Maisie?"

"I don't want to be a burden—or another mouth for you to feed."

Aiden made a shushing noise, splaying both hands across Maisie's back as though to bring them close enough for two to merge into one. "The last thing you are to me is a burden." She kissed Maisie's temple, then released her, backing away until they no longer touched. "Listen, why don't you take a shower and try to relax? I saw a sign for a gas station a mile and a half from here, so how about I go out and grab you a few necessities, maybe some dinner?"

A little space sounded like a fine idea, even if Aiden leaving her didn't. "You don't have to do that."

"But I want to." Aiden blew her a kiss and pointed at Major lounging on the bed. "Major Badass here will watch over you while I'm gone. Believe me when I say he'll bite anyone who so much as looks at you funny." She bent to give him an approving pat. "Not a bad quality in a travel companion."

In the end, Maisie agreed to let Aiden go only because she needed the guilt-free time to stand under the hot spray of the shower and think about the days ahead. By the time she stepped out from behind the curtain and slipped on the fluffy white bathrobe provided by the hotel, her brain still hurt, but her heart had found some measure of peace. She'd rather face an unknown tomorrow than suffer through another day of lying to her mother, herself, and everyone else about who she was and what she wanted. To have Aiden in her life, she'd give up everything a thousand times over.

By the time she emerged from the bathroom, Aiden had returned from her hunting-gathering expedition. Seated on the bed alongside a couple of plastic bags filled with gas-station necessities and a paper sack from a sandwich shop Maisie had heard of but never tried, she stopped petting Major to greet her with a tentative smile. "Hey."

"I missed you," Maisie said, gathering the robe tighter around her nude body. She hadn't appreciated quite how much until she saw Aiden's adoring gaze and remembered the safety she always felt when they were together. Eyeing the bounty Aiden had collected, Maisie went to the closet where her purse was hanging and retrieved the lone bill from her wallet. "I have only twenty dollars at the moment, but I promise to pay you back as soon as I can."

Aiden tilted her head and gave Maisie an odd look. "Huh?"

"For the food, and supplies, and…" She withdrew the cash when Aiden made no move to accept. "Everything."

"Maisie." Exhaling, Aiden scooted to the edge of the bed and placed her hands on her knees. "Look…don't worry about the money, okay? I can afford to help my friend out of a bad situation. And if you're worried about what I might expect in exchange…" She shook her head. "Don't. I'd love to have someone to talk to on the road, but even if you choose to sit next to me in complete silence…I'd be cool with that—and only that."

"Why?"

Aiden bit her lip, an internal battle playing out on her expressive face. Maisie held her breath while she waited for whatever admission Aiden found so difficult to make. When she finally spoke, her voice was barely louder than a whisper. "I know it's crazy to say, given how little time we've spent together, but…I'm almost positive I'm in love with you. That's why I'm willing to do absolutely anything if it means you might one day love me back."

Maisie put her hand over her heart, laughing at the absurdity of her relentless self-doubt. Aiden loved her, and wanted her, and didn't care how much or little she had to offer. The steady, unconditional devotion Aiden had shown her was real—as real as her own head-over-heels crush and dreams for a shared future. Walking to the bed, Maisie stood in front of Aiden and cupped her exquisite face in delicate hands. "I'm almost positive I already do."

With that, Maisie urged Aiden's head forward to rest on her belly so she could play with the short, dark hairs at the nape of her neck. Aiden moaned into the thick robe, a low rumble of contentment mixed with longing that went straight to Maisie's clit. She scratched her fingernails over Aiden's scalp, shivering at the instinctive power she seemed to hold over the woman below her. She brought her free hand up to cradle the back of Aiden's head, hips rocking into the sturdy shoulders and chest that were keeping her upright. Though Maisie realized she was extending an unconscious invitation, she didn't regret offering it.

Aiden bent to nuzzle the shallow indentation between her terrycloth-covered thighs, and Maisie could practically feel the hot breath on her clit, the wet heat of a mouth where she'd never been kissed. She groaned at the big hands sliding up the outside of her thighs, then bucked against Aiden's face when those hands reached around and grabbed her ass for leverage. "Aiden," she whispered, unsure what to say. She needed Aiden to know that whatever she wanted to do next was all right—*more* than all right—because without this Maisie might never sleep again. "I want you. Please."

Aiden tightened the fingers on her bottom, spreading the cheeks enough to expose her anus to the robe's plush fabric. Then she drew away to stare up and into Maisie's eyes. "Tell me what you want."

Too shy to say the words out loud, Maisie untied the robe's belt from around her waist and dropped it onto the floor. The sharp inhalation Maisie received in response emboldened her to lower the robe halfway down her shoulders and expose even more bare skin to Aiden's riveted gaze. Entranced by the rapid rise and fall of her chest, Maisie caressed Aiden's flushed face, then reached around to take hold of the base of her skull. Feeling almost out of her body, she guided Aiden's head into the narrow space between her thighs.

A sultry rush of air washed over her stomach, then her vulva. Maisie closed her eyes, shaken by her own boldness and the fervor with which she prayed Aiden would fulfill her greatest fantasy. She jumped when soft lips brushed her lower abdomen, teasing the flesh less than an inch above the subtle rise of her mound with the tip of her tongue. Eager for more, Maisie set her slippered feet farther apart on the hotel carpet.

The insane gratification she expected didn't materialize. Opening her eyes, Maisie looked down to see why Aiden had stopped, and the loving smile that greeted her sharpened Maisie's already painful arousal to near-intolerable heights. She dug her fingernails ever so carefully into Aiden's scalp, letting the hint of their bite communicate the depth of her disappointment. Aiden's smile stretched into a grin at the punitive gesture.

"A kiss?" Aiden asked, holding Maisie's eyes while she pressed her lips right above the defined border of her pubic hair. "Is that what you need?"

Maisie encouraged Aiden to move lower, bumping the slick labia she yearned to have sucked against Aiden's stubbornly positioned chin. "Yes." When Aiden didn't protest the forceful overture, Maisie tilted her hips to rub her clit from Aiden's slippery chin to the bottom lip now within her reach. "More than one, though. *Kisses.*"

Aiden shocked her with a long, languorous lick up her slit, followed by a return trip that ended at her still-untouched hole. Maisie latched onto the shoulders holding her in place, releasing a hoarse cry as she tried and mostly failed to stay on her feet. She jolted at yet another pass of Aiden's tongue over the responsive folds, unsure how much more of this divine bliss she could withstand before she fell forward and drowned Aiden in her unbelievable wetness.

"Oh!" Maisie pushed against Aiden's shoulders, helpless under the onslaught of yet another pass of her talented tongue. "I can't...I..." She moaned, shuddering at the even-better-than-expected jubilation of sharing her body this way. "*Aiden,*" she whimpered. "I'm afraid I—"

Aiden backed off in a flash, straightening to meet Maisie's wide eyes and study her face. "Afraid of what, baby?" She moved her hands from Maisie's ass to the back of her thighs, careful not to let her fall. "You can tell me if we're moving too fast. I won't be upset."

Touched by Aiden's resolute dedication to her comfort and emotional well-being, Maisie stroked her flushed face, then bent to kiss the crown of her head. "Not too fast. Just...more precarious than anticipated." At Aiden's puzzled look, she elaborated. "I didn't realize how hard it would be not to fall on my ass once you...started." She shrugged, still too shy to name the act despite her recently acquired experience. "Maybe we could..." She waved at the bed. "Lie down and try again?"

Wrapping Maisie's lower body in a protective bear hug, Aiden swept her off her feet and onto the bed by her side. Then she snapped her fingers at Major, sending him to the corner of the room with a stern look. Maisie frowned at his grumbled protest, almost sorry for the poor guy as he searched for an acceptable spot on the floor.

"He's fine," Aiden said, rolling her eyes good-naturedly. She moved the plastic bags from the bed to the nightstand. "Tonight is about you."

"And you." Maisie flushed at the huskiness of her own voice, now rougher and deeper than ever before, thanks to the absolute rapture of Aiden's lively tongue. "*Us*."

Aiden stood up and drew back the comforter to reveal the crisp, clean sheets below. She shoved the heavy blanket down to the footboard, then helped Maisie stand. Sweeping her up into possessive arms, Aiden kissed her forehead, then laid her down on the bed. Maisie propped herself up on her elbows to watch Aiden swagger to the foot of the bed and unbutton her jeans.

"Know what would make me happy?" Aiden lowered the zipper on her fly.

"What?" Maisie asked, breathless for the answer. She would do practically anything for Aiden, her strong, noble savior.

"My mouth on your pussy." Blue eyes sparkled at Maisie's audible gasp. "Sucking and licking my beautiful girl until my tongue is covered in her cum."

Maisie moaned at the fresh wetness that gushed out of her at Aiden's graphic language—words Maisie had never spoken out loud, too dirty—and taboo—to include in her squeaky-clean lexicon. She'd had no idea how powerfully affecting a simple word or turn of phrase could be. She held out her hands, beseeching Aiden with an exaggerated pout. "Then come here. No more teasing."

Aiden lowered her jeans to reveal a pair of black boxer briefs that hugged her perfect ass like a second skin. Another rush of juices flowed out of Maisie to join the growing wet spot on the underside of her robe. Flustered by the copious fluids coating her vulva and inner thighs, Maisie mustered a shamefaced smile. Aiden frowned, climbing onto the bed to join her. "Everything okay?"

"Yeah," Maisie said without thinking.

"Then why do you look like you're afraid to tell me something?"

Astute as ever. Maisie let her upper body drop onto the mattress and hid her face behind her hands. "I'm, um…well, I've never been this wet before. I'm not sure *anyone* has."

Aiden grinned, chest puffed out with apparent pride. "I'll be the judge of that."

Maisie's breath hitched at the firm pressure of large hands on her inner thighs. Aiden pushed them apart just far enough to allow for a lengthy visual inspection, drinking in the sight of Maisie's outrageous arousal with lustful, hungry eyes. Guiding her legs down against the mattress, Aiden spread Maisie's legs farther than they'd ever been spread, exposing her swollen, slippery *pussy* to the cool air and—as she drew closer—Aiden's steamy breath.

Rattled by the silent appraisal, Maisie curled her fingers around Aiden's wrist and squeezed. "Am I normal?"

Aiden blinked, eyes glossy and reverent as she bent to kiss the edge of Maisie's groin. She lifted her head, then reached up to press Maisie's chest until she lay flat on her back. After shoving a pillow under her head, Aiden reclaimed her place between the widely spread legs Maisie hadn't dared to close. "You're extraordinary," Aiden murmured, wrapping her toned arms around Maisie's upper thighs to hold them open. "Let me show you."

Aiden lowered her head and fitted her open mouth over Maisie's clit and labia, waiting until Maisie strained to break free before running the flat of her tongue from the tight pucker between her cheeks to the tip of her clit. Maisie's mouth fell open at the euphoria of indulging in what was once forbidden, of luxuriating in the hedonistic thrill of being worshipped in the most intimate way possible. A loud moan burst from her, the only option she had to ease the pressure building deep inside. She squeezed her eyes shut, abashed by her overenthusiastic performance.

The tongue buried in her labia withdrew, leaving Maisie to search for Aiden with her hips. She sucked in a ragged breath when wet lips ghosted over her quivering belly, unsure what to expect from the sudden shift in mood. After a lot of writhing and thrusting, Maisie gave up the hunt and opened her eyes to an infuriatingly calm Aiden smirking at her from just beyond her reach.

"Aiden!" She tried not to sound like she was pleading or like she lacked the authority to direct Aiden's next move. "I'm *begging* you."

So much for asserting her power.

"Eyes open." Aiden brought her shiny face close to Maisie's center, blowing gently on her throbbing clit. "I want you to pay attention. Watch what I'm doing to you."

The implication of her request was clear. This was to be both an offering and a lesson. Breathing faster at the prospect of returning the favor in kind, Maisie asked, "So I'll know how?"

"So you can see how much I love you." They locked eyes, and Aiden rewarded her outer lips with two tiny kisses. Not bothering to hide her delight at the uncontrolled twitch of Maisie's lower body, Aiden whispered, "How sexy I think you are."

Maisie clenched deep inside, a near-orgasmic spasm that curled her toes and sent her hips into the air. She could feel her nostrils flaring and knew she must look like a woman possessed, like the shameless sex maniac she'd always known lurked beneath the thin veneer of her chaste respectability. Dying for Aiden to continue, Maisie folded the pillow under her head to give herself a better view of the oral mastery that was about to unfold. She tightened her fists at the slight dip of Aiden's head as she positioned her mouth above the folds she'd already licked swollen.

The interminable wait was almost too much to bear. As though sensing her distress, Aiden placed a loving kiss on the hood of her clit and reached up to lace their fingers together. "Ready to come for me?"

Too on edge to speak, Maisie gave Aiden's hand a vigorous squeeze, certain she would pass out from the novelty of having an orgasm that wasn't self-induced. When Aiden did nothing to end her suffering, she forced herself to take a deep breath and answer. "I'll die if I don't."

Aiden's affectionate laughter shot through Maisie like a fast-acting drug, easing the tension in her muscles and further priming her body for a legendary climax. Doing as she was told, Maisie watched—the sensual slide of Aiden's tongue over and between her labia; the thrilling suction delivered by the tight circle of her full, diligent lips; the ardent devotion expressed in every kiss, every lick, every breath she bestowed on Maisie's receptive flesh. It didn't take long for Maisie to crescendo into full-throated exultation and shaking, shuddering release. Set free by the proficiency of Aiden's clever lips and tongue, she raised her hips off the bed, then grabbed Aiden's head and thrust into her mouth.

Aiden moaned around her clit, triggering an aftershock to rival the quaking pleasure from which Maisie had yet to recover. She was shocked by how easily Aiden coaxed a second orgasm from her exhausted body, then a third, until finally Maisie had no choice but to grab Aiden's hand and squeeze until she winced and backed away.

"We'll have to come up with a safe word. For next time," Aiden said, surging up to capture Maisie's half-open mouth in a heated kiss.

Maisie wasn't sure what she meant and didn't have the energy to ask. Instead she sucked on Aiden's tongue, only mildly scandalized by the knowledge that the new flavor she detected was her own. Less than a minute later Aiden broke away, trailing wet kisses from Maisie's neck to her nipples. She spent long, languorous moments tasting both in turn, sucking the painfully tight nubs like a pair of extra clits. Maisie threw her arms around Aiden's shoulders and, with a weak, upward tug, beseeched her to return for another kiss.

Aiden left her breasts with one final, hearty lick apiece, then nibbled her way up to Maisie's lips. After another lingering, head-spinning kiss, Aiden rolled their bodies so they were side-by-side and face-to-face. Maisie stared at the swoon-worthy woman in her arms, astounded that anyone could believe what they'd just shared was somehow wrong. She'd never felt so cherished and accepted, so *seen*, by another human being. With Aiden, she was safe. She could do or be *anything* and still be worthy of love.

"Talk to me, sweetie." Aiden tucked a lock of hair behind Maisie's ear, appearing anxious for feedback. "Are you okay? Or was that too much, too soon?"

Maisie grinned, amused by the unnecessary concern. "More than okay—and not even close to too much."

Aiden exhaled, then beamed at her, eyes welling. "Maisie, you're…" She shook her head, seemingly at a loss about which adjective to choose. Finally, she said, "Everything."

"I love you, too," Maisie whispered. She molded her body against Aiden's and closed her eyes, reaching under the familiar flannel shirt to caress the bare, smooth expanse of her lower back. "You're my favorite."

"Customer?" Aiden teased. "Trucker? Butch?"

"Person." Maisie drew away, wanting Aiden to see how sincere she was about her next request. "So, hey…"

"Anything." At Maisie's puzzled look, Aiden broke into a bashful smile. "Anything you want, baby, just tell me."

"I really *would* like to know." To clarify, Maisie rubbed her thumb over Aiden's top lip, then the bottom. "How."

Aiden swallowed, then captured Maisie's thumb in her mouth

and bathed it with her tongue. She let go after a few moments, never taking her eyes off Maisie's. "Then I'll show you." She gathered Maisie closer, enveloping her in a warm hug. "Tomorrow."

"Tomorrow?" An involuntary yawn hijacked Maisie's pout. "But I want to make you feel good *now*."

"You did," Aiden murmured, rocking her back and forth as though to lull her to sleep. "You do."

"But—"

"Shh." Aiden breathed into her ear. "You've had a long day and no dinner. Tonight, let me take care of you. Tomorrow…" She nipped the edge of Maisie's earlobe, then soothed the tender flesh with a suggestive lick. "I'll teach you how to make me come. Deal?"

Exhaustion now settling into her heavy limbs, Maisie wasn't inclined to put up a fight. It felt nice, having someone she trusted to relieve her of the burden of always being on guard. She turned her face to press a kiss against the side of Aiden's neck, savoring the steady thrum of the pulse beneath her lips. Grateful to the universe for the precious, flannel-wrapped gift in her arms, Maisie whispered, "I can live with that."

ABOUT THE AUTHORS

MEGHAN O'BRIEN is the author of ten lesbian romance/erotica novels published by Bold Strokes Books, including *Thirteen Hours* (2009 GCLS Award, Lesbian Erotica), *Wild* (2011 Rainbow Award, Best Lesbian Novel), *The Night Off* (2012 Rainbow Award, Lesbian Erotic Romance and 2013 GCLS Award, Lesbian Erotica), *The Muse* (2015 Foreword INDIE Bronze Medalist, 2015 Lambda Literary Award, 2016 GCLS Award in Lesbian Erotica), and *Her Best Friend's Sister* (2018 GCLS Award, Erotica and 2017 Foreword INDIES Silver Winner for Erotica). She lives in the Bay Area with her wife Angie, their son, and a motley collection of lovable pets.

AURORA REY is a college dean by day and award-winning lesbian romance author the rest of the time, except when she's cooking, baking, riding the tractor, or pining for goats. She grew up in a small town in south Louisiana, daydreaming about New England. She keeps a special place in her heart for the South, especially the food and the ways women are raised to be strong, even if they're taught not to show it. After a brief dalliance with biochemistry, she completed both a BA and an MA in English.

She is the author of the Cape End Romance series and several standalone contemporary lesbian romance novels and novellas. She has been a finalist for the Lambda Literary, RITA, and Golden Crown

Literary Society awards but loves reader feedback the most. She lives in Ithaca, New York, with her dogs and whatever wildlife has taken up residence in the pond.

ANGIE WILLIAMS, winner of a third-grade essay competition on fire safety, grew up in the dusty desert of West Texas. Always interested in writing, as a child she would lose interest before the end, killing the characters off in a tragic accident so she could move on to the next story. Thankfully as an adult she decided it was time to write things where everyone survives.

Angie lives in Northern California with her beautiful wife and son, and a menagerie of dogs, cats, snakes, and tarantulas. She's a proud geek and lover of all things she was teased about in school.

Books Available From Bold Strokes Books

A Turn of Fate by Ronica Black. Will Nev and Kinsley finally face their painful past and relent to their powerful, forbidden attraction? Or will facing their past be too much to fight through? (978-1-63555-930-9)

Desires After Dark by MJ Williamz. When her human lover falls deathly ill, Alex, a vampire, must decide which is worse, letting her go or condemning her to everlasting life. (978-1-63555-940-8)

Her Consigliere by Carsen Taite. FBI agent Royal Scott swore an oath to uphold the law, and criminal defense attorney Siobhan Collins pledged her loyalty to the only family she's ever known, but will their love be stronger than the bonds they've vowed to others, or will their competing allegiances tear them apart? (978-1-63555-924-8)

In Our Words: Queer Stories from Black, Indigenous, and People of Color Writers. Stories Selected by Anne Shade and Edited by Victoria Villaseñor. Comprising both the renowned and emerging voices of Black, Indigenous, and People of Color authors, this thoughtfully curated collection of short stories explores the intersection of racial and queer identity. (978-1-63555-936-1)

Measure of Devotion by CF Frizzell. Disguised as her late twin brother, Catherine Samson enters the Civil War to defend the Constitution as a Union soldier, never expecting her life to be altered by a Gettysburg farmer's daughter. (978-1-63555-951-4)

Not Guilty by Brit Ryder. Claire Weaver and Emery Pearson's day jobs clash, even as their desire for each other burns, and a discreet sex-only arrangement is the only option. (978-1-63555-896-8)

Opposites Attract: Butch/Femme Romances by Meghan O'Brien, Aurora Rey & Angie Williams. Sometimes opposites really do attract. Fall in love with these butch/femme romance novellas. (978-1-63555-784-8)

Swift Vengeance by Jean Copeland, Jackie D & Erin Zak. A journalist becomes the subject of her own investigation when sudden strange, violent visions summon her to a summer retreat and into the arms of a killer's possible next victim. (978-1-63555-880-7)